THE MYSTERY OF THE HOMELESS MAN

SEEMS DETECTIVE SERIES
BOOK 3

GINA CHEYNE

First published in 2023 by Fly Fizzi Ltd
Pyers Croft,
Compton, Chichester
West Sussex PO18 9EX
www.flyfizzi.co.uk

www.ginacheyne.com
Cover design by Kari Brownlie

ISBN 978-1-915138-08-8 ebook
ISBN 978-1-915138-09-5 paperback
ISBN 978-1-915138-10-1 hardback
ISBN 978-1-915138-11-8 audiobook

❀ Created with Vellum

This book is dedicated to Keith and anyone else who finds themselves homeless and living on the streets

A soul needs something more than four walls and a ceiling
    Munia Khan

Homelessness is not a choice but rather a journey that many
find themselves on
    Asa Don Brown

CONTENTS

CHAPTER 1
OWLY VALE VILLAGE VORTEX

When Neil was thrust into wakefulness he was immediately aware of two things: one was the intense cold, even though he was pretty sure he had fallen asleep in the summer, the other was the dog licking his face.

He opened his eyes and the dog sat back on his haunches and barked. Neil's sore eyeballs alighted on a ball by his arm, and the dog pushed it harder against him; in case he had missed it.

'Phew, dog!' he muttered. 'Have you chosen the wrong moment.'

Carefully he put up his hand and rubbed his aching head. As he did so he noticed the trees: there were trees everywhere. He rolled onto his back and, ignoring the dog's plaintive cries, stared at tall branches and a heavy over-growth of leaves which almost obscured the sky. Did he really fall asleep here? His normal playground was the streets, this looked like countryside, a wood even. Where was he?

'Well, hello!' said a rather too loud and jolly voice. 'You stealing my dog?'

A slightly overweight young woman hovered into his vision grinning happily. No, he thought, hovering was the wrong word, she collided with his vision: she was the sort of person who was *there* when she was there, and left a hole when she went. He pulled his beard. He wasn't making sense even to himself, he wished they would all go away.

'Well,' said the woman again, 'you look like you need help. You OK?' And she gave a schoolgirl laugh. 'Up you get.'

Neil shut his eyes. This was a bad dream. He was really in a doorway in Brighton. He was not here, wherever here was, and he had a bottle of whisky in his hand. He opened his eyes again, but there were no bottles anywhere round him. Nothing except cracked earth, bushes, and wild garlic: which smelt. This was not Brighton.

Apparently this idea had also occurred to his female persecutor, as she said, 'How did you get here, anyway? You homeless? You're a long way from civilisation. Mind you,' she continued suddenly becoming surprisingly literary, 'I'd rather be down and out here than in London or Paris.' She laughed again. 'You need a bath.'

He sighed. Yes, she was the sort of woman who 'spoke as she found' and he wished she hadn't found him. He made an effort to get to his feet and found she was there too, leaning in, helping him. And she was strong. Surprisingly so.

'Hum, you don't weigh much. Don't you eat?'

He said nothing, scrambling to get up before she damaged one of his street-weakened arms.

'You'd better come with me and have something to eat,' she said, still in that rather too loud voice. 'The children are having breakfast, you can join them.'

'Where am I?' he asked.

'Owly Vale,' said the woman. 'You're in the woods behind a house called Wild Garlic.' She gave a guffaw of laughter. 'You can smell why.'

He nodded carefully. 'How far from Brighton?'

The woman stared at him, eventually she said, 'Brighton? Over an hour by car. Did you walk here?'

Neil shrugged and shook his head.

His new friend giggled nervously. 'Well! I'm Miranda, this is Pugwash.'

'And I,' said Neil, 'am your pilot on this flight.'

He expected her to laugh and say something meaningless but instead she looked at him quizzically and said, 'Are you? Well that explains a lot.'

She put her arm under his shoulder and led him out of the wood and towards the kitchen where the children were having breakfast.

The children who were having, rather than actually eating, breakfast, were two girls. Miranda introduced them as Poppy, a dark-eyed girl around ten years old, and her aunt, Agata, a sixteen-year-old girl who was reading a book while pretending to eat. The kitchen was full of unopened boxes and Neil wondered if they had just moved in.

'Hello,' said Poppy, eying him curiously.

Agata ignored him until Miranda said: 'Agata, manners.'

Sighing, Agata looked up. 'Witam!' she said, raising an eyebrow as though challenging Neil to do something about it.

Miranda also sighed. 'Agata only speaks Polish these days,' she said. 'It's just a phase.'

Neil sat down on a kitchen chair and pulled at the chain

around his neck. He shut his eyes and imagined he was in a doorway in Brighton, under a blanket, a bottle of whisky in his hand: unfortunately it had just started to rain, his cover was getting wet and he smelt a dog peeing on him. He snorted. Perhaps he was better in the kitchen for the moment, even with two antagonistic children.

'Coffee?' asked Miranda, and then, as a man walked into the kitchen, 'this is Phillip, my husband.'

Phillip stared at him blankly and Neil imagined he might be wondering how this man had suddenly appeared in his kitchen, but instead it seemed that Phillip hardly noticed his presence. He said, 'I'm off, I'll be late tonight. Want anything from London?'

'Yes,' said Poppy, 'take me. I'm fed up of living here. I want to go back to Grandma.'

Miranda frowned. 'We've only been here two weeks, darling, give it time, OK. Anyway, I thought you were going to spend the day with that girl from the next-door village.'

'Julia. Yeah. OK,' said Poppy. 'But I'm registering a protest.'

As Miranda started shaking her head, Neil said, 'Er yes. Could you drop me in ... some big town?'

Phillip looked his way and nodded. 'Sure. I'm Phillip. You a friend of Miranda's?' He walked out of the door without waiting for an answer.

Neil gave Miranda his hand. 'Thank you, my friend, I'm afraid I'm irredeemable. But thank you for trying.'

As he followed Phillip out of the room Miranda followed him, she pushed twenty pounds into his hand. 'OK, but take this then. And be careful. London isn't always friendly.'

Miranda turned back to the children. 'So girls, what shall we do today?'

'I'm going out with Julia,' said Poppy, raising a lip, 'you just said.'

'Oh, yes,' said her mother. 'OK, sis, how about we spend some quality time together?'

Agata yawned. 'I'm studying,' she said. But then had a slight softening of heart, perhaps remembering that Miranda had left school and started working simply to allow her sister to continue at school. 'Why don't you go and bother that tall woman whose husband has just died. She probably needs your mothering instincts.'

'Cat,' said Miranda, nodding her head. 'That is a good idea. I haven't seen her for a long time, several days at least. I hope she's OK. Yes, Agata, that is a good idea.'

And she hurried out.

CHAPTER 2
KING'S CROSS

N eil went out of the front door to where Phillip was getting into an elderly Mercedes. He climbed in and pushed back the seat. *The suicide seat*, he thought, *that's what they used to call it when I was young.* He shivered suddenly as his body remembered: His life had shown this was only too true.

The two men drove the whole way to London in silence. Phillip listened to the radio but made no comments even when the announcer said that Enron former Chief Executive Jeffrey Skilling and founder Kenneth Lay had been found guilty of conspiracy and fraud. Neil had no idea who these people were, but the stiff way Phillip sat gave him the impression he was listening to that part of the news intently.

He wondered if Phillip worked in the city.

As they left the M25 at the A40 exit, Phillip seemed to become aware he had a passenger. 'I'm going to pick up a client at King's Cross,' he said. 'Would you like me to drop you there?'

'Yes, please,' said Neil. He hadn't been to King's Cross for many years but he remembered there used to be shops there that sold unbranded drugs very cheaply, he could use Miranda's twenty pounds for some solace.

Phillip dropped him at the station and Neil took the underpass to the chemist. As he passed a man shooting up he suddenly laughed. Phillip, he thought, would shoot up into the sky; this man shot up into his arm: an odd homophone. He went into the chemist.

After buying a large amount of paracetamol, Neil went into the station to buy a bottle of whisky. Then, happily ensconced in an alcove, his feet on a cardboard box, he settled down to forget again. Very soon, he thought, even his own name would be a distant memory and certainly not the past which right now was hovering on his conscience. It must have been those damn women, he thought, that brought back all the memories. That and that dreadful house in that dreadful village: Wild Garlic in Owly Vale. How had he found his way there again after all these years? Nearly twenty years ago. He pulled at the chain around his neck, and took a long swig from the bottle.

Just as Neil was sinking under the ether the voice came again. A strong London voice, West End rather than East End.

'You're back are you? Found your way. Come back to haunt me!'

He opened his eyes fast but saw only the passing feet of shoppers. A cold shiver cascaded across his body. He shut his eyes, and the voice started again.

'You took my life away!'

'NO! No! It's not true,' he screamed and sat up, but his movement hardly caused a ripple in the endless passage of feet. A random dog sniffed interestedly but was pulled away by its owner.

He got up and staggered across the station, nearly falling on top of a woman in a wheelchair. 'Sorry! Sorry!'

There were mutters and frets but people moved out of his way, complaining loudly about the smell. He found his way outside and sank down under a statue of someone unknown, tipping the bottle down his throat. Relaxing as its powerful medicine filled his body. He was going to forget. He refused to listen.

'Sorry, mate, you can't stay here.' The voice wasn't unfriendly, but it was demanding. He looked up and a policeman was standing over him, with a small colleague by his side. 'Up and off, or we'll have to take you in,' the man said. But he smiled.

Behind them the woman in the wheelchair was watching.

Neil clambered up and dragged himself down the road. The fat woman from Owly Vale was right: London was not friendly. He pulled out the remains of Miranda's money. He could walk to Waterloo, he could take a train. He would go back to a village he remembered from long ago: Billington. He would go there. There would be no policeman, no passing feet and there he could finally end his life. In peace.

As he walked down the road a silver Toyota Sienna drove up beside him and slowed to his pace. It seemed to be shadowing him. He tried to look inside but the windows were blacked out. He walked faster, the car accelerated. He stopped, the car stopped. Other traffic hooted behind the Toyota but the driver ignored them. Only when Neil reached the underpass did the car swerve away and pass on towards the west. From the safety of the underpass steps, Neil watched it go. Had he been imagining it? Was someone following him? Why? Why would anyone care about a drunken homeless man?

By the time Neil got off the branch line train at Billington it was dark, and the station lights gave an eerie glow across the forecourt. Neil forced himself out of the warmth of the station, and stopped dead: the Toyota was waiting for him outside.

He considered running but what was the point? Whoever it was would get him eventually. He opened the door and looked in. It was dark and the driver's features were alienated by the coloured forecourt lights, but one thing he knew for sure was that this was not a ghost.

He got into the suicide seat. 'Where are we going?' he asked.

'To the scene of the crime,' said a London voice: definitely West End, not East End.

CHAPTER 3
GARLIC IMPROVES MEMORY

I t was fifteen years later, when Miranda was reminded of the homeless man she found in the wood. Poppy had grown up and now lived in London and Agata was employed by the police. Only Miranda was still in the village, with her two younger children and the detective agency she founded with her tall, currently redheaded, friend Cat.

'Password?' said Stevie's mother as Miranda and her dog entered the SeeMs Detective Agency office.

'Morning, Blinkey.'

'Wrong! But you may pass this time,' said Blinkey and suddenly dashed off upstairs.

Miranda raised her eyebrows at the dog and walked on into the office. Stevie their young colleague, an airline pilot who did all their internet research, was already there.

'Hi, Miri, we have a great new job on.'

'Oh good. What?'

'Clive Creamer came in this morning. Know him? The bloke who owns Wild Garlic. It won't sell and he's paying us to find out why? Lots of research there.' A broad smile spread across her thin face.

'Oh, honestly!' said Miranda, collapsing down on the sofa followed by her dog. 'What a crazy job. OK, good to have the money but why on earth use a detective agency, surely an estate agent would be more rational?'

Stevie was about to answer when they heard: 'Password?'

Followed by Cat's kindly voice. 'Hello, Blinkey darling. I love your new jewellery. So pretty! Was it a family heirloom?'

Miranda rolled her eyes. 'She knows it's costume jewellery! Why does she do this all the time?'

Stevie's laugh was admiring. 'Because she's Super Mum, mother of all.'

Cat came in and gave the girls a coffee each from the shop. 'I've got doughnuts in the bag.'

Miranda rolled her eyes again. 'I'm on a diet. We're not all six foot and stick thin. You cow!'

'Sorry, darling. I was going to bring chocolate this time, but my daughter popped in while I was away and snaffled the lot. Right of the young: what's Mum's is mine!'

She looked around, obviously waiting for them to laugh.

'Oh,' said Miranda, pushing the dog off the office sofa. 'I wish you were my mother.'

Cat opened her eyes wide. 'Yikes!'

'But seriously, Cat,' said Miranda, 'is she depressed again? That's when she hoovers up chocolate like it's going out of fashion.'

At the same time Stevie asked, 'Which one?'

'Caroline, of course. But never mind all that, I've got some fascinating news.'

'What?' asked Miranda, leaning forward, her eyes shining.

Stevie stared into her coffee. Her colleagues had a way of exaggerating everything, so a whistle turned into an orchestra.

'You know that house on the corner, Wild Garlic, the one with the smelly plants? Well, last night someone drove a car into it, through the gate, knocking down part of the wall and ending up in the garden. I just went past, and it looks like a work of art amongst the trees.'

'Wow,' said Miranda. 'Who was it? Some drunk on his way home from the pub?'

'Apparently not. Police are there, and they are saying unlikely. Pub closes at eleven, and the neighbours say they heard a noise around three a.m.'

'The police are there already?' said Miranda. 'That's novel. When we had a burglary, it took a day and a half before anyone even returned our call.'

'Yes, but apparently, that's to do with the owner. He's a person of interest.'

'Person of interest?' Miranda's eyes flared. 'Why?'

'They wouldn't tell me, but it made it more urgent.'

'Blimey! Do you think he's a murderer? Smashed the car and murdered the occupants? Dragged them out and buried them? All here in Owly Vale? How exciting!' She jumped up and did a little dance around the office, followed by her barking dog.

Stevie sighed and turned back to her computer.

'Maybe,' said Cat, 'but let me finish, there's more. For a start, there's a wheelchair in the boot.' She stared at her colleagues. 'I mean, how can someone leave the scene of the crime if they leave their wheelchair behind?'

'Sounds like a stolen car,' said Miranda. 'Kids. Joyriders. They probably didn't even know there was a wheelchair in the boot and certainly nothing about the owner being a *person of interest.*'

Stevie looked up from the computer and stared at Cat. 'What sort of car was it?'

Miranda stuck out her tongue. 'You're asking the wrong person. Cat won't have a clue! What colour was it is more her line.'

'Ha,' said Cat, 'actually I do know! It was a Yaris, green colour. I'm not a detective for nothing.' She grinned happily.

'Really?' said Stevie, now staring at Cat with an abstracted look on her face. 'A Toyota Yaris? I think I'll just pop over and have a look. Back in a sec.'

And she left, sidestepping Blinkey, and leaving her colleagues staring at the void.

'What do you think that was all about?' asked Cat.

'Well, she was doing some investigation into that house, although why she would care about the type of car, except she always does, you know what she's like about machines. But you were saying something about Caroline feeling depressed.'

Cat frowned. 'You said that, not me. She's much better. She been allowed to keep Anthony as her therapist. There was talk about her having to change, and it made her desperately anxious.'

'Good,' said Miranda. 'Although I'm amazed she was allowed to keep the same one for so long.'

Cat was about to reply when they heard: 'Password!'

'It's me, Mummy.'

'Why do you call me Mummy? I'm not Egyptian.'

Stevie rushed back into the office so fast she collided with Miranda's dog. 'Just as I thought! It's a green Toyota Yaris. One nearly hit me last night on my way back from Heathrow, going at least sixty down those tiny roads. Pity I didn't note the registration, but it passed me so fast I didn't have time.'

'Oh dear,' said Cat, her eyes widening. 'How lucky it missed you, sweetheart.'

Miranda frowned. 'Last night? Must be the same car then… Sounds like joyriders buzzing through the country at top speed. Smashing into things and legging it. Did you see who was driving?'

Stevie shook her head. 'No, it was dark.'

Cat frowned and drank her coffee thoughtfully. 'It could be a coincidence, but it does seem unlikely there would be two Yarises speeding through the local area in the middle of the night. What time did the car pass you, Stevie?'

'I finished my shift at midnight, but I stayed to do a session in the simulator: I've got a test coming up and I liked to work through with an instructor a few days before. I left just before one a.m., the tunnel was closed so I was diverted and would have been on the Lea Coach Road fifty minutes later. If I turned off the A3 at quarter to two, I would be at the Billington turn twenty minutes later, so say just after two a.m. That's where it nearly hit me.'

Cat nodded thoughtfully. 'And Billington to Owly Vale would take you ten minutes?'

'Less, around seven usually, but on this occasion there was a deer on the road, or rather what I thought was a deer that had been hit by a car. I thought it had been hit by the Yaris.'

'Had it?' asked Cat.

'No. And it wasn't a deer but a man.'

'What? The joyrider had hit a man,' said Miranda, sitting down again, 'that makes it much more serious. No wonder the police were there.'

Stevie frowned. 'No, it wasn't like that. He wasn't hurt, at least I don't think so. He got up and ran towards me crying and yelling, I thought he was going to attack me. But instead, he sunk down by my door whimpering: he kept saying, "You are alive, you are alive!"'

'Weird,' said Miranda, while Cat frowned and looked into her cup.

'Before I could fathom what was happening,' Stevie said, 'a young woman came out of the bushes screaming. She ran up to the old man and put her arms around him, comforting him like he was a child. She kept saying soothing things to him like, "she's alive" and "that's good, isn't it" and so forth.'

'Did she say anything to you?' asked Miranda.

'Only what a bad corner it was and that I should drive slowly round it. And then she lead him away.'

'At least he wasn't hurt,' said Cat. 'So then what happened?'

'I drove home. I did pass Wild Garlic, but there was no sign of a Yaris in the garden at two fifteen.'

Cat bit her lip. 'I wonder where the Yaris went between two fifteen and three a.m.?'

Miranda spread her arms. 'More wild driving perhaps? Did he run out of fuel, do you think? That why he ended up in Wild Garlic?'

Stevie moved back to the computer.

'Why are you investigating the history of Wild Garlic, anyway, Stevie?' asked Cat.

'Oh, yes. I was about to tell Miri when you arrived. The freeholder of the house came over early this morning. He wants to employ us to find out why it won't sell. He's agreed to our terms, signed the contract, and paid the deposit.'

'Ah,' said Miranda, her voice lyrical, 'so, he's committed to the agency that finds out the reality behind what seems to be true.'

Cat nodded, then her phone rang, the *Ghostbuster*'s tune cutting through their conversation. 'Hello, darling. What? Really? Wow! That was quick. Right, OK, let me know if anything arises.'

She turned to the others, snapping her phone cover shut. 'That was Frank,' she said, adding unnecessarily, '*my boyfriend*. He's joined a group of fit young men rounded up to look for the owner of the car.'

'Really? Why?' said Miranda. 'I mean... if they think it's a joyrider, the owner's probably at home trying to buy another wheelchair on eBay.'

Cat shook her head. 'Frank doesn't know. He was merely asked to join the search. They're looking for a woman and she may not be alive. And, they were told to look out for a homeless man who has been hanging around Billington. He might be dangerous.'

The girls looked at each other.

'A homeless man!' said Miranda. 'Like that one I found here all those years ago? He wasn't dangerous at all. I felt rather protective. I remember I warned him to be careful.'

Stevie frowned. 'How long ago?'

'Um. Maybe fourteen or fifteen years.'

Stevie snorted. 'I'll check the internet but I think the average lifespan of a man on the streets is about forty-five, so I imagine the time on the streets itself must be about five years, tops! Pretty unlikely to be the same homeless man after all this time.

I think it's more likely to be the man lying in the road. The one I nearly hit. He was pretty dishevelled. Easily could be homeless.'

'Yes,' said Miranda, 'and no.' She pinched her chin thoughtfully. 'Talking of homes, we'd better go and look at Wild Garlic soon since we've got to find out why it won't sell.

Maybe our super-sleuthing noses will be able to tell something all the estate agents have failed to find out. I'll book an appointment to visit the *Doghouse* for tomorrow. Who's coming with me?'

'I'll look it up on Rightmove,' said Stevie, turning back to the screen.

'I'm coming,' said Cat enthusiastically. 'I love looking at houses.'

CHAPTER 4

FRANK THE LIVERPUDLIAN DETECTIVE

When Cat got home, Frank and his two Labradors had returned from the search and he was cooking, closely watched by his two friends.

'Alright, babe,' he said cheerfully. 'Welcome to the sleuth house. I'm the detective now, next time you go *geggin* in I'll be way ahead!'

Frank's determinedly Liverpudlian phrases always made Cat crack up, but she pressed her lips together and kept her voice serious. 'We are not being nosy—or geggin in, as you say. We are an important detective agency with a history of success. So there!' she added, ruining the effect.

Frank blew her a kiss. 'OK, don't get a *cob on*! I've got news for you and you're going to be calling me boss.'

She sighed. 'OK, OK, never mind the jokes; tell me the news.'

'You would've been proud of me, right proud. We went out to look for this lost lady and they'd only given us two bizzies to help in the search. One of them was a sergeant; the man in charge. So, Agent Frank and his dogs were in there. He saw what fine detectives I and my two friends were and asked if we were good at scenting.'

Cat looked at the two fat Labradors now lounging on the sofa and raised an eyebrow.

'And you said?'

'Well, I told him the truth, they were like bloodhounds and could follow any scent to a dead squirrel.'

Cat snorted. 'Bet he was impressed.'

Frank blew her a kiss. 'Well, as it happened, he'd been to one of my gigs and he loved my style. Anyway, long story short, he told me about the car.'

Cat cocked her head. 'What about the car?'

'The bizzies have been chocker with joyriding recently and wanted an arrest, so they brought forensics in to do a fingerprint search on the car, and guess what?'

'What?'

'No fingerprints at all. None, *nada*!'

'None? How odd. You mean, not even the owner's?'

'Nope, nothing. Wiped. Steering wheel, the strange adapted driving arrangement it's got for accelerator and brake, all clean. No prints.'

Cat frowned. 'But why? Why would a joyrider—some teenage boy out for a thrill—do that? They're not cold, calculating fingerprint-hiders. What do the police think?'

'The DS said they were keeping an open mind. That's bizzi-speak for got another idea.'

'Like what?'

'Patience. Do you interrupt like this when you're interviewing?'

Cat laughed. 'Sorry.'

He kissed her, and she had the opportunity to ask another question. 'Did you find the owner?'

'Yes,' said Frank, shaking his head mournfully. He

returned to chopping the onions, tears dripping down his face.

'Was she alive?'

'Wait! How can I build up the joke if you keep asking for the punchline first?'

Cat put her hand flat on her lips and opened her eyes wide. He went on.

'The DS and I left here, behind the dogs, sniffing the ground like super-sleuth adjuncts. The dogs that is.' He stopped but she flashed her eyes and waited for him to continue.

'So, he said it was likely some kind of domestic. "People",' Frank said, changing into a Sussex accent, '"never cease to shock me in the way they bring the police into their private disputes, as though we hadn't got enough to do with serious crime. Makes you wonder, don' it".' Back in his own accent Frank said: 'He had a right cob on! We'd walked the whole way along the Owly Vale part of the road, left the village and past the farmhouses where they keep all the cockerels that start yelling early in the morning—'

'Crowing,' put in Cat, unable to keep quiet any longer.

'Hah! Got yer!' He laughed, and she shook her head.

'So, we were almost in Billington when we saw what looked like a funny little crumpled sack on the side of the road. The verge is a bit wider there, because there's a long drainage ditch running into a stream at the bottom of the hill, and if you were going to stop for a kip that would be a good place to go.'

Cat rolled her eyes, fingers pressed to her lips.

'As we got closer, the crumpled sack lifted its head like a monster, except, and now I'm speaking as a highly trained detective and not as a man you understand, a very beautiful female monster with long blonde hair. Sort of thing to tempt Odysseus.'

'Ah,' said Cat.

'As we got up to the bird, we could see she had bruises all over her face and neck, and there was some blood on her right arm. It certainly looked as though she'd been in a fight, and I thought the DS's idea of a domestic seemed pretty sound.

"You OK?" he asked back in a Sussex accent. "Are you Rebecca Finlater?"

Frank put on a West End London accent. "She's my sister. The car is registered in her name, but I drive it." That seemed kind of odd to me.'

Cat moued. 'As long as she's on the insurance it wouldn't matter. You drive my car.'

'Yes, but, I dunno. Anyway, at that point the bird was keen to tell her story. She said: "I gave a homeless man a lift. He was hitchhiking. I often pick up homeless. They usually make the journey more fun, they have great stories, but this guy was a git! And drunk. I hadn't noticed the alcohol smell over the other smells.

We hadn't gone far before he asked me to stop. I thought he was going to get out, but he leant over and punched me in the face, then he opened my door and pushed me out of the car. I was lucky I wasn't more hurt! He hopped into my seat and drove away fast, the brute!"

"I see",' said Frank, now in the Sussex accent, '"did you know the man?"'

Back to the London accent. '"I might if I saw him again, but there wasn't anything special about him. Except the smell!"

'The DS shook his head and asked if she had a phone. She said she had but had left it at home.'

'Really?' said Cat, her voice riven with suspicion.

'Really what? You do.'

'Yes, but I'm not paralysed. Besides, who hitchhikes in the middle of the night?'

'Party goer,' said Frank, getting the marinated chicken out of the fridge, putting the onions on top of the potatoes, and grating some cheese. He put on the oven. 'Someone who had too many bevvies.'

'Also, how could a hitchhiker jump in and just drive away in an adapted car? How did he know how to use the controls? And how did she know he was homeless?'

'Dinner will be about eight, all right?'

'Lovely. What did your DS say about that?'

'About the cooking? I think his wife does that.'

'Funny man, not! So, what happened to the so-called homeless hitchhiker? Weren't you supposed to be looking for him too?'

'No idea. Unless you think they mean the owner of Wild Garlic. That man is a right blert. He passed me the other day wearing the sort of clobber you'd be embarrassed to be gardening in and when I asked him where he was going, he said he'd been invited to the palace and was off to see the Queen.'

'Hmm,' said Cat, 'odd, maybe that's why he's a person of interest. So the police think it's a domestic after all?'

'Yes, my friendly plod said his lips were sealed, but, as I'd been helpful and all in confidence, that he thought the woman was driving a boyfriend. He reckoned they probably had a row, he hit her, she fell out the car and he drove it off. But it's not an easy thing to drive an adapted car if you're not used to it, and hence why he ended up in the garden at Wild Garlic. Probably took her phone as well... I reckon he wasn't taking this very seriously.'

Cat got a bottle of wine out of the fridge and waved it, saying in a phoney Liverpudlian accent, 'Hey, Frank, fancy a bevvy?'

Frank snorted. 'Betcha!'

'I'll ask the girls tomorrow what they think. It certainly looks a bit suspicious to me. What did they do with the woman?'

'Took her home. She was very cold. They were going to ask her some questions but apparently the DS said it wasn't worth going all the way to Worthing to interview her, and the local cop-shop is being refurbished.'

'Refurbished?'

'Yes, he gave me to understand it was turning into more of a PR station than a hard-nosed police place. They don't have cells or anything there.'

Cat sighed. 'No wonder the world needs amateur sleuths.'

'Reason not the need...'

'OK, King Lear, what else did you discover? Did you talk to the woman?'

'I tried to, when I helped the DS put her in the panda car, but she didn't say a word once we started lifting.'

'Perhaps she was shocked,' said Cat, 'especially if she'd had a row with a boyfriend.

Poor thing. Incidentally, Stevie thinks she recognised the car?'

'How come?'

'Last night, on the way home from Heathrow, she was passed by a green Yaris going a top speed and shortly afterwards saw a man lying in the road. She thought the Yaris might have hit him.'

Frank raised his eyebrows. 'No wonder the driver wanted to ditch the car, manslaughter as well as theft!'

'No, the man got up. He was crying but it was to do with something else ... Stevie said it was something to do with a past accident or possibly more than one ... and then a girl came and took him home.'

Frank raised an eyebrow. 'Ever thought of performing confusing comedy? You'd be a star.'

'Ha, ha. My Watson!'

'Watson, indeed,' said Frank, miming placing a deerstalker on his head. 'And now for the pièce de résistance...'

'What? A delicious pudding!'

'No. You and your stomach. I took a picture of the lovely lady.'

Cat gave an exaggerated frown. 'Why? Apart from her beauty, that is.'

'Ha,' said Frank, pouting seductively, 'lucky I'm a quick thinker! It is evidence, my lovely. My Super-Watson brain is super-intuitive.'

Cat laughed and kissed him. 'Oh yeah. Well I'll WhatsApp it to the girls and we'll discuss it tomorrow, but now for dinner. I'm starving.'

CHAPTER 5
TASTING THE GARLIC

The house on the corner of Owly Vale village was an ordinary 1980s cottage, the only unusual feature being the collapsed wall, which was now shored up with wood and plastered with safety notices. A wicket gate, with Wild Garlic emblazoned on it, leant against the crashed wall, and a pebbled path led up to the door. As they walked in, they were assaulted by the strong smell of the growing garlic, forcing its way up through the gravel.

Cat leant down and breathed deeply. 'I love that smell. Reminds me of wonderful holidays in France when the children were young. Staying with my mother when Charlie was still alive. She said I was an awful cook, so she did everything and she was superb. Local wine. Lazy days in the sunshine for the first time in my life.'

She realised she was crying and hastily brushed away her tears. Silly to try and recall a past now so long gone. Particularly now she had Frank, who was both closer to her own age and to her own temperament, and her children were leading happy, fulfilling lives: sort of!

They met the estate agent outside the door of the property. A young man from a small, local agency, he danced towards them with the large bunch of keys in his hand, his voice singing a welcome. He said nothing about the fallen wall. Perhaps he hoped they hadn't noticed.

'Hi, I'm Jasper, you must be Miranda, and, er, is this your mother?'

'Yes,' said Miranda, before Cat could speak. 'Mummy's thinking of getting rid of me at last. She's buying me a house.'

'Welcome, both. What a nice mother you must be.' He laughed ingratiatingly. 'Wish my mother would buy me a house.'

He went ahead and Cat twisted her head to glare at Miranda who whispered, blinking innocently, 'Ssh, *Mummy*! Don't make such a fuss.'

Jasper unlocked the door, pointing out the pretty garden but still ignoring the signs of the crash.

Miranda walked in behind him, but Cat stopped, suddenly overwhelmed by an overpowering sadness. As she stood there a heavy weight descended on her shoulders making it an effort to move forwards. Breathing deeply, she forced one leg after the other until she got into the house.

Miranda and Jasper were already in the front room, chatting away about children. Jasper had a daughter the same age as Miranda's daughter Peta. As Cat walked in, Miranda noticed the drawings on the wall. 'Oh!' she said. 'How old are these children? What an odd drawing.'

Cat looked where she indicated and saw a picture of a family, except it was a family separated by a wall, the father one side, the mother and two children the other.

Jasper nodded. 'Yes, they are in the midst of a divorce, and I believe it's not amicable.'

'Is that why they are moving?'

'Yes.'

'I've been looking on Rightmove,' said Miranda, almost truthfully, since it was Stevie who'd looked, not her. 'It does seem to have had rather a lot of tenants in the last few years.'

'Yes.' Jasper nodded his head, smiling happily. 'Just unlucky, I guess. Like this divorce. They moved in eighteen months ago, ready to start a new life with the kids. They moved down from Manchester, but now they are splitting and she's taking the kids back to Manchester. He's staying here, but he wants a smaller house. He's got a brilliant job. Apparently, she missed her family.'

'So, the picture ought to be a road dividing them, not a wall,' said Cat.

'Yes, right, right, very clever,' said Jasper, his gaze dropping to his appointment list while his mouth continued to smile. 'Shall we see the rest of the house?'

As they trailed through the kitchen, bathrooms, bedrooms and so forth, none of which were anything unusual, Cat felt fine, if a little tired, until they entered the attic bedroom.

'This is rather clever,' said Jasper, opening what appeared to be a cupboard door in the furthest wall. 'See, inside is the en-suite bathroom ... rather neat ... and this cupboard—Oh! Are you OK?'

Cat, stepping into the cleverly concealed bathroom as he opened the cupboard door, had suddenly shot forward and collapsed on the floor in front of him. She gave a muffled sob.

'Blimey! Has your mum had an attack?'

'Cat! Are you OK?'

Their voices sounded miles away. In their place was the

noise of rushing water. Cat had the strangest feeling she had fallen into a ditch. Water was seeping into her clothes. She was going to drown! She was trapped! She wanted to scream but nothing came out of her mouth.

'Cat! *ARE YOU OK*?'

The noise stopped and Cat's anxiety receded.

'Yes, yes, I'm fine.' Cat breathed deeply. She rolled over. She touched her clothes. They were dry. 'Must have tripped.'

Miranda and Jasper looked at the flat sill between the rooms, exchanged glances and said nothing. Miranda gave Cat her hand to help her up.

Leaving the house Cat felt her spirits lift; it was a beautiful day.

As Jasper drove off to his next appointment, Miranda looked questioningly at Cat. 'What happened? How could you trip over a flat surface?'

'I don't know. I felt … it felt … honestly, Miranda, something awful happened in that house.'

Miranda stared at her. 'You mean something more awful than a car crashing through the wall into the garden?'

Cat nodded. 'Did you feel anything?'

'Sorry, no. But, if I was really thinking of buying a house, this one would not be on the list. It was damp.'

Cat bit her lip. Stevie would be even less credulous. Cat knew she was on her own with this one.

'But,' Miranda added in her child-friendly voice, 'you may just be more sensitive than me. I'm not much of a feng shui-type person. You did go down like a blow to the head.'

'Neck.'

'What?'

'It was a blow to the neck, as though I was caught in a car with a stuck seat belt and sinking into water. You know, like a ditch. Perhaps there was a ditch here once, before the house was built.'

Miranda twisted her mouth. 'Ah. Yes. How odd. A ditch? I know I said our super-sleuthing noses might find something special but I hadn't thought we'd become ghost hunters.'

Although Miranda kept her eyes still, disbelief was written there as clearly as if she'd rolled them round their sockets. 'Do you think someone died here?' she asked sweetly. 'Their ghost is trying to tell us what happened?'

Cat nibbled her lip. This wasn't the first time she'd had a sudden sixth sense, but, as a child she'd learnt to keep it quiet since adults usually thought you were telling lies.

Stevie, when told about the house visit, was even more forthright. 'Carbon monoxide.'

'What?'

'Carbon monoxide. It's very common in empty houses. Gas leaks are usually the cause. If you were really going to buy the property, I'd suggest you had it tested.'

'But what does it do?' asked Cat, refraining from pointing out Owly Vale did not have mains gas.

'There are a range of symptoms, but usually feelings of fatigue, even to the extent of falling asleep. You can feel cold, occasionally you faint.'

'But Miranda wasn't affected at all, or the estate agent. Just me.'

Stevie shrugged. 'Some people are more sensitive than others. For example, smokers tend to be less immediately affected but with worse long-term results.'

'How do you know?' asked Miranda. 'You haven't had time to make love to Terry Terminal since we told you.'

'Ha, ha. I've had it. You remember when I was employed to bring a twin-engine plane back from Florida and fly it across the Atlantic to the UK? Terrible company that didn't give me enough money for lodgings, so I had to sleep in the plane?'

'Sort of.' Miranda looked down at the dog and avoided Stevie's intense look. Stevie had so many flying stories.

'OK, well, anyway, I got stuck in Wabush, in Labrador. Weather turned nasty and we had three days of constant snow. I wasn't going anywhere in that.

'Since I had nothing to do, I ran up the engine to keep it warm. I taxied around the airport, and I started to feel this pressure on me ... like a weight ... and tiredness. It was difficult to keep my eyes open. I could hardly taxi back to the hangar. But when I got back, I had the engineers check the exhaust and I had a leak: carbon monoxide. Once it was fixed, no more spooks!'

Cat smiled in a pained way that lifted her upper lip and showed her teeth.

'Look, Cat,' said Stevie, facepalming, 'if you think something dreadful happened in the house, ask around about a ghost story, or get Miranda to ask Pete Drayton. After all, he built the place. But, meanwhile, since Clive Creamer has paid the deposit for our work, we need to find out everything we can about the disappearing tenants and failed house sales. I'll have a look at all the purchasing transactions and see if I can find anything unusual.'

'OK,' said Miranda. 'I'll go and ask Pete again. I think we should sign him up for the agency as a freelancer. He is our chief go-to in every case!'

'And,' said Cat, 'I'll go and chat to a priest.'

The other two exchanged glances. Cat had been an altar cleaner in her youth; in her generation it was the girl's version of an altar boy in the Catholic Church. Cat smiled naughtily.

'The first tenant was a vicar. Apparently, the vicarage was being done up after the last incumbent, and he rented the house for six months.'

'Well,' said Miranda, 'if anyone is going to have felt a ghost it must be a man of the spirits.'

Cat scowled at her. 'Is that what you atheists think vicars are? Men of the spirits?'

Miranda's eyes shot open. The nearest her family ever got to churches was as tourists when visiting her father's relatives in Poland. 'Well, yes.'

Cat sighed. 'Let's just call him a man of the cloth, shall we?'

Stevie and Miranda exchanged glances. Cat was a bit ferocious on the subject of religion.

'So,' said Miranda, 'any news on Clive Creamer's wicked past yet?'

'Sort of,' said Stevie. 'I did find he has an ASBO against his name for harassing the Queen.'

'What? Are you serious? *The* Queen? Not Queen the pop group or…?'

'Yes, the citation said he had sent her over one hundred letters and phoned Buck House almost as many times.'

'Come on. So, he's a nutter—there must be plenty of them around without becoming a person of interest. Anything else?'

Stevie shrugged. 'I'll keep looking.'

'Meanwhile,' said Miranda, trying not to smile at Cat, 'I'll go ghost hunting in the pub.'

CHAPTER 6

OWLY VALE'S FINEST BUILD: THE PUB

Miranda met Pete Drayton in the Owly Vale pub. He preferred meeting in one of *Drayton's finest builds*, the Cock and Pheasant, but they were refurbishing at present and wouldn't reopen until next week. It made more sense to Miranda to meet in the same village as the haunted house anyway.

'Funny you should ask about that house,' said Pete. 'It's always been a bad 'un.'

He took a gulp of his beer. 'It were a dreadful house.'

'Really? How so?'

'It were built on a marsh, and it couldn't hold the warmth long enough for the concrete to set. It took twice as long as normal houses. Then there was problems with corrosion. And we found an underground well. The archaeology boys had to come over and they dated it way back. In the end we was allowed to continue. But it was always a struggle.'

'Oh, right.' Miranda took a gulp of her wine. Hardly relevant, was it? This was going to be another dead end.

'And then, of course, they found the stiff, and even more hold ups.'

He took a long draught of beer.

'*Stiff*? What? What stiff?'

Interviews, thought Miranda, were the weirdest things. One moment you were about to ask for another glass of wine to tide you over the boredom, next moment you were jumping with joy.

'Tell me! About this stiff?'

'Yeah. It were funny, really. I was just dropping Charleen, that's my youngest, back in the cottage she shared with her boyfriend; he's a chippy and a nice lad. They never married but they've got two lovely girls. I don't know what the young have got against making it legal ... Mind you, after the trouble we had with That Bitch, Anastasia, it's a pity my brother wasn't so sensible!'

He drank deeply and shook his head.

'Anyways, I was dropping her home after a night in the Cock and Pheasant over the other side of Chai, when we heard the sirens.

'"Rozzers!" I said, fucking amazed. "Rare as rocking horse shit in a village these days. Shall we follow them and see what's at? Better go on foot in case they get bored and want to solve another crime at the same time."'

He chuckled, stroking his chin.

'Charleen thought it was coming from the house we built. Wild Garlic, they named it. Too right! It stinks like a Frenchman's breakfast! As we walked over, half Owly Vale came too. It was probably one of the most exciting things to happen in the village since they pulled up the train line. People were flocking over to see what a policeman was doing in Owly Vale, like twitchers following an unusual bird.

'The freeholder arrived and opened the door, and a PC stopped the hordes going in. He was shoving that stripey crime tape they use everywhere. I couldn't help thinking it was lucky he had it with him and wondering if they always carry that sort of thing, just in case. You know, the way I always have my tools to hand.

'Well, anyway, my Charleen, she always was a nosy bint. She eased her way around to the back and peered in the window.

'Inside, slumped against the living room table, she saw a huge sack. As she moved to a closer window, she saw it was a dead body. She got the back door open and rushed over to have a look. The smell, she said, was graphic!

'The policeman jumped out of nowhere, right over the top he was. Mind you, he was clearly way out of his depth and people were nosy as hell, pushing up against the tape left and right. Trying to see what was what.

'He yelled at her. "Get out at once, you are destroying evidence!"

'Charleen beetled out the back and saw the PC putting up more tape to prevent people walking around her way. He muttered as he moved, something about villages being full of savages!'

Pete laughed and drank some more beer. 'Poor old copper, lived in Worthing and Owly Vale seemed to him like the depths of darkest Africa!'

He took some pork scratchings.

'When was this?' asked Miranda, amazed there should be a local policeman any time after the 1970s.

'2007 or 8. Charleen's Angie was born a year later and she's eleven now, or is she fourteen? They grow up so quick. Around then, anyhow.'

He knocked back some more beer and went on talking

but Miranda stopped listening. Why didn't she know about this? They moved into the village in 2006; how could she have missed such an event? And then it hit her: it must have been 2008.

2008 was the year her baby died.

She and Phillip had been so pleased when she got pregnant again, twelve years after Poppy was born. A beautiful little boy, but then at just a few months old he died: cot death. She was devastated, hardly left the house, Phillip started working even harder than ever, and Poppy refused to stay in this 'house of doom' and went to live with her grandmother and Agata in London.

Miranda shook herself hard and had a long gulp of her wine. That was then, she told herself, she'd had two more children since then and now had a detective agency and a client. Even though she still thought about the little boy she mustn't allow herself to dwell on the past. If she went there the accumulation of trauma would knock her over, maybe for ever. She forced herself to listen to what Pete was saying.

'Well, nosy old Charleen asks the gathering crowd what happened. Roderick, you know him? Sits at the back of the bar with his mongrel and talks to anyone who will listen. Blah. Blah. Blah. He told us he'd heard a noise in the empty house and reported it.

'"How come the police got here so fast?" asked Char.

'Roderick laughed. "Oh, that's Paul. He's Willow's friend and was at her house on the Green when the call came through, so he came over ASAP. Took him all of half a minute to drive over but must have been fun playing the siren. Bet he doesn't get to do that often!"

'Later I had a word with Paul, the copper. Said it was a drunk. Strong smell of alcohol and vomit in the house, empty bottles all round. Vomit all down his beard and chest (sorry, Miri), completely dried but stuck to his jumper like a bib. Probably choked on it. Not a nice way to die. There was blood on his head, too, probably hit his head on the table when he fell.

'You know, they never found the name of the stiff. But,' he added, 'there was a couple of funny things, Cha told me. The stiff had one of those nicotine e-cigarettes in his hand. I always thought it was a bit sad if you were giving up smoking and you dropped down dead that your last gasp wasn't the real thing. But you lot, nowadays, you all like replacements, don't you!'

Miranda smiled and had another drink.

'An e-cigarette, eh? What is that replacing?' He winked wickedly.

'And the other thing?'

'Eh?'

'You said there were two things.'

'Oh yeah. They found the stiff's clothes were wet, as though someone was trying to drown him!'

'But,' said Miranda, 'do you mean he wasn't alone when he died? Or he poured water over himself?'

Pete shrugged. 'Who knows. But as I said, it was a damp house!'

CHAPTER 7

BLINKEY LEARNS TO PLAY BRIDGE

As Miranda headed through Stevie's house to the office, she noticed the dining room door was open and Blinkey was pouring wine into various glasses laid out round the table. Glad to avoid today's password hunt, she hurried on by. Stevie was in the office.

'Blinkey having a lunch party?'

Stevie didn't look up from the computer. 'Three friends, and their carer, coming over to play bridge.'

'Play bridge? Dementia bridge?'

'Yes, my mother thought she'd learn. Apparently, someone told her it stops dementia. One of the women has played and she thought she'd teach her. No idea about the other two, but the carer seemed on for it.'

'Wow,' said Miranda. She looked out the window. 'Looks like they're arriving.'

Stevie sighed and giving up her work joined Miranda at the window. Three elderly women were climbing out of an equally elderly Rover. One woman had a stick, which she was using to draw pictures in the air, rather than for walking.

'Will you let them in, please, Miranda?' said Stevie. 'I just want to finish something here.'

'No problem,' said Miranda, hurrying to the door. Anything for a bit of social interaction; Phillip was constantly working, and the children were at school. Made her long for the pandemic again. She threw open the door.

'Welcome! Come in.'

The carer looked rather surprised. 'Oh,' she said, 'I was warned to expect a password session.'

Miranda wondered if she was disappointed. 'Blinkey's in the dining room, pouring out wine'—she giggled—'again. She's been doing it for the last few days, but her carer kept pouring it away.'

The woman sighed sympathetically. 'Come on, girls, in you come. Careful with that stick, Annie.'

Annie paraded into the room, the stick held out in front of her like a machete cutting corn. 'Careful! Annie!'

'What a pretty stick,' said Miranda admiringly, noticing the engraved silver head.

Annie immediately cuddled it to her. 'I found it,' she said. 'Finders keepers.'

The carer said quietly, 'Show us what it does, Annie.' To Miranda she added, 'You'll like this, it's amazing.'

Annie turned the knob on top of the stick and the inside shot out, doubling it in length. On the bottom was a small knife.

'Oh!' said the carer putting out her hands to grab the stick. Then stepping back as Annie turned towards her defensively. 'I didn't know about the knife. I just thought doubling...'

'Watch that,' said Stevie, coming into the hall from the office. 'I think you need to put something on the end. You could hurt someone with that.' She smiled at Annie and took the end of the stick in her hand, lifting it gently. 'Um, I could get a cork and fix it on safely, so although you might bruise someone with that, you won't cut them.'

'Thanks,' said the carer, smiling at Stevie. 'You're good; she wouldn't let me touch it. She found it yesterday on a walk, and it's been her constant companion since then.'

Miranda looked at Stevie, but she was busy attaching the cork and missed Miranda's glance.

'Where did she find it?' asked Miranda.

'Just outside the village.'

Miranda moued. 'While they're playing bridge, will you show me where she found it?'

'Sure, it's not far away. We usually walk up to Billington and back on a sunny day. Takes about half an hour, which is enough for the others, although Annie's a good walker.'

Half an hour later, Miranda, her dog and the carer walked up the lane towards Billington.

'We walk along the road, partly because it's easier for the girls, but also so I can get help if something happens or it rains. They are wonderful at the home, come out at once if you call for help. Best place I've ever worked. Mind you, the old girls, or their families, pay through the nose.'

She stopped and indicated the drainage ditch. 'This is where she found the stick. We're walking a lot faster than the girls do.'

Miranda nodded. The ditch was slightly back from the road, and she murmured that she was surprised Annie had found the stick in the long grass that covered it.

'Yes,' said the carer, 'but she walks ahead of the others and then stops and noses around. You should see some of the things she brings back. This one was rather a find. I do hope she doesn't have to give it up to the owner. She's very attached to it and it's a lot cleaner than the pieces of flint or pottery she usually gets.'

Miranda laughed. 'Was she an archaeologist before she got dementia?'

The carer shrugged. 'No idea. Nice one, though. I'll ask her daughter when she visits. It would fit.'

Miranda took pictures of the site and the local area and trees. Her phone told her the distance from Owly Vale.

'Good things, these phones,' said the carer. 'You doing this for any reason?'

Miranda pursed her lips. 'I'm not sure; put it down to instinct. Do you remember the car that crashed into Wild Garlic, the house on the corner of Owly Vale?'

'Do I! We made several trips there. Annie loved it, she insisted on visiting often until they took the car away.'

'Well, I just have a feeling there is a connection between this stick, the car and the house. I can't explain why.'

The carer laughed. 'You'd better have a look at the CCTV. There's a village one. We find it really useful when the residents go wandering.'

'Thank you,' said Miranda. 'I had no idea.'

'Yes, they put it in in 2008. Up until then there was a lot of petty vandalism, which pretty much stopped once the camera was in place.'

CHAPTER 8

WILD GARLIC'S GHOSTLY HISTORY

'So,' said Stevie, 'I've been looking into the background of Wild Garlic, the house, and, interestingly, the freehold of the land originated from the Domesday Book of 1086.'

'Oh,' said the other two, exchanging glances. Miranda stifled a yawn and signalled her dog to come over and get brushed, while Cat put on the coffee.

'And,' said Miranda, 'this is relevant to Clive Creamer's ASBO, how?'

'Yes,' continued Stevie doggedly, compressing her lips like her Domesday forebears praying in church. 'And the Magna Carta ensures that a person cannot be *"disseised of his Freehold"* without *"lawful judgment of his Peers, or by the Law of the Land."*'

'Oh, right,' said Miranda, pulling a couple of ticks off the dog, squashing them and putting them in the bin. 'Well, who knew?'

'But, in the Middle Ages, rich barons who held the land wanted to get every groat out of it, so they created a leasing system whereby the serfs or villeins would lease a portion of land and give a part of what they grew to the landlords who owned the land proper. Later, in the eighteen hundreds, there was less need for food and so landlords or freeholders started leasing out property for lengths of time, ninety-nine years for example. That way they got money in and no costs, while the tenant had to give the land back eventually. Clever, eh?'

'Fascinating,' said Cat, handing around the coffees. 'And this is relevant to the dead body in the house or Clive Creamer's ASBO in what way?'

'Hang on,' said Stevie, 'dead body investigation is a side-line. Clive's paying us to find out why the house won't sell. And you do know there were one hundred and fifty unidentified bodies in 2008 alone? Think how many there must have been since then.'

Miranda rolled her eyes. 'And *you* don't think that having a dead body in the house, and an unsolved crime, is enough reason for the house to become a pariah? Let alone a visiting car in the garden.'

Cat muttered, 'how can a dead man be a sideline?'

'So,' said Stevie, ignoring them, 'it seems the village was on the edge of a forest in the mediaeval era and the King hunted here. One of his ministers was killed hunting by the local landlord. Who was then sent to the tower. And who do you think the landlord was?'

The girls shrugged.

'Only Clive Creamer's ancestor!'

'Oh!' said Miranda, rolling her eyes. 'No wonder he has an ASBO!'

Cat laughed.

Stevie made a low noise. 'No, I didn't mean...'

'Perhaps,' said Cat, 'the homeless man's ancestor was

killed by Clive Creamer's ancestor, and that's why he's haunting the house and why it can't be sold.'

Stevie sighed. 'Ha, ha,' she said, reluctantly giving up her history. 'OK. I'll ring the police records in Brighton. Find out if they've still got the body. By the way, heard any more about the search for the ghostly hitchhiker?'

'Nothing,' said Cat. 'Perhaps we should ask Miranda's sister. How is her police job going?'

'Great,' said Miranda. 'I think she's on a training course at the moment—she wants to be a detective—but I'll see what she can find out. By the way, Stevie, did you manage to get hold of the village CCTV?'

'I did,' said Stevie, 'and I saw the car drive into the village careering wildly, but then when it gets to Wild Garlic it goes out of the picture. The car is out of sight of the cameras.'

'I wonder if he knew that,' said Cat, 'or was just lucky.'

Next day, Stevie came back with the news that the homeless man was indeed still in the hospital and there was still no identification. However, she had discovered that the doctor who did the examination was not only a pilot but also flew from Goodwood. So, she had flown over there in her Tiger Moth and met him for a coffee.

'He was so helpful,' she said. 'There really should be more pilots in the world. It would solve so many problems.'

Miranda rolled her eyes. 'What did he say? Once you got off the subject of ancient aircraft and on to the point?'

Stevie wrinkled her nose at Miranda. 'Well, at first he was a bit edgy, didn't want to admit the body was still in the hospital.' She raised her eyebrows at her colleagues, smiling slightly. 'Turns out that they'd been using him in the physio school for anatomy lessons. Bit of a grey area he said, but if I could not spread it around it would be appreciated!'

'Hmm.'

'Anyway, he said there were past injuries to the medulla, which indicated he might have had a job that included high "G" manoeuvres, so there was a good chance our John Smith was an aerobatic pilot or a diver. But although the police had made some investigation in that direction, they found nothing, and the doctor wasn't sure how seriously they were taking it. There was also an unexpected puncture mark in the groin, which would indicate drugs, but none were found in the system at the time of examination.' His arms and legs, the doctor had told Stevie, had no signs of previous puncture marks so they had ruled out drug use.

'A pilot?' said Miranda. 'The homeless man I found ... he made some joke? I can't remember exactly what but something about being my pilot. Should I go and have a look at him? He might be the same man.'

Cat and Stevie glanced at each other. 'Sure,' said Stevie shrugging, 'can't see why not. I'll call the mortuary and let you know. But you don't *actually know* that man's name, do you?'

'What about DNA?' asked Miranda, ignoring that irrelevance: a trip to the mortuary was exciting.

'They took some, and it's preserved, but they couldn't find any matches with the men reported missing at that time.'

'Oh, right,' said Miranda. 'So, presumably, he wasn't reported missing.'

'Isn't that odd,' said Cat, 'that no one reported him missing?'

'You think?' said Stevie. 'When I walked out of my parents' home no one reported me missing.'

'True.'

'Yes. Lots of people don't want to get the police involved, or just don't think about it. They assume, as my parents did, that I would come back in time.'

'Yes,' said Cat, 'and of course, in your case, they were right.'

However, as all three girls knew, Stevie would not have been all right if Cat's late husband, Charlie, hadn't been so impressed by her bullish spirit that he'd decided to support her. Clearly no one had cared about the late John Smith's spirit, bullish or otherwise.

'I was homeless, too,' Stevie reminded them. 'Living in my car.'

Cat nodded. Stevie had loving but old-fashioned parents, who wanted her to live her life their way but not the way she chose for herself. They'd completely opposed her desire to be a pilot.

'It all could have been very different,' said Stevie. 'There really is a fine line between living a full life and having no life at all.'

She got up the pictures of John Smith the records office had sent.

'Sad,' Stevie said. 'He doesn't look super old. Perhaps fifty-five-ish? Could be younger.'

'That might be the man,' said Miranda guardedly, 'but I still think I'd better visit the mortuary.'

Cat looked over Stevie's shoulder. 'Yes. Drinking makes you look older. I've noticed excessive drinking makes your face swell, as though it was holding liquid.'

Miranda grimaced, cautiously prodding her own face to see if it was swelling.

Cat laughed. 'Oh, come on, Miranda. You do drink too much, but not to this level. This guy probably drank until he passed out every day. You have a job. A full life.' Her eyes filled with tears. 'It is so sad. Especially when you hear that the injuries point to him once having had an exciting job.'

She stared sadly at the pictures, then frowned. 'So, Stevie, was the doctor suggesting all airline pilots have medulla damage?'

'Oh, no,' said Stevie. 'That would be caused by aerobatics. He said John Smith must have done aerobatics, or else was in some kind of car crash that caused the injuries but never got treated.'

'Interesting,' said Miranda. 'Another car crash. Makes you wonder if they are all related.'

CHAPTER 9
THE JOY OF FACEBOOK

For the first week after posting the picture on Facebook, Stevie got no responses. But, after Miranda's visit to the morgue she focused on homeless sites.

'It is the same man,' Miranda said, although her colleagues made sceptical faces. 'OK, he's changed a bit by the formaldehyde, but you know I'm good with faces. I remember people. But why, why did he keep returning to Owly Vale? When I met him he couldn't wait to leave, to hitch a lift with Phillip away from the village.'

'No idea,' said Stevie, flicking away on the computer keys.

'Village vortex,' said Cat, getting out a doughnut.

Miranda rolled her eyes and tried to remember more about her homeless visitor. She took herself back to 2006 and their meeting in the wood behind Wild Garlic. Had he said something about Bognor or was it Brighton?

'Stevie,' she asked, 'is there an airfield at Brighton?'

Stevie looked up from the computer quickly, mouing. 'Yes, there is, it's called Shoreham. Do you think our homeless man might have had some connection there? I have some friends at the airfield I can ask, at least I could if we knew his name.'

Halfway through the following week Stevie got a message.

'Hello,' said the DM. 'Hope you're well. I'm Julie. I saw the picture on the homeless site. Looks like a guy who used to come to St Botolph's soup kitchen. I volunteered there from 2004 to 2006, when it closed, and then at another site until 2008. Give me a number and I'll call.'

Ten minutes later the girl, Julie, was on the phone. Her young voice sounding sad.

'I remember him,' she said. 'Awesome brain. I never understood why he was living on the street. He could've been somebody. Name was Neil.'

'Did he come to the centre often?' Stevie asked.

'Several times. Usually with a junkie, Robin, but he's dead now. Drug OD right there in the church.'

'Did you talk to him much? Neil, I mean.'

'Yes, a lot. He liked young women. He was charming. Funny. He said he was trying to get off the booze, and when he did, he said, he'd come and find me and take me out to dinner. I'd have liked that.'

'What did you talk about?'

'Books. He was the one who put me on to the book *Perfume* by Patrick Süskind. It always seemed funny to me, to be recommended *Perfume* by a man who oh my Lord needed it.' Her laugh sounded like a gurgle on the phone. 'Oddly, he usually smelt of garlic sausages.'

'Any idea what he used to do for a living, before he was homeless, I mean?'

'He said that he'd been a pilot. You can't always believe

what people living on the streets say, they often fantasize, or have mental problems, but he talked intimately about flying. He explained the principles of flight, of lift and drag, to me in simple terms. If he wasn't a pilot, he certainly knew a lot about it.'

'You remember him pretty well for someone you knew so long ago,' said Stevie sceptically.

Julie was quiet for so long Stevie wondered if they'd been cut off. Then she said, 'yeah, well, I left St B's not long after that to get married. Nuf to say it didn't work out and we parted, so I often think back to that time and wonder what happened to Neil.'

'Oh,' said Stevie, feeling her stomach tensing. 'I'm afraid he's dead.'

'Yeah,' said Julie so quietly Stevie could hardly hear her. 'I figured. When I saw your post, I thought I was going to be sick. I sent the message, hoping, but not believing, if you know what I mean.'

'I'm sorry,' said Stevie.

'Yes. I sort of wish ... maybe I could have helped him. I volunteered with the homeless for four years and I talked to a lot of people on the streets. There's always a story behind why they're there. Some stories are heartbreaking. Several men and women end up on the streets after a divorce makes them homeless. There used to be an ad which said:

Homelessness is only a paycheque away.

I often think of that.'

Stevie bit the inside of her cheek. She hadn't really thought about the effect of her post. She'd just wondered who he was, but, of course, he could have had friends, relations, people who would now feel guilty, hurt, upset. It should have occurred to her. But it hadn't.

'If I arrange it for you,' she asked, speaking gently,

'would you like to come in and see the body? See if you could identify him. I realise you are not a relation, but we haven't found anyone else.'

Julie made a strange noise. 'Oh. Well then, sure,' she said, and this time Stevie could hear the emotion rising in her voice.

* * *

Stevie waited for Julie in her car outside the hospital. She liked sitting in the car; that way you didn't have to talk to anyone. It wasn't that she didn't like people, she did, but she really couldn't understand why anyone would chat about the weather, their dogs, all sorts of things that nobody cared about. Why converse about them just to make human inter-action? It made no sense to her.

A girl who looked like the picture on Julie's FB page approached the entrance and Stevie jumped out.

'Hello? You Julie?'

'Yes. Stevie?'

'Yes.'

They went down the corridor to the vault without speak-ing. Stevie put in her passcode and the steel doors swung open. Behind the door a young assistant was waiting, and he went and fetched the body, leaving them with it and going to another part of the room where he could do other things while observing them.

'Could be,' said Julie, gagging at the smell of formalde-hyde. 'It could be Neil. It's a bit hard to tell now, especially with the discoloration.'

Stevie nodded. She knew people were often overcome by looking at bodies, but it didn't worry her at all. It was just a dead piece of meat.

However, when Julie saw the small collection of things sitting at the bottom of the body, a chain, shoes and a few odds and ends, his whole life's possessions, her body crumpled, and her eyes filled with tears.

'Ah!' she said. 'That's making it more likely, certainly. He always wore that chain around his neck. He said he'd been engaged three times, twice to the same girl, and that she gave him the chain.'

'Can you remember her name?'

'He didn't tell me. As I said, he was a very private person. He never said anything about his family or friends, only about books and aerodynamics and the like. That was the only time he said anything personal and then only because I asked about the chain.'

'Are we any wiser?' asked Cat when Stevie told her the story. 'We know he was called Neil, but not even a surname.'

'Soup kitchens don't usually like to ask for names, especially not surnames. Too revealing.'

'Still,' said Miranda, 'goes along with what the doctor said about stress injuries to his medulla. Sounds like he was a pilot … at least for a while.'

Stevie nodded. 'I'll investigate pilot sites. And I'll ask around at Shoreham if there was a Neil there, but don't hope too much, there might be lots of pilots called Neil.'

Cat sighed. 'So sad. A man who loved books and flying, dead from drink.'

'Don't look at me when you say that!' said Miranda. 'I hate flying!'

CHAPTER 10
CAPTAIN OF THE CRAFT

A few days later, Stevie received a Facebook message asking if there was an email address the writer could use to contact her. The result was an email from a man called Tim who said the pictures looked like his physics teacher back in the 1980s, Neil O'Banyon. He attached a rather fuzzy picture from his school magazine. It showed a man looking about twenty-four or twenty-five years old, with wide, rather red cheeks in a round face and short, curly blond hair. The redness of the cheeks and the presence of a moustache made Stevie wonder if he had once had a beard like their body. The accompanying piece said he had recently left London University, where he originally studied dentistry before changing to physics in his second year. He did a PGCE at King's College. This would be his first teaching post.

In the picture, the man looked healthy and hopeful: a man setting out on life with an exciting new career in teaching. If this was the same man as their homeless body, what could have happened to reduce him to this level?

· · ·

Stevie emailed Tim back, to see if he could remember anything else about the teacher.

'Thanks, Stevie. No, not much. He was a quiet guy, not like some of our teachers. Didn't say much. Never took assembly or anything. I can't remember a single thing about his classes, but I will ask around my school friends. Perhaps they can remember something. It was rather a long time ago.'

Noting it had been a grammar school, Stevie looked it up only to discover it had been changed to an academy in 2010. She contacted the school secretary, but although she had been employed by the original grammar school for its last three years and had lists of teachers, when asked to find a teacher who had worked there in the 1980s, the secretary laughed.

'I'm sorry, love. No chance of finding anything that far back. We have enough trouble finding records of people in the nineties, but the eighties? Lucky if they even kept the records.'

'Are you in contact with any teachers from then?' Stevie asked, looking for another angle.

'Sorry, no, but you could try Friends Reunited. If you know which school the guy was at, it's a great help.'

'Thanks,' said Stevie, wondering why she hadn't thought of that herself. Would it tell her any more about the dead man?

Amazingly, even though Google told her that Friends Reunited had 23 million members by the end of 2010, it had closed down in 2016. There were a variety of other sites where you could contact old school friends, but Neil O'Banyon was not on any of them.

'Underlines,' said Cat later, 'that he really was a very private man. Any other internet presence?'

'Nope. No sign of him anywhere.'

Cat nodded. 'Not really surprising if he was born in the sixties, like me. I don't either, or only for the agency.'

'But,' said Miranda, 'a lot of people in their sixties use LinkedIn. Have you tried that?'

Stevie nodded.

'Bear in mind,' said Cat, 'most homeless people don't have a computer!'

Stevie stared at her colleagues, her eyes blank. Hell on Earth!

The next day, as Stevie surfed through the internet, she found an entry on a site called PPRuNE. An aviation-related site, Stevie knew of it but, because its posts usually descended quickly into abuse, it never occurred to her to use it to find the lost man. The post read:

Anyone else think the picktur floating on Facebook looks like Neil O'Banyon? Is it? I remember him when he dated the Blonde Bint who wanted to be an airline pilot.

There was only one reply in the thread it said:

I suppose you mean me by the Blonde Bint. I AM an airline pilot: Captain. Amazed to be doubted.

The name of the posting woman was Amy Earhardt, which Stevie found extremely unhelpful. When she looked up

"Amy Earhardt pilot" there appeared to be about 100 claimants to the name both with the American and German spelling of Ehrhardt and several between the two.

It seemed liked a dead end, but then, a few days later Stevie was sent a message through Facebook from Amy Earhardt.

'Hi, can you email me on BloWoPil@gmail.com I've studied your FB post and I think I know the man you are looking for.'

Three days later they met in the café in One Tree Books in Petersfield.

Amy Earhardt, which apparently was her real name, was a BA pilot. She had long blonde hair neatly tied up in a bun. However, as Stevie arrived, she was busy pulling out the pins to release it. She shook her head and then plunged her hand into the hair, twisted it into a bunch and dropped it. Stevie, whose hair was short and restrained, watched, fascinated as Amy's hair billowed behind her. Stevie could imagine plenty of young men becoming obsessed by Amy. She had a little scar on her temple, which somehow added to her sense of allure.

'People didn't understand Neil,' Amy said, looking at Stevie angrily, as though she might be one of those nefarious people. 'They said I used him. That all I wanted to be a pilot and I made him help me up the ladder, but it wasn't true.'

She sipped her coffee. Even that, thought Stevie, was done elegantly and without the coarseness of the normal slurp-and-replace with spillings. Amy transferred her gaze to the staircase behind Stevie's head, staring at the descending shoppers.

'It's usually other people's hang-ups that cause their judgemental words,' she said. 'The reality was he wanted to help women become pilots. It was an obsession for him.'

She looked back at Stevie. 'I don't suppose you believe me, either. No one ever does.' The sharpness of her voice made Stevie suddenly feel guilty, as though Amy was right.

Stevie shook her head. 'Actually, I do believe you! Been there! If it wasn't for a friend's husband, I'd still be fighting my parents and trying to get enough money for training. I worked in a factory, I did deals and I got a free house from my friend Cat's husband. I know it is not easy to become a pilot for anyone, let alone a woman.'

Amy nodded, looking away, and then back at Stevie. 'We started going out when Neil was a private pilot, but it wasn't until he became an instructor that I could log the hours. He taught me for free.'

She sighed and spun her spoon across the table. 'He was the one who suggested I became a pilot. We met at a party and he started laughing at my name, saying I ought to be a pilot with that name. I didn't know what he was talking about, then he told me about Amy Johnson, amazing British pilot, and Amelia Earhart, legendary American pilot. I said I'd give it a try. And it was awesome. I was hooked.' She shrugged and stroked her hair.

'That's why everyone thinks I sponged off him, but I didn't, really, I didn't. He wouldn't take payment. Refused. He let me buy him drinks and food and even presents but nothing else.'

Stevie nodded. She was starting to like this Neil guy; he sounded sympathetic in a way she found few men were.

'After I got my pilot's licence, my basic commercial licence,' said Amy, 'he persuaded a school to take me on as a photographer, glider tower and general gofer pilot. They had a no women pilots rule before that, but he made it possible for me.'

'What!' said Stevie, clenching her fists on the table. 'No women pilots! Stupid school! Was that even legal?'

'Probably not. This was the late eighties, and life was much less regulated then. I doubt anyone asked. I don't suppose it was written; it just was ... well, you know.'

'So, you got engaged?'

'Yes,' said Amy, again fiddling with her hair, her eyes now following a woman buying a book. 'He was so kind. I'd never met anyone so interested in me, so willing to help me.'

'If he was so kind to you, why did you break off the engagement?'

Amy snorted and turned her attention back to Stevie with a sudden sharp swing. 'Drinking!'

She examined the end of her hair, shrugging. 'When he was sober, he was a lovely man, when he was drunk ... Look, he didn't do anything horrible, he didn't beat me or anything, but he just kept drinking until he collapsed. Not really the night out of choice, is it, to carry your fiancé home ready to mop up the inevitable vomit and wait until the hangover kicks in.'

'No. But you got engaged to him twice.'

Amy frowned at her. 'Who told you that?'

'A girl he met at St B's.'

'St B's? What? The down and out place in London? Did he end up there? On the streets? Oh shit! Poor Neil! I had no idea.'

Amy's eyes filled with tears, and Stevie thought they were probably genuine. 'That's awful. Poor darling. However awful he could be, it wasn't his fault.' She shook her head so her hair flew around her face. 'It's an illness ... did no one care enough...?'

She gave a deep sighed and wiped away the tears, carefully, so she didn't disturb her make-up.

'What about the father?' Amy said, sudden hope in her voice as though she could bring Neil back to life. 'I met him once. Bit of a cold fish, and his mother died years ago but his father could've...'

Stevie shook her head. 'Dunno.' It was the first time she'd heard of a father; they'd better investigate that angle.

Amy shook her whole body like a wet dog, but she dropped her hair and leant forward. 'OK. The first time, we broke up completely. I didn't want to see him anymore. He was part of my past life. I went to work for a charter company and later married the boss, Graham. Neil and I completely lost contact then. I didn't even hear of him or anything, although we had friends, well, colleagues really, in common.

'Then one day, when Graham and I were having a break, you know what I mean... We were on a marriage sabbatical, as it were. I was taking an Embraer to Lyon. The client was a freak. He kept trying it on, you know how they do, even in the air. Lots of money makes them think the pilot is theirs. I can deal with it, but it is irritating. He didn't stop even when we had landed. You know, blah blah, let me buy you a drink to thank you for keeping me alive. Oh, your skill is amazing ... to think I had a woman pilot ... blah, blah!

'I had got away from the client by saying I was meeting my boyfriend in a bar but then, of course, I had to go and find one. A bar, I mean.

'I left the hotel and found a smart-looking place where I hoped I wouldn't be hassled. I had just sat down at a small table in a window alcove, where I reckoned I'd be out of view, when I heard. "Well, hello. Do you come here often?"

'I looked up, furious, and was about to make a stinging

reply, when I saw it was Neil. He'd shaved off his beard, a good sign because when he was in a drinking mood he always let it grow.

'He said something like, "Well, ships in the night, eh?" That was clever because when we were both flying, we used to laugh about passing at thirty-thousand feet in the night and not knowing the other one was there. So near and so far.

'Anyway, he sat down, and we started catching up. He'd got a job with BA. He'd given up drinking completely. Done AA and all that. Got his medical back. He was totally clean and had been, he told me, for several years. And, well, you know, Neil was a sexy man, and so attentive.

'I thought wow, he's a changed man. He's going to be OK. Of course, we went to bed together that night. It was wild. It had been a while since I left Graham and I was ready for some fun.

'Neil suggested that I apply for BA. Apparently, they were keen to employ women, especially ones with a good record like mine. He knew someone I could meet. Have a quick, informal interview. You know how it is.'

Stevie said nothing. She did not know how it was. She'd joined BA through the formal channels.

'Before long, I agreed to divorce Graham and get engaged to Neil again. Of course, it had to be a secret until my divorce came through.'

'Tricky,' said Stevie, 'when you were still working for Graham.'

'Hmm,' said Amy, wrinkling her nose. 'Thing is,' she took a sip of coffee, 'you have to understand what sort of person Graham is.' She waved her cup around and then replaced it neatly on the saucer. 'He's a bit military, know what I mean? Bit naïve when it comes to women.'

Stevie looked blank and Amy bit her lip, thinking.

'OK, look, I'll give you the picture. I went for an inter-view with Graham in 1992 and he was all oh so posh and important. Interview in a suit and all that. I knew they'd never ever employed a woman and were proud of it.'

She looked at Stevie, eyebrows raised.

'His whole family had been pilots. His grandfather was one of the early pioneers, his father flew in the war and later started a flying charter business, which quickly got a name for well-trained, efficient pilots. Graham started flying at fourteen and it was understood when his father retired he would take over the business.

'Everyone wanted to use their company and all the pilots wanted to fly for them, meaning they could choose the best of the best. And, of course, I was the best.' Amy smiled, showing her teeth. 'But he hadn't realised that yet.'

'Got a list of interviewees for today?' Graham asked his secretary as he arrived at the office. His eyes automatically scanned the office board for out-of-date licences. All up to date. Just one would need a recency check next week.

'Yes, sir,' she said.

Like his father, Graham insisted on being addressed as 'sir'. It was old-fashioned, but he felt it instilled a sense of military discipline and that could never be wrong in such an edgy profession.

'This morning you have Sam O'Malley, four-hundred hours, CPL, working as an instructor at Blackbushe for Cabair. Followed by James Fanie, five-hundred hours CPL, teaching on Cessnas and Tiger Moths at Goodwood, and finally Amy Earhardt, six-hundred hours of photography, glider towing and aircraft deliveries.'

Graham yawned. Usual run of young instructor pilots hoping to make good in his firm before moving on to the airlines. 'Any of them have twin ratings?'

'Yes, sir, Amy Earhardt. She has a twin rating on a Duchess and a conversion onto an Aztec. Half of her hours are on twins doing second seat on commercial deliveries across Europe. She's noted that although she is often the handling pilot, she has only logged a percentage of the hours flown according to CAA guidelines, so she has considerably more stick time than is logged.'

'The boys?'

'No, sir, no twin time. Most of their hours are instruction.'

Graham frowned. He didn't think women made good pilots: far too emotional, and then there was the baby angle; they always got you there, lulled you in with their expertise and then got pregnant and you had to pay them for time off. Very manipulative, women. Neither he nor his father had ever employed them. 'Why leave the kitchen empty?' was their catch phrase. Still, he'd better interview this one, since somehow, she'd got through the paper round. But he would floor her with questions about her future, boyfriends and how she would balance her life. She'd be putty in his hands.

First, he had Sam and James to interview.

Sam arrived promptly, wearing a slightly shiny suit that Graham recognised from Burton. As he came in empty-handed, he had clearly refused coffee. Graham instructed his secretary to offer coffee just before they came in, so he could see what they would do with the cup.

'Morning, sir. Thank you for interviewing me.'

Graham held out his hand and Sam shook it. Nice clean, firm handshake. Boded well.

Graham looked at the form in front of him. No military

experience, which was always a deficit. Both Graham and his father much preferred ex-military pilots: good sense of discipline.

'So, Sam, got your PPL in exactly forty hours. Excellent. Solo in five. Good. How do you like instructing?'

Sam laughed politely. 'Well, don't really, sir, but needs must. Most of the guys are nice chaps but usually middle-aged and quite slow; we seem to do the same lesson over and over again. Personally, can't wait to get onto proper flying. Must say, hate sitting there seeing them doing it all wrong and having to show them all again.' He grinned. 'Still, we can't all be aces.'

Graham smiled back. 'Like you, you mean.'

'Oh well,' said the boy, dropping his eyes modestly. 'Don't like to brag but did take to it like a bird to the sky, as you might say.' He laughed happily.

'Yes. No twin time, I see.'

'Umm, no, pockets rather to let, know what I mean. Had to borrow from my sister for my original licence. Not that she'll miss it, her old man's rich as Croesus, know what I mean?'

'I see. In the advert we did ask for twin time if possible.'

Graham raised a polite eyebrow. He knew what would come next.

'Yes, absolutely, but I'm a quick learner. Thought if you took me on and trained me up, I'd be quickly ready for the fleet. Shouldn't take long at all. Know what I mean?'

'Yes,' said Graham. 'I do.'

The next interviewee was James, who had a cup of coffee, which he switched to the other hand when Graham offered a handshake, spilling some on the carpet and then dropping down in panic, trying to mop up the stains with his handkerchief.

'Thank you for interviewing me, sir,' he said, following Graham towards the chairs, holding his damp, smelly hand-kerchief crunched in his left hand.

James did have military time, but not as a pilot, as a navi-gator. 'Of course, I'd be happy to have been the pilot, but the navigator is really in control,' he explained, laughing, while his feet did a little jog along the floor. 'He's the man in the hot seat, know what I mean?'

Graham smiled, knowing very well this would have been a service choice. 'No twin time?'

'Sadly not. The army paid for my basic civvy CPL, but they didn't cough up for the rest. Shame, because I'm a quick learner. I'd have done them proud.'

Amy laughed. 'When I walked in I was wearing the shortest skirt Graham had ever seen, and of course I have the longest legs.' She stretched them out, her eyes smiling defiantly at Stevie. 'He didn't notice that I brought the coffee cup with me and placed it on a coaster on his desk.

"Hello," he said, and I tell you, Stevie, he leered at me. I knew I was in then.

"How nice to interview a pretty girl after all the boring old blokes I've been seeing all day. What a pleasant change."

"Thank you," I said. "I saw you had James and Sam before me. How did they do?"

"You know them?" he asked, as though I didn't know everyone in the flying world; made it my business to do so. I said yes, alluding to the fact they were on the easier CPL course when I was doing my ATPL without actually saying so.

'He glanced down at my application form. "Ah, I see you

went straight to Airline Transport Licence. Why did you do that?"

"Cheaper. It's risky to go straight to the harder licence but I was prepared to work hard. I still need to build hours, though. It's frozen for the moment, so I've been building hours glider towing and taking photographs, and I've been lucky enough to get second seat twin flying on commercial trips all over Europe. Basically, all the usual ways."

"But not instructing?"

"No."

"Any reason why not? Most women tend to do that ..."

"And end there," I said.'

Amy made a face at Stevie. 'Of course he had no idea. This was just chit-chat for him. So I told him.

'I'm aware of that. I didn't want to teach; I wanted to fly. How much actual flying do you do when teaching? You didn't teach either, did you?

"No," said Graham, "but it is different for me."

" Why?"

"Well, for one thing," said Graham, as though we were back in the nineteenth century. "I'm a man..."

"So?"

"Well, I won't have to look after children."

"Why not? Don't you like children?

"I didn't mean that."

"What then?"

"Well, that's a woman's job, child rearing ... How many male pilots have to alter their schedules to change their children's nappies?"

He laughed. I didn't. I thought this man's an idiot. I wasn't going to let him patronise me.

"Oh," I said, "so you don't believe in progress? Clearly, your father does, or he wouldn't have moved on from the

Dakota he used to fly to the Embraers. Good move, incidentally. They look like being a very progressive company and not many people are aware, so the price is still very good."

Graham stared at me. "You seem to know a lot about our company."

It was now my turn to look amazed, and my goodness did I layer it on. "Of course. You don't think I'd come for an interview if I didn't think the company was a perfect fit, do you? It would be crazy to do that." I think I even tilted my head.

Graham said nothing, he must have been fully aware that most of the men who came for interviews had only the barest notion of what they used to fly here and how they had moved on. He hesitated. Then he made a last-ditch attempt to save himself and his biased ideals.

"So, what if you have children? Won't you want to stop working for us and go and look after them?"

"No. I'll get a nanny. Whoever employs me I will do that, so it really depends on if you want to try me out, or if I go somewhere else. I'm going to work as a commercial pilot and neither you nor any other people's old-fashioned notions are going to stop me."

Amy laughed.

'And poor old Graham found himself offering me a job subject to a flight test and six months' trial. But I passed all of those easily. I did come top in the ground school exams, although I didn't bother to mention it.

'So,' said Amy, swishing her hair and laughing. 'I soon became chief pilot, but it wasn't enough. I wanted to work for and with the best of the best, and at that time that was BA.'

Stevie said nothing.

'Well, I had my interview at BA ... they loved me. I was

always good in interviews; the secret is research. If you know more about the company than they do, you can impress them. Anyway, I got right in.'

'And Neil?'

'He was well on the way to becoming a captain.'

'Which he never did?'

'No. He started drinking again. I threw him over ... much more quickly this time.'

'You went back to Graham?'

'Yes, he came and begged. I thought I'd give him another chance. Then I got preggers.'

'Pregnant? Who?'

'Graham, of course! I don't think he knew anything about Neil, anyway.' Amy threw her hair behind her and shook it into a fan.

'So, you had to stop flying?'

'Only briefly. Luckily, I had twins. We got a nanny, and I went back to work. I'm a BA captain now.'

'And Neil?'

'Yeah, well, silly fool went back to the booze, and then he got stopped by the police, driving in for a day's work still pissed from the night before.'

Stevie looked a question.

'BA kept him on for a while, but they made it obvious he would never become a captain.' She put her hand up to her hair again and whipped it out behind her like a whirlwind. 'I guess the pointlessness of a job without chance of promotion made it worse ... and from there he was sacked again ... Poor Neil.' She blew out heavily. 'OK. He had a lot of charm,' she added, almost as though she was talking to herself. 'He did have something, but, you know, once a drunk always a drunk. He was dangerous. He would drive drunk. I'd never do that.'

Her hand automatically moved to the little scar on her hairline. Stevie wondered if she got that from Neil, but Amy was still talking.

'Apart from the fact it mucked up his career, it mucks up lives.' She shrugged. 'Anyway, Graham and I and the twins are fine now. The boys enjoy flying, too.'

Stevie sighed quietly. 'I wonder, did you give him a chain, something to remember you by?'

'With *allium ursinium* on it?'

Stevie frowned, thinking. 'Is that wild garlic?'

'Yes. Its real name. When we were first engaged, we were going through a Sunday market at the airfield. I saw the chain and recognised it immediately. It made me think of him. You know, *ursa* is a bear, and he was like that, a great big bear of a man, innocent like those big men tend to be. *Allium ursinium* comes from bears waking up from hibernation and looking for bulbs. That was Neil: a big teddy looking for things he could never find, never be satisfied. A perpetual rover. You know the type.'

'I guess,' said Stevie politely, although she thought this case sounded rather different. If anything, Amy appeared to be the rover here.

'Well, that's wild garlic. Grows and thrives where it wants. Delicious but no good when domesticated!'

Amy laughed but Stevie felt incredibly sad.

'Hey,' said Amy, looking at her watch and getting up, 'back to work. Who knows, you may find yourself with me as your captain one of these days!'

As Amy picked up her bag Stevie said, 'Just one more thing.'

Amy raised an eyebrow.

'Sorry to ask, but your scar ... did you get that from Neil?'

Amy raised both eyebrows. She stood still for a moment, looking at Stevie.

'Funny question, but yes, I did. You remember I said he drove drunk. One night, after we'd been engaged for a while, we went to this fabulous café near Chichester. I was living in a village nearby then, so I knew the place. It doesn't exist anymore, but it was run by a couple of old girls, from their house. Food was mega, and their wine to die for.'

Stevie raised her eyebrows wondering if Amy was being ironic, but Amy just glanced at her and continued with her story.

'We both got legless. I refused to drive. I never drive drunk. Too much respect for myself. But I was too drunk to notice he was wrecked too. We were nearly home when, out of the blue, he starts crying, talking to someone as though he'd seen a ghost. Suddenly he was yelling, "Sorry! Sorry! I didn't know! I'm so sorry! It wasn't my fault. I was pissed."

'I started laughing. I thought it was a joke, but then the car began swerving from one side of the road to the other. I reached over but before I could do anything the car went into a slide. It was terrifying. It all happened so fast. It catapulted over the verge and into a huge drainage ditch. I screamed. I thought he was going to kill me. The car fell onto my side, half in the ditch, and I pushed the door as hard as I could, but it wouldn't open. My seat belt was locked. I was stuck and around me the water in the ditch was rising. I looked over at Neil, but he'd gone. Legged it. I shouted for help, loud as I could, but all the time the water was rising. I was terrified.

'Then, out of the blue, this chap stuck his head in. He was crying. He leant in and cut the seat belt. He can't have been more than eighteen or nineteen, but he was incredibly strong. He leant into the car and dragged me out. I owe my life to him, but he ran away before I could thank him.'

She sighed.

'I'd cut my head, but otherwise I was OK. I broke off the engagement. You can't marry a man who would do that to you.'

She gave a small wave and walked out of the café.

CHAPTER 11
SON OF THE FATHER

A few days later Stevie got an email from a 'Hugh'.

'Hello, detectives,' said the email. 'My name is Hugh as you can see from the email. I am neighbour to a man called Donald O'Banyon who is ninety-six years old, not that I am much younger.

'My children are on the social network known as Facebook. When you put the name of Neil O'Banyon on a picture there, they contacted me. Donald is prepared to believe it is his son. They lost contact in 2001. Do you have a phone number? We could ring you. Landline please. No mobiles. Too expensive. Yours, Hugh.'

The two old boys phoned together. Stevie wondered if they had one of those phone extensions that allowed two people to talk. She hadn't seen one since she was a child, but they might well still exist. She put the speaker phone on at her end.

'Neil,' said Donald, his voice clipped either by emotion

or habit. 'If it is him, I'd like to take him home. Would they let me?'

Stevie said she imagined so, but wondered what he would feel about his son being doused in formaldehyde?

'Would,' she asked, 'you be happy to do a DNA test?'

'Happy,' said Donald. 'Odd word, but I'm willing.'

'When did you last see your son?' asked Miranda, thinking of how heartbroken she would have been if any of her children had broken off with her. Even though they were dead tiresome, she would probably pursue them until they let her back into their lives.

There was a clunking noise on the end of the phone as though one of the men had dropped the extension, then Donald said, 'Hard to remember. Probably around the time of his mother's death. You think of anything more recent, Hugh?'

'No.'

'Oh,' said Miranda, her eyes filling with tears. 'How awful. What happened?'

'Nothing special,' said Donald. 'Not much in common... apart from our genes.' He gave a brisk laugh. 'We just drifted apart, after his mother died, when was that, Hugh?'

Hugh said, 'It was 2001, right after the fall of the Twin Towers in New York. Not,' he added in case the girls might be confused, 'that there was any connection. I just find that it is a very good date to relate to, don't you?'

* * *

The two old men arrived at the mortuary in Hugh's car. A VW Beetle from another era it still had the remains of a flower painting on the door panel. A wheelchair was strapped to the back. Miranda, who was waiting to guide them to the morgue, wondered if they'd tried and failed to fit the wheelchair in the boot. She rushed out to help them, but Hugh was already unstrapping the chair and putting it on the tarmac. He laughed delightedly when he saw Miranda.

'You've got to be quick to beat me,' he said cheerfully, wheeling the chair around to pick up his friend. 'Marry in haste, repent at leisure,' he intoned happily; Miranda stared at him, puzzled.

Donald O'Banyon got out of the car and into the wheelchair without speaking. He took off the brakes and wheeled himself around the front but allowed his friend to push him over the doorsill into the hospital facility and on down the corridor.

They were both slim old men with an upright stance that made them look like elderly soldiers. Miranda wondered if they had met in the war and been friends ever since.

As Miranda and Hugh walked along, Hugh pushing the chair, Donald silently examined the passing walls. Hugh, it seemed, had been in hospital many times recently and clearly realised that Miranda would be interested in every detail. Having delighted her with the minutiae of his two knee operations, twenty years apart with very different surgical procedures, he continued with his more up-to-date entries.

'... So, only two years after my second knee operation, I had the hip done. The doctors said I was a modern miracle the way I could keep having these procedures and recovering so well ... they brought in all the students to look at me ... then I was in again for my prostate, now that really was a success, no problem in the lower department now, not that the old girl was very responsive even before she died.' He gave a great guffaw of joy. 'Necrophilia rules OK!'

Miranda blushed and led the way into the PM examination room. John Smith's body was lying on the clinical steel table with his few possessions on a small table by his feet.

Hugh stopped talking and both men regarded the body silently. Miranda wondered if Donald was upset, but when he spoke it was in the same clipped voice he had used on the phone.

'Yes, that's him. Are those his things?'

The clinician said they were, and Hugh pushed Donald's chair over to them. He picked them up and gave them a cursory look. 'Do you want them, Hugh?'

'No, thanks. I have pictures to remind me of your son.'

Miranda wondered if there was disapproval in his voice, but if so, Donald didn't appear to notice.

'You then, girl detective, you keep them. May be clues for you. Presumably you're trying to find out something about him. Think he was murdered, do you? One of his street colleagues or a street employer.' He gave a rasping laugh.

Miranda nodded, but she didn't answer the last part of the question, assuming it was rhetorical. 'Yes, thank you, we'll take them. If you're sure.'

'No use to me, are they? I hardly remember him, let alone the rubbish he accrued on the road.' He turned to the clinician. 'When can I have the body? I'll need to arrange a funeral. His mother was buried; she'd like him beside her. All a load of rubbish but she believed it. I'll just be burnt; no one will care about my old ashes now they're both gone.'

His laugh was as dry as his future ashes. Miranda watched him and wondered if anyone could really care so little about their own flesh and blood. It was anathema to her.

The clinician said quietly they could arrange for the undertaker to pick up the body and everything further could be done through them. Nodding, Donald turned his chair.

'Well, that's it, Hugh. Shall we go? Unless you have any further business with this nonsense.'

Hugh looked at Miranda and for a moment she wondered if he looked slightly apologetic, then he said, 'That it? Anything else we need to do?'

The clinician stepped forward with a form asking for a few details and soon both men were traversing back the way they had come, towards Hugh's car, which he had left outside the door, ignoring the signs requesting cars to be left in the car park. Donald pointed at the notice.

'Ha, Hugh, looks like you'll get a fine. Silly old boy. Should've moved the car. They have cameras now. Not like the old days when you could get away with murder.'

Miranda gave him a sharp glance but immediately realised he didn't notice the irony of the phrase.

Hugh shook his head. 'Oh,' he said to Miranda, 'I expect you lot will pick that up, won't you?'

She wondered how to answer without being rude, but, as Donald was already climbing into the passenger seat, any reply seemed unnecessary. She watched them leave before walking back to her own car, in the car park. Dealing with these members of the older generation certainly had its humour, but she wondered if they were as clinical as they seemed. Was Donald hiding a deeply wounded heart under that cold performance or did he really, truly not care about his son? And if so, was that the underlying reason his son cared so little for himself? Had that spurred on his descent into drink and homelessness? Miranda felt a weight of sadness and incomprehension settle on her body; she needed a strong drink, and she wasn't even related to Donald.

When Miranda got home, she hugged her children and told them she loved them. Peta squealed in delight, but Felix said pertly, 'OK, Mum! Bad day, was it?'

Perhaps the younger generation were going to grow up like their grandparents, she thought sourly.

When Miranda told Cat about the visit, Cat said, 'Oh dear, I'd better call my stepbrother and see how he is. I probably wouldn't know if he had died. Life can be callous if families don't stick close.'

Miranda said nothing but wondered if Cat had listened to her own words: Cat's children only spoke to her when they wanted something, and they were the least close family she knew. Maybe, Miranda thought, she meant life can be callous, but now Cat had found Frank her life was so much happier than it ever had been.

CHAPTER 12
STREET LIFE

Cat sat down with her coffee. 'You know, none of the people we've talked to had seen Neil in the last five years, and only the St Botolph's volunteer knew he was on the streets. Isn't that odd? He must have had some recent acquaintances. Where did he live? Where did he go when he wasn't on the streets? How did he get money to drink? Did he beg? Where?'

'And,' said Stevie, remembering they had a client, 'why did he go to Wild Garlic to die? Did he ever live there? If he was killed, did the killer live there?'

She printed out the list of people who had lived in the house since 1990.

'Shall we have another look at these? See if any one of them might have crossed paths with him for any reason.'

'Well,' said Cat, 'I've already interviewed the vicar. Nothing there.'

'Did anything he said help us?'

Cat frowned. 'Only that he told us again that story about the freeholder getting an ASBO because he wouldn't stop writing to the Queen.'

'Unbelievable,' said Miranda. 'I do think he's dotty enough to have stolen the car and crashed it into his own house. Was there an insurance claim, Stevie?'

'Apparently so. The insurers of the car agreed to pay for the wall in Wild Garlic. According to my "friends" it was settled out of court.'

'Poor old Clive Creamer, missed his day in court!' said Miranda. 'Bet he was annoyed about that. He could have brought up the Queen's negligence while he was at it.'

Cat laughed.

'OK, so what other suspicious people do we have on the list?' Cat asked, picking up the list.

Stevie swung on her computer chair. 'From time to time, when he couldn't get tenants, Clive made it a holiday rental. We'll never find all those people. Do you think the free-holder even has a list of them? It is possible Neil stayed there. He might have gone to Wild Garlic because he had had a happy holiday there, and returned there to try and find happiness, the way older people revisit the places of their youth, hoping to rejuvenate themselves.'

'Maybe,' said Cat, 'but let's concentrate first on the longer tenants for the moment. Here's one for you, Stevie,' she added, her eyes travelling down the list. 'Victoria Bell, owns an aviation-themed nightclub in Clerkenwell. She lived in the house for a year from 1998 to 1999, so just after a couple called Haydon. It doesn't say why, with a nightclub in Clerkenwell, she rented a house over an hour or so away from London. Perhaps that's suspicious?'

'A nightclub,' said Miranda thoughtfully. 'I think I'd better pop up to Clerkenwell and interview—'

Stevie's dagger dart speared her friend. 'Know much about aviation, do you? I'll take any pilots, OK?'

'Have you ever been to a nightclub?' asked Miranda doggedly.

Stevie said nothing.

'I see. Look, Stevie, I think it's better if I go. I'm much more streetwise than you,' said Miranda, her words lengthening with longing.

Stevie again stared at her silently. Eventually she said, 'No, I'm going. It is aviation-themed. As the owner of the club obviously is, or was at some point, a pilot, I'm going to be able to talk to her pilot to pilot. There's no debate.'

'Interesting thought, that,' said Cat, nodding her head. 'Are you once a pilot, always a pilot, like a priest, even if you don't have a ministry?'

She drew out her lipstick and painted her lips thoughtfully.

'Cat,' said Miranda, pleading, 'don't you see how silly this is...? I mean, Stevie, why do you even want to go? You don't like people.'

'I'm going,' said Stevie. 'No debate.'

Cat shrugged. She tapped Miranda's should. 'Leave her. She wants to go. You know how she likes talking to other pilots. It worked well with Amy. Probably this woman will open up to her in a way she never would with us.'

Miranda muttered about safety issues and gangs, but neither Cat nor Stevie took any notice.

'OK,' said Miranda, 'then I'll take this one, then, from 1997 to 1998, whoever it is ... Oh! As long as it's not a pilot, that is.' Her shoulders sashayed into a sarcastic shrug. She picked up Stevie's notes and read them in a loud voice. 'John and Humphrey Haydon. They were planning to buy it but then refused and it reverted to the freeholder. That's odd. Could it be 'coz of the ghost, do you think, Cat? They still live locally, so they obviously like the place...'

'Chichester,' said Cat drily. 'Not quite a village, though, is it?'

'Look,' said Miranda, her eyes skidding on down the list. 'Look at this! Your pilot Amy lived there for a year. When did she say she broke up with her husband, Stevie?'

'It was around 2007 or 2008, I think. I'll look at my notes.'

'Odd,' said Miranda, 'she didn't say anything about that, considering the body was found in her house and when she was living there. She must have been interviewed by the police at the very least. I mean she knew him.'

'Yes,' said Stevie. 'Although she, and they, might not have made the connection between an unknown homeless man who broke into her house and Neil, whom she hadn't seen for years. If she was away on a long-haul flight she might have just had rudimentary contact from the police. I'll send her an email and see if she remembers.'

'OK,' said Cat, but she nibbled her lower lip thoughtfully.

'Also,' said Miranda, 'I wonder who the other person was he was engaged to? Did Amy have any idea, Stevie?'

'No. I asked her, but she said it must have been after her time. She said that once he left BA, she never saw him again.'

CHAPTER 13
STEVIE AND THE QUEEN OF
THE SPINNERS

When Stevie arrived at the Spinners Nightclub, its gentle, pale atmosphere took her by surprise. This was more like a visit to Legoland than a nightclub. She had spent hours researching nightclubs: what they were like, what to wear, what to expect. Most appeared to be darkly lit places with bouncers outside, long queues and cross-faded clubbers dancing long into the night. Stevie had dressed in black leather trousers and jacket, with a black tee-shirt, hoping to blend in with the clubbers, however, even dressed in back and as a young woman alone, she immediately felt welcome.

There were model planes hanging from the ceiling, propellers over the bar. She recognised one model aircraft as a Sopwith Camel, and one of the propellers as that of a Curtiss Jenny. The booths had been designed to look like cockpits from ancient aircraft, and even the bar was reminiscent of a first-class airliner.

Stevie bought a tomato juice and took a seat at a table near the bar, somehow feeling that would protect her from any unwelcome advances. The table was patterned with comic air show scenes and ground crew under helicopters getting hit by buckets. Stevie examined it. *Humour can be very individual*, she thought.

Before long, someone approached her. 'Buy you a drink?'

'Thanks, no,' Stevie said. 'I already have one.'

'Cute,' he said, smiling and sitting down at her table. 'Come here to listen to the music, did you?'

'Yes,' she said, wondering if it would look odd if she read a book sitting at the table. It was probably too dark to read anyway, but even if she couldn't see the text, it might make him go away.

'What do you like best?' persisted her tormentor.

'Pink,' said Stevie. 'I like her humour and the fact she doesn't give a damn what anyone thinks. Adele's got a better voice, though. I don't mind this one, all the same.'

'Don't you?' he said, sneering slightly. 'What is it?'

'"Learning to Fly" by Pink Floyd,' said Stevie. 'Don't you recognise it?'

In response he got up and asked the barman. 'You're right,' he said, slumping down in the chair.

'I know,' Stevie said, sitting upright. 'Did you doubt me?'

'Do you want to meet my sister?' the man asked, curling his lip.

Stevie stared at him. What an odd man. 'Your sister? Why? Is she a pilot?'

He sniggered. 'You are a funny little one, aren't you?'

Stevie hoped he would move away. She pulled out her phone and started scrolling; surely that would persuade him to take himself off.

He got up abruptly, nearly knocking over the chair. 'Well, you're a laugh a minute, aren't you?'

Stevie smiled quietly. However, it seemed her lack of

interest was like a magnet and a few moments later another man sat down at her table and offered her a drink.

When a third man left with a similarly disgruntled expression, the bartender approached the table.

'Come and sit at the bar,' he said, smiling in a fatherly manner. 'Safer!'

'Thanks.'

He went off to serve a couple of customers and Stevie watched him work. He was a short man, surprisingly muscular for a bartender and, as she now noticed, had a small scar under his left eye. He laughed with the clients and seemed almost protective to them. Stevie was wondering how a man like that ended up working in a nightclub when a tall woman, wearing the highest stilettos Stevie had ever seen, walked over, slid across onto the next stool and kicked off her heels. She rubbed her feet together under the bar.

'Oooh, sooo much better.' She smiled at Stevie. 'Hi! It's so difficult being female in a club, isn't it?' she said.

'I guess,' said Stevie. 'I've never been in one before. But there is a nice atmosphere here. I like it.'

The woman's smile widened. 'You a pilot?'

'Yes.'

'It figures. Most solo women here are pilots. They come for the ambience.'

'You a pilot too?'

'Yup, Embraer. You?'

'Nice. Seven-seven-seven, BA. You biz jets?'

'Yup.'

The woman drank her vodka and orange, twiddled with the umbrella, and looked around the club. She turned back to Stevie, who was now staring at the bottles.

'I'm Jenny. You?'

'Stevie.'

'Stevie? Boy's name.'

Stevie frowned. She didn't know why but this struck her as a bit creepy. She hoped the barman would come back soon. However, a quick glance found him at the far end of the bar chatting to a customer.

'It's short for Stephanie.'

'I figured. I didn't think you were male.' The woman laughed and her mouth opened widely, reminding Stevie of a donkey. She lifted her drink and read the labels on the bottles behind the bar.

The hands on the clock behind the bar moved, Stevie had another sip of tomato juice and a man walked over and asked Jenny for a dance. Giving Stevie a saucy wink, she got back into her high heels and followed the young man on to the dance floor wiggling her hips. Stevie read more labels. Should she have let Miranda do this job after all? She really wasn't cut out for social chit-chat.

The barman came back. 'You OK? Miss Victory doesn't like her customers hassled. She asks me to keep an eye open for when it looks tricky.'

'Thanks,' said Stevie. 'Is she here?'

He looked over her head at the opposite wall. 'Do you know her?'

'No. But I heard she was a pilot. I am too. I'd like to meet her.'

The barman nodded. 'I thought you might be a pilot,' he said slowly. 'Most of the girls like you are. OK, I'll ask. She doesn't often come on the floor, but she'll be watching.'

Stevie stared at him, wondering what he meant by that, then turned to see where he was looking. Above them was a mirror.

'No way! A reciprocal mirror? Like a James Bond film? She can see us, but we can't see her?'

The barman nodded, his smile slightly twisted. He glanced at his phone and as he did so Stevie noticed there was a small discreet plug in his ear; perhaps he was deaf.

'OK,' he said, 'she agrees. Come. I'll show you.'

Stevie jumped off the stool and followed him up a small spiral staircase behind the bar.

'Miss Victoria doesn't use this,' he said. 'There's a lift, which is why the stairs are so spiral.'

'Oh,' said Stevie, not understanding.

However, when the door opened into the office it was suddenly clear: Victoria, the owner of Spinners, was sitting in a wheelchair; hence the lift. If she had been a pilot, she was not anymore.

The woman had her back to them and was looking through the looking glass. The barman coughed discreetly and melted away to serve the customers.

Victoria turned and looked at Stevie silently. Stevie felt a shock run through her like a cold shower. This was the woman with the Toyota Yaris. The owner of the car that had crashed into Wild Garlic. Frank's picture was still sitting in her phone.

'Oh!' she said.

'Oh?' said Victoria. 'Not used to cripples? Is that it?'

Stevie stared at her, uncertain what to say, feeling guilty although she hadn't thought any such thing, but unable to admit Frank had passed her photo around their WhatsApp group.

'No. But, you drive a Yaris,' Stevie blurted out, before realising that might sound a little strange.

'Blimey,' said Victoria. 'You're smooth. I'd love to hear your pick-up lines. Yes, I drive a modified Yaris. Not that odd in my book but better than being the dame on wheels, I suppose. And you are a TAP. No question of that.'

Miranda would have laughed, thought Stevie, said something soothing that would cool the issue but she herself felt petrified. Why did people say such strange things? It was frightening. She'd obviously offended this unknown woman.

'Hi, I'm Stevie,' she said, putting out her hand appeasingly. 'Sorry. I didn't mean to be rude...'

The woman snorted. She didn't take her outstretched hand. 'Welcome to Spinners. I'm Victory Bell.'

Stevie withdrew her hand, wondering if she'd just made another mistake. 'Thank you. Oh, but actually I'm with BA, not TAP.'

Victoria stared at her. 'What?'

'I was told you are happy to meet pilots and I am a first officer, but not for TAP, for BA.'

Victoria's brow crinkled for a moment, then slowly she started to laugh.

'Oh heavens! What an out-and-out pilot you are! What I said was you were a T-A-P – a temporarily able person. Unlike me, that Dame on Wheels. I didn't mean that you flew for TAP.' She blew out sharply. 'I guess we are all strange in our way. What do you fly?'

Here at least was a question Stevie could answer without problem. 'A seven-seven-seven.'

'The triple seven. Nice.'

Stevie looked at her silently, gauging her age. She was older. It also could be that living in a wheelchair made you look older. But either way she was too young to have retired. Did she have an aviation accident? Something so bad it prevented her continuing.

Victoria was silent and Stevie tried to say something

useful. 'Er ... would you like me to get you a drink? I could drop down to the bar ... I mean ... do you drink alcohol?' Stevie blushed.

Victoria looked at her, eyebrows wrinkling and gave a sudden short laugh. 'Well! It's the first time I've been offered a drink when I'm the host. You must be gasping. Or do you think I can't lift a wine bottle? I'm disabled. I hurt my back in an accident. I haven't come from another planet!'

Stevie felt distraught, yet another mistake. 'Sorry, I didn't mean to be rude.' She realised she was shaking.

Victoria laughed properly this time and her shoulders relaxed. 'It's OK, Stevie. I'm teasing. Sorry! I don't mean to be ... well, abrupt, but you aren't the first able-bodied person to feel frightened by my injuries.' She burst into song:

'I used to walk just like you. Talk like you. Now I'm the Queen of the Spinners.'

She stopped singing. 'In fact, if you close your eyes and just talk to me, you'll see I'm exactly like you except I no longer have a pilot's licence!'

Stevie didn't see any humour here. She felt that horrible, cloying sense of embarrassment, of upsetting someone and being unable to do anything to undo it. She tried to act normally.

'But I'm not,' she said, 'that is, I'm not frightened by your injuries, except of course I wouldn't like to have them ... I mean ... looks like you've done really well here...'

Victoria gave a flat smile and slightly shook her head. Then, she shrugged. 'Yes, OK then. Get me a glass of white wine, thanks. And to make up for your manners you can have one too. OK? I have a bar up here,' she added as Stevie turned to head downstairs.

'Oh, yes.' Stevie smiled with an effort. She wished she was up in the clear blue sky, miles away from this difficult situation. She looked around the room, wondering where to find the drinks. Along one wall was the mirror she had seen from below and through it a clear view of most of the bar and dance floor. Next to it was a square box with controls; it looked like something you might find in a small airfield air traffic control tower.

'Good view.'

'Yes, when you can't run around and be somewhere, it helps to watch instead. My guys on the ground are my legs, but since I can see the aerial view, I'm their eyes.'

'I see.'

'Was that a joke?' asked Victoria, and although Stevie had her back to her, she knew she was smiling. *God*, thought Stevie, *I'm useless without a machine and I never know what to say. If Miranda was here, she'd be sharing Victoria's life story by now.*

'What? No. Sorry, I didn't think…'

'I know,' said Victoria in the same flat voice. 'Found the booze yet? Getting thirsty over here!'

Stevie crossed her arms across her chest while her eyes searched on. The rest of the room had been designed like the interior of an old-fashioned flying school, with planning maps on the wall, a low desk on which were whirly wheels, a compass and various other bits of navigation equipment. Perhaps Victoria was like someone whose child had died, keeping their room in the state it was when they were last there: her planning room just as it was when she could still fly. If so, it must have been a long time since she last flew since much of this equipment had been superseded. She looked down at the nightclub floor.

'Oh, there's that girl who was talking to me, back at the bar again.'

Victoria wheeled over her chair and looked. 'Girl?'

'Um, she said her name was Jenny. Flies Embraers.'

'You are a little country mouse, aren't you?'

There was something in Victoria's voice that made Stevie glance back at her.

'What?'

Victoria shrugged. 'Yes, she sometimes comes with her partner, another pilot.'

Stevie stared down at the woman drinking at the bar, now flirting with the barman, waving her hands provocatively.

'Yes, she's a hoot,' said Victoria. 'Pity about her partner.'

Stevie wasn't listening. Her eyes traversed on, searching until, finally, she saw the bar. It was set below her eyeline, in the corner of the room, where it would be both protected from moving wheels and easily reachable. The bottles all had screw tops, which might be significant. Perhaps it was difficult to remove corks if you were sitting in a wheelchair.

'It's a nice place,' said Stevie, opening the wine and pouring some into two glasses. 'Empathetic.'

'It reminds me,' said Victoria, 'of someone I knew when I could still fly.'

Stevie wouldn't have asked, but since Victoria had mentioned it, she did. 'What happened?'

Victoria picked up the glass. She looked at it. Took a sip of wine.

'This is nice. What is it? The guys bring them up from downstairs and sometimes I don't recognise the taste.'

Stevie looked at the bottle. 'It's from Chile; does that help?'

'You don't know much about wine, do you?'

Stevie shook her head. 'Not really. I have friends who drink but I don't find it does anything for me. It's a bit like sugary water. I much prefer tea.'

Victoria smiled.

'Flying,' said Stevie, 'you said you used to fly. Does that mean you weren't born in a wheelchair, or you flew in a modified plane?'

Victoria stared at her, then she laughed sardonically. She echoed 'born in a wheelchair' adding almost in a whisper, 'The opposite of born free, I'm guessing!'

She took another sip of her wine. 'Well, it's nice, the wine, probably Sauvignon Blanc. But, yes, OK. *As I said*, I was born walking in the normal way, like you.' She looked away from Stevie and down into the club. She gave a deep sigh. 'OK. My therapist said I should talk about it if I got the chance. He said it would help me. So, OK.'

She gave a snorty laugh. 'Everyone in my family flew. Both my parents. We had a couple of Piper Cubs. We went camping all over France and Spain when we were young. My sister and I both learnt to fly as soon as we could touch the pedals. Just like some kids learn to drive as soon as they are tall enough, but with us it was the Cub. To us it was the norm.'

'Your sister,' said Stevie. 'I'd love to have had a sister.'

Victoria snorted. 'She's dead! Killed by some arsehole drunken driver. The bastard!' Victoria shook herself. 'But sorry, we are off the point, aren't we? Why are you here, Stevie? What was it you wanted to know?'

'Oh, yes,' Stevie bit her lip. Whatever the therapist might or might not have said, she was actually a detective and here to interview a witness, if that wasn't too pompous a term.

'Owly Vale,' said Stevie. 'We're looking at the case of a homeless man killed in a house there. We're just going back through all the people who lived there. You rented the house in 1998.'

She wondered if she ought to mention the car crash but

left it. Possibly Victoria didn't even know where the hitch-hiker crashed her car.

Victoria looked surprised. 'Are you a policewoman? I thought you were a pilot. You told Oscar you were.'

Stevie thought her voice sounded rather annoyed and felt guilty. Of course, she should have said that too, but she thought of herself as a pilot, not as a detective. She attempted to explain how she felt.

'I am. A pilot that is. My friends and I have a private detective firm. Normally we look for lost dogs, fly-tippers, that sort of thing, but we've broadened our remit. The house you rented has had problems selling and the freeholder hired us to find out why. But then we discovered the story of the dead homeless man and the two cases seemed inter-linked. Police aren't really interested. Well ... it happened more than fourteen years ago.'

Victoria nodded.

'When exactly was he killed?'

'March 2008.'

'Oh,' said Victoria, 'long after I lived there then. How was he killed?'

'The police think he probably OD'd on alcohol. He appears to have choked on his own vomit.'

Victoria shuddered. 'Ugh. But if the police think he OD'd, why do *you* think he was killed?'

'Reasonable question, but my friend Cat has a sort of sixth sense, and she got hung up with ghosts and the like...'

'Whaaat? Ghosts? Oh, come on! Are you a serious detective agency or Ghostbusters?' She laughed and, even as Stevie tried to outline the other reasons for thinking Neil had been killed, began singing again, this time the movie theme song.

Oh hell, thought Stevie, *I'm losing control of the interview*.

Did this always happen? Or was it just her own incompetence? She breathed deeply.

'OK. So, tell me about how you came to rent the house. It was a long way from Clerkenwell ... from here.'

Victoria sighed. 'Three days after my younger sister was killed, I went out in the Cub. I wasn't concentrating. I was thinking about Bella, and I flew into a tree.'

Stevie stared silently. She knew that people used to fly low in the past but hitting a tree! Wow.

Victoria shrugged. 'The only good thing about my accident was that my parents stopped obsessing about Bella's death because they had to focus on me. I was in hospital for months.'

She shook her head before continuing and moved in her seat.

'I tried to go back and live with my parents, but that was impossible. They live and breathe flying, and I couldn't even climb into a cockpit. It was a bad time for our family.'

Victoria stopped and breathed heavily, before going on. 'In the hospital, my surgeon saw how badly I was dealing with everything, and he suggested this excellent therapist, Anthony. Anthony was still training, he was really a social worker, but he wanted to go further. He had so much insight into the psychological effect of trauma, he was brilliant. He immediately saw that being with my parents was holding me back, was preventing me taking control of my own life.'

She stared down at the club and fell silent. Stevie said nothing, waiting. Victoria took a deep breath and went on. 'So, he suggested I left my parents' house and start a new life, one outside all the things I previously held dear. And of course, he was right. As soon as I left my family and their influence, I was able to regather my thoughts and plan a life away from flying. But, since I left home just like that, I needed to rent something immediately. In fact, my therapist found the house for me. Apparently, he knew Owly Vale for some reason and he knew about the house where two men had moved out at short notice.

'The freeholder was prepared to give me a discount if I moved in straightaway. I did. But I hated it almost immediately. Everywhere there was the smell of wild garlic. I should have got a plough and destroyed the whole lot forever. Would have done if it had been my property. Even now I can't smell garlic without feeling angry.'

She moved restlessly in her chair.

'However, my therapist said that anger was good, now it was channelled away from my parents and family and into a house. A non-receptive house that could never be hurt by my pain.'

'Why was your therapist so knowledgeable about Owly Vale?' asked Stevie. 'It's a tiny place.'

'No idea and I no longer have any details for him.'

'What did you say his name was?'

'Anthony.'

'OK,' said Stevie, writing it down. 'It may mean something to someone in the village. Thanks.'

CHAPTER 14

HOUSE OF THE RISING HUSBANDS

John and Humphrey Haydon lived on a modern estate on a former farm outside Chichester. There were a couple of clearly signed parking spaces. There was a piece of cardboard hanging from the parking sign which said: 'Please park tidily. Think of your neighbours.' There were several exclamation marks after the writing.

Interesting, Miranda thought, parking her Polo, *how what seems like convenience becomes a rule. No freedom here.* She left two wheels over the lines as her part of the rebellion and walked up to the door. The bell, sitting next to a highly polished milkmaid knocker, worked. Unlike hers, which had been replaced by a dung-encrusted fox that Felix had found in the sheep's field. She must remember to get the bell fixed, sooner or later.

The door was opened by a slight man in his late forties. His hair had the salt-and-pepper look of middle age. He smiled broadly and Miranda noticed he had the straight, white teeth of good dental work.

'Miranda, is it? I'm John. Come in. Shall I take your coat?'

Miranda shrugged it off and let him take it. He hung it in a cupboard by the door. These developers had thought of everything: in her house the walk to the cloakroom was so far that everyone left their coats on the stairs.

She followed John into the lounge where another man, this time bald, relaxed on the sofa with a cup of coffee, looking at his iPad. 'Hi,' he said, without getting up or taking his gaze away from the fascinating screen.

'Would you like a coffee?' asked John.

Miranda nodded and sat down beside the other man who, presumably, was Humphrey Haydon, although he didn't say.

'Are you brothers?' Miranda asked, bouncing heavily on the sofa so Humphrey's iPad dislodged, and he was forced to look up. 'Or just friends who have the same name? I had a friend like that, moved in to share with another girl through SpareRoom and they both had the same surname, even though they'd never met and weren't related.'

Humphrey laughed and let the iPad slide down by his side. 'What was the name? Smith?'

'Patel,' said Miranda, also laughing.

'No,' said John, coming back with the coffee. 'We're actually married, but I changed my name to Humm's because mine was such a joke.'

Miranda raised her eyebrows expectantly.

John grinned. 'It was Blow-Forthgas, the result of too many people marrying and merging their names. Besides, my father was a shit, and I didn't want to be reminded of him every time I went to a trade show! The badge,' he added, as Miranda looked a bit nonplussed. 'I work in publishing, loads of trade shows, meetings, etc., and we wear these horrid little badges so I'm constantly being reminded of my own name.'

'Hi John Blow-Forthgas,' said Humm in an American accent. 'I'm Randy Diver. So, John Blow-Fordgas, did you read my submission? What did you think about it, John Blowford? Will I become an overnight best seller, John Blowme-Downgas?'

Both men collapsed in laughter while Miranda tried to join in politely, wondering what was so funny. Here again was a man with father problems. Luckily Felix and Phillip got on well; they seemed to enjoy fishing together.

'Sorry,' said Humm, wiping his eyes, 'it's just American writers love to repeat your name, in case they forget it, and then, even if they get it wrong, they go on repeating the error. It's hilarious.'

'Ah.' Miranda kept her eyes still. 'So, why did you leave Owly Vale? It seems like a friendly village to me.'

The boys exchanged glances. 'Well,' said Humm, 'you know how it is. We worked in London, came down to relax at weekends and well, frankly, we were a bit young for the village.'

'Too many wild parties?' asked Miranda, wishing they were still residents. 'Too much noise at night?'

'Yeah,' said Humm, 'that sort of thing. We much prefer Chichester; it's got a uni and a real night life.'

Miranda bit her cheek, hoping the pain would quell her spurt of envy. 'Umm.' She changed the subject but had to bite her cheek harder to prevent herself smiling. 'Did you ever notice a ghost in the house?'

The men again exchanged glances. Humm raised an eyebrow. 'You know our house was only built in the eighties, don't you?' he said.

Miranda snorted. 'Yeah.'

'Don't ghosts like places with turrets and history and things?' asked John, clearly trying to repress a smile. 'The only problem we had was damp, which the freeholder insisted was condensation...'

'We're very sensitive to the occult, aren't we, Humm?' said John, by now also fighting to keep a straight face. 'So we'd've noticed. Honest!'

Miranda let one side of her face smile, but it was too late. Both men had hysterics, laughing until they cried all the while apologising for not being able to control themselves.

'Actually,' said John, raising an eyebrow at Humm, 'we did have a ghost, didn't we? Great trouble getting rid of it.'

'Her, please!' said his husband, wiping his eyes. 'Yes, it was so long ago I'd forgotten about the ghostly Phylida.'

'Phylida?'

'Yup, she haunted us daily for about six months,' said Humm, trying hard to keep a straight face. 'Then she disappeared never to return. Odd that!'

Miranda gave them a dark look. 'OK, come on, explain.'

'Clive Creamer: only explanation you'll ever need.'

'The freeholder? What happened there?'

'Our Clive,' said John, 'who really is a couple of gallons short of a full tank, told his girlfriend to spy on us. So, she spent six months creeping around our garden, in our sheds, hiding behind trees trying to see what we were doing.'

'Sounds like she wasn't the full load either,' said Miranda.

The boys shrugged in unison.

'Anyway,' said John, 'eventually we caught her and tackled her with it, and she told us Clive had told her we'd stolen her bicycle and only by spying on us would she get it back. So, we had it out with him and guess what he said?'

John started laughing. 'He claimed she'd died, so it must be her ghost!'

'Died!'

'Yes. Only we saw her two days later, so she was a very corporeal ghost!'

When she got back to the office Miranda said, 'I doubt if there'd be much reason for them to kill a homeless man, and they didn't know anything about Cat's ghost, although they did have one of their own...' She glanced at Cat, sniggering.

'No,' said Stevie, 'but if Clive Creamer dies suddenly, they could look guilty.'

'Why?'

'Apparently, they had a huge bonfire which smoked out the whole village and Clive Creamer went over to complain. Somehow, they got into a serious dispute and Clive Creamer, well, we know by now he's a bit eccentric, hit John Blow-Forthgas. The upshot was they got into a huge fight, which spilled out into the street and the whole village came to watch.'

'Wow, bit extreme for a bonfire matter.'

'You'd think!'

Stevie made a face. 'Well, it went to court ... I found it on the internet. Blow-Forthgas versus Creamer. The freeholder represented himself, and John got a barrister from London. Result: Clive Creamer was fined fifteen hundred pounds and bound over to keep the peace for eighteen months.'

'Hmm,' said Miranda, 'must have made for interesting relations when they came to returning the house back to him. Starts to explain why he's got an ASBO if that is his normal way of sorting out a small problem.'

'Yeah!'

'And' said Stevie, 'he does look a bit guilty anyway. I mean why didn't he mention the body in the house when he asked us to investigate why it wasn't selling?'

Cat nodded. 'Good point. Good point, indeed. Someone needs to interview him soon.' And she looked pointedly at Miranda.

CHAPTER 15

THE LIFE AND LOVES OF A PHYSICS TEACHER

C at had asked Tim, whose surname she now discovered was Tom, to arrange a meeting with as many members of Neil's physics classes he could find. She suggested they met in a café near Sir John Soane's Museum in Lincoln's Inn. She liked that area of London. The square was beautiful at this time of year, sunny with pockets of shade and full of happy people walking dogs or discussing squirrels. Tim said that the last time he was there, the square had been taken over by a homeless camp.

'When was that?' asked Cat.

'Couple of years ago or more,' said Tim. 'It was interesting. I used to go and talk to the guys, a lot of them had fascinating stories. In the end I wrote an article about it. Got published in a Japanese magazine under the title, "Stop Homelessness before it becomes Hopelessness". Good, eh? All got cleared away by the police in the end; lawyers didn't like seeing real people outside their windows.'

'Did you ever see Neil there?' asked Cat, thinking how little they still knew about Neil O'Banyon.

'No,' said Tim. 'Did he become homeless? Poor fellow, but he always was an oddity.'

When Cat walked into the café, the five former students were already assembled. One got up to greet her and the others gave a collective intake of breath.

'You're tall,' said Paul, whom she discovered later was a lawyer.

Cat laughed, once that comment used to annoy her, now she lived with it. She asked the former students what they would like to drink: they had waited for her before ordering.

As Cat tended to confuse the names of people in groups, she had asked Miranda how she differentiated one from another.

'Easy,' said Miranda, with the suavity of one who remembers faces without difficulty. 'As you are introduced to each one of them, describe them to yourself in your mind.'

So now Cat tried to do that.

Karl—who wore a brown corduroy jacket, reminding Cat of another era, and had brown hair, with slightly elephantine ears—worked in the museum as a volunteer, so he had been delighted at the choice of venue.

Paul, the small one who jumped up when she arrived, was almost bald and had a laughing face. He was a lawyer here in Lincoln's Inn. Then there were two men with names beginning with D, Don and Dee, and Tim Tom, who was almost as tall as Cat and had a full head of wavy grey hair.

Paul, the solicitor, did most of the talking.

'Neil was an eccentric teacher,' he said. 'Sometimes he would sneak into the room without your seeing him. You would turn round and there he was like a ghost at the feast. Weird. I always felt there was something slightly fey about him. I sometimes wondered if he might not internally combust before our eyes.' He laughed, his hands waving theatrically.

Cat, whose daughter was also a solicitor, thought Paul might have been more suited to being an actor than a solicitor.

'True. True, Paul,' said another man.

Cat thought it was Don the teacher, but it might have been Dee the accountant, their names were already starting to get mixed up in her head. She wished she'd ignored Miranda's advice and given them labels.

'There was something spooky about him. I remember those times when he came in and slumped in his chair, didn't say a word.'

'That was later,' said Tim. 'That was when he started arriving in class pissed as a newt.'

'He came to school drunk?' Cat was shocked. 'How did that happen?'

Paul laughed. 'Things weren't so strict in the eighties, and it was hard to get physics teachers. The one before Neil was an architect who couldn't find a practice—he left when he got one—and before that we had a man who taught physics in Kenya and got caught up by the Mau Mau. He told us so many stories about atrocities on both sides, we were all longing to join up.'

'No, wait,' said Karl. 'The drunken happenings were after that girl threw him over.'

'What girl?' asked Cat. Now, finally, the interview seemed to be getting useful.

'Don't you remember?' Karl looked round at his colleagues his arms open, pleading. 'He was fine in the early eighties ... enthusiastic, made us love physics ... then just like that everything changed. He was fine on the Tuesday, then, on the Wednesday he came in drunk. It was so sudden I put it in my diary. Ninth of March, it was. That Wednesday he just sat there for the whole hour staring at the classroom as though there was a ghost at the end of the room. At first, we were spooked, then we just ran riot.'

Paul shrugged. 'Was it like that? He was quiet, yes, he was often drunk, but when he was sober, he did stick to the subject. I got physics 'O' level because of him and I'm not a natural scientist.'

'Why do you think a girl was involved?' asked Cat. 'Did he ever talk about anyone, or did you ever meet anyone he knew?'

The others shook their heads, but Karl said, 'Just once, about a week after he started to drink. I'd had a really bad day; I think I might have been crying and he found me in the locker room. He tried to cheer me up, in that funny way he had, sort of patting me on the shoulder like I was a dog and mouthing like a rabbit...' Karl made a nibbling movement with his teeth and lips. 'He often reminded me of a guinea pig, and of course he smelled of garlic like a guinea pig. Anyway, we started talking and he said, "You know, Karl, I've been having a pretty rough time too. Women let you down. They lead you on, and then they kick you in the balls." Sorry,' said Karl, glancing at Cat, 'I'm quoting. I remember he said, "they kick you in the balls".'

Cat smiled. 'Go on.'

'Well, I thought he fancied the maths teacher, so I said, was it her?'

'What?' broke in Paul. 'The mouse? That little skinny one with no boobs?'

Karl nodded. 'Yes, that's her. She wore long, flowery skirts, almost to the ground, Jesus sandals and did her hair in a ponytail.'

'Sounds like you fancied her yourself,' said Paul. 'I just remember she couldn't keep order and people talked all through her lesson. You had to sit at the front to be able to hear what she was saying.'

Karl shrugged. 'Yes, that one. I did sit at the front. Not that it did me any good. I got an F in maths 'O' level.'

'And,' Cat broke in testily, 'was it her? Any idea of her name?'

'Marianne de Laney,' said Karl, while the others exchanged knowing looks. 'But, no, it wasn't her. He said this girl was a pilot and he would have died for her, but she didn't even remember him. That's all I remember. Honestly, you know what kids are, I was more interested in my problems than his.'

'OK,' said Cat, thinking the maths teacher might know more about this and be quite helpful. 'What about the maths teacher, were they friends? Do you know where she is now?'

Four men shook their heads.

'I did go out with her a few times,' Karl volunteered, ignoring the smirks of the other men, 'but she was keen on Neil and talked about him the whole time! It didn't work. I've got an address somewhere, but she might have moved. I'll send it to Tim, and he can send it on to you.'

Cat nodded. 'So,' she asked, 'have any of you ever been to a place called Owly Vale?'

Karl laughed. 'Nice name. Are there lots?'

Cat stared at him. 'Lots of what?'

'Owls. Presumably the name was because of them ... Owly Vale.'

Cat went red and pressed her hands to her cheeks. 'Yes, of course, what an idiot I am. I get so used to calling it Owly

Vale I forget what the name means. Anyone ever been there?'

'Where is it?' asked Paul.

'Oh. Yes. In Sussex, near Chichester.'

'Nice part of the country,' said Karl, while the others murmured about preferring towns, pavements and so on.

'Mud and all that, not much up my street,' said Paul, and laughed. 'See what I did there?'

CHAPTER 16

KNOWLEDGE IS NOT UNDERSTANDING

As Cat drove home, she felt a sense of defeat. Nothing had come from that interview. She knew nothing more about the man, Neil, except the maths teacher might have fancied him and he was a good, if drunken, teacher. No idea of why he stopped teaching. No idea of any friends. Could she find Marianne de Laney, the maths teacher, and interview her? She might know who his friends were and what he liked doing. Cat could imagine them chatting together in the staffroom. If she did fancy him, and it wasn't just an adolescent boy's dream, would he have told her about his love life?

Why would anyone want to kill an ex-physics teacher and ex-airline pilot so much they would lure them to a house in Owly Vale to do the deed? What was special about Owly Vale? Or indeed Neil himself?

Perhaps, she thought, as she turned the wheel into her own drive, she ought to go and interview Neil's dad. He might be ninety-six, and not have seen his son for years, but he still could have some light to throw on Neil's behaviour, even if not his killer. Perhaps there was something in his past? Perhaps Stevie would have some further information from Amy Earhardt, alias BloWoPil. Could anyone normal really call themselves that?

The other two detectives were in the office when Cat walked in, neatly sidestepping Blinkey, who was digging a hole outside the front door watched by the elderly dog.

Cat put down the doughnuts and looked for the kettle, telling her colleagues about the interview with Neil's former students. 'I suppose one of us should go and interview Marianne de Laney,' she said. 'Maybe she was the other person engaged to him. Seems she liked him a lot.'

'Hmm,' said Miranda, waggling her head, 'did she? Do you think she haunted him, perhaps?'

Stevie nodded sagely. 'I'm afraid there's not much on the internet about failed engagements years ago!'

'Ha, ha. Both of you.'

'You know,' said Miranda, 'we keep thinking that the second engagement must have been after Amy, but think of his age.'

'What do you mean?' asked Cat.

'We now know he was born in 1960, so by the time he met Amy he was already twenty-nine. He could have been engaged before Amy, and then that finished somehow. Especially if he was talking to his physics students in the 1980s about a girl who didn't remember him.'

Stevie looked surprised. 'Wouldn't you remember someone you'd been engaged to? I mean, how often does someone get engaged? If a girl didn't remember him, it seems more likely he fancied her, but she wasn't even interested.'

'Good point. Do you think his dad would know?'

'It's possible, although the way he was talking about Neil

it didn't seem like he even remembered who he was. He relied on Hugh to tell him when his wife died.'

'He is ninety-six.'

'Just my point,' said Miranda, although she knew Cat would know it wasn't her original point.

'So,' said Cat, 'just to clarify, you are thinking he might have been engaged to … let's call her Jodie, then something goes wrong, and something happens between them, but she waits until 2008, at least twenty years later, before killing him? Sounds likely to me.'

'Ha, ha, Cat,' said Miranda. 'Very funny. But when you are brainstorming you have to look into all possibilities. Right?'

'Yes, sorry, right.' She blew Miranda a kiss. 'OK, friends again!'

Miranda, seizing the opportunity, said. 'OK. You take the dad, Cat, and I'll interview the Hippy Schoolteacher.'

CHAPTER 17
SPUD THE SHARP POTATO

Marianne de Laney lived in a village outside Chelmsford in Essex. She had recently retired and there was a bicycle leaning against the wall of her flint cottage but no car in sight. Miranda half smiled: she had bought an e-bike as part of her diet and get fit regime, and it sat in the shed waiting for that moment when she had enough time to lose weight.

The small garden was divided into flowers on one side and vegetables on the other. A bench sat half-hidden by the flowers, and a hat and partly drunk cup of tea were balanced on its seat, which shone as though recently oiled.

Miranda walked up to the door just as it opened and a slim, grey-haired woman wearing a caftan walked out. She started when she saw Miranda.

'Oh, sorry. I was just...' She waved at her recently vacated bench. 'I mean, would you like a cup of tea?'

'Yes, please,' said Miranda, more because she wanted to see inside the house than because she wanted to drink tea. 'Thank you.'

As they stepped into the house the woman slipped off

her shoes, so Miranda did the same, saying as she did so, 'I'm Miranda. Are you Marianne de Laney?'

The woman turned around. Gave a sudden spurt of laughter.

'Oh yes, I'm so sorry. Yes, I just assumed you were … given the time. But yes, indeed I'm Marianne, but you can call me Spud, everyone does.'

'Thank you, Spud.'

Miranda stared at her. With her small, thin body and long, girlish hair she was as unlike a potato as any person she had ever seen, but school nicknames were always odd. Miranda was known as Bready, which came from Bread-Roll (Pole), not from wealthy.

'It's short for potato,' said Spud, reading her mind. 'It comes from the Dutch spyd, which first meant a dagger and then a digging instrument. I think my schoolfriends thought I was rather sharp,' she laughed, 'not potato shaped.'

The house was full of flowers, and the women walked through a cacophony of smells to the kitchen, where a large basil and several parsley plants filled the window ledges.

'What sort of tea do you like?' asked Spud. 'I have camomile, mint, rosebush, ginger, lemon and ginger, green tea, Chinese and India teas.' She stopped and waved her hand towards the shelf. 'Do you want to have a look?'

Miranda looked at the cupboard where boxes and boxes of teas stood in line, their labels outwards and their tops neatly shut. She couldn't imagine such a lack of chaos in her kitchen.

'Green tea,' she hazarded, wishing she had asked for wine, but she saw no indication that Spud was a drinker.

'You worked with Neil O' Banyon in the eighties?' Miranda asked as they carried their teas outside to drink in the sunshine, surround by the smell of jasmine and in sight of hellebores.

'Yes, I was so sad to hear he was dead. He was such a kind man.' She paused. 'I saw it on the internet.'

Her pause made Miranda look at her more closely. Did she actually find out some other way, and, if so, why pretend she saw it was on the internet? Was it on the internet? She'd have to ask Stevie. She thought that they had been keeping it low key.

'Did you know him well?' asked Miranda, attempting to put down her cup and finding nowhere flat. She balanced it on a stone under the bench; if it fell over it would save her drinking it.

'In a way. We often met after class. He was an excellent teacher, and he gave me many tips on how to deal with the boys. It wasn't easy in the eighties, teaching a bunch of unruly boys, but he really understood my problems and showed me how to get them in line. I missed him so much when he left, but I understood his dream was not in teaching.'

'What was his dream?'

'It will sound odd.' Spud looked at Miranda and waited for her encouragement.

'Go on.'

'He wanted girls to realise they could fly ... Sorry, I'm not putting that clearly.' Her smile looked sad. 'He would have caught me up for that ... pointed out if you confuse people, they stop learning.' A wave of pain enveloped her face. 'I mean it literally. He wanted more girls to learn to fly, to become airline pilots, or helicopter pilots or something.' She stopped and drank her tea. 'In those days women couldn't fly in the armed forces in the UK, that didn't happen until the late nineties, and even then, opportunities were limited because the police, air ambulance and other outlets preferred ex-military pilots. But Neil was different, he thought women made excellent pilots. He wanted more of them to realise their opportunities.'

Miranda frowned. 'What an odd desire. Why? Did he have a sister or mother or something who wanted to be a pilot and couldn't?'

'No. You have to try and put your mind back to the eighties and nineties.' Spud looked at Miranda and made a face. 'Sorry, you are too young for that, lovey, but even I, who lived through it all, sometimes forget how different times were then, how women struggled to get recognition in any field. Maths teachers, especially ones in caftans and sandals like me, were laughed at. One student said, "If I was a girl like you, Miss, I'd be a hippy too." And he meant it kindly.'

She stretched out her legs. 'Sorry, getting off the point. The point was he, Neil, wanted to encourage women to be more like boys, to think about careers not marriage.'

'But why? And why flying?'

Spud looked around her, and for a moment Miranda thought she might slip off the bench and start weeding, but eventually she looked back at the detective and went on.

'Well, I suppose, since he's dead, it won't matter if I tell you.'

She stopped again and this time Miranda said, 'Go on' immediately.

'He killed someone. A girl. A pilot. He didn't mean to. It was an accident. He left the scene of the crime and ran away. No one ever found out it was him.'

'What? He told you that. And you did nothing?'

'Don't judge me,' said Spud, turning sharply towards Miranda. 'You don't know the facts.'

Miranda bit her lip. 'Sorry! Go on.'

Spud wiggled herself into a more comfortable position on the seat. She moved her hat, so it shaded her face more. Miranda wondered if she was thinking things through, her mind unaware of her automatic movements. Eventually she spoke almost in a whisper, as though there were people in the garden who might be listening.

'The girl was drunk. So drunk she couldn't walk properly, but she was determined to drive home. She got into the driving seat of her car and was fumbling around, trying to start the engine. She had just got the key into the ignition and the engine was turning over when Neil got to her. He thought if she drove, she would kill herself … So, he thought he'd drive her home. He was sober, he told me. Anyway, as they started driving, she fell asleep. Then, after a few minutes, she woke up and tried to climb onto his lap. He was trying to push her off when the car spun out of control. The car rolled over, he couldn't remember how many times, and finally came to a halt upright but in a ditch. She had broken her neck; he could see she was dead by the odd angle she was lying and the blood on her lips. He panicked. Jumped out of the car and walked home. For weeks afterwards he was expecting to be contacted by the police, but it never happened.'

'But what about the accident? Didn't he report it? Or at least try and find out what happened?'

'No.'

She got up and started weeding. After a short pause Miranda went and knelt down beside her. 'Can I help?'

Spud looked up and Miranda saw tears were dripping down her face.

'One of the boys saw him crying in the lockers,' she said, pulling out the weeds and passing them to Miranda, who collected them in a little pile.

'He didn't stay much longer at the school. He told me he was bored of teaching and he was going to fulfil his ambition of becoming a commercial pilot.'

She pulled out more weeds and Miranda added them to the pile.

'He'd started it years ago but ran out of money. He took another loan and went and finished it. I didn't know he was running away until much later, when he told me about the accident.'

She picked up some secateurs and began dead heading.

'When he came back a year or so later and still hadn't heard anything he guessed it was all over. He came back to teaching but he'd lost the spark.'

'When was the accident?'

'Eighth March 1988, he said. I guess you don't forget a date like that.'

'So,' said Miranda slowly, picking up the pile of weeds and passing them back to Spud, 'he was still a physics teacher then?'

Spud put the weeds back on the path and walked back to the bench.

'Yes. He came back in time for the 1989 summer term. But he left the following September anyway, by then he'd got a job as a pilot. The school was annoyed; it's hard enough to find physics teachers, let alone at short notice.'

Miranda frowned. Leaving the scene of the crime was an offence, but in this case it might have changed the outcome from injury to death.

'You say he saw from the angle she must be dead. So, he didn't know for certain she was dead. She could have been alive. If he'd reported it, she might have been saved.'

Marianne wrinkled her nose and shook her head.

'Oh, yes. No. Maybe. But a couple or more years later he

was at a dinner, and he ran into the girl who had given the 1988 party. He asked her whether the girl in whose honour the party was given was a pilot now. His friend looked very sad and said no, she'd got so drunk at the party that she'd been killed driving herself home. Which of course explains why they weren't looking for him. They thought she was driving herself. Which she would have been, if he hadn't intervened, so the outcome was the same.'

Miranda looked at Spud to see if she was being ironic, but there was no trace of it on her face. Indeed, the way she was looking down at the flowerbeds Miranda got the feeling her mind had gone back to weeding.

'Can you remember the name of the woman who gave the party?'

'He didn't tell me.'

Figures, thought Miranda. *If Spud did tell anyone about the incident, he could just deny it, and without facts Spud would just look like an idiot.*

'So, when did he tell you about it? While you were still working together?'

'No.' Spud shook her head. 'Not until years later. We kept in contact; we had dinners...' Her voice drifted away, and she seemed to be reliving some of the dinners. Perhaps she was walking along the Thames, chatting with her old friend, laughing about their teaching years. Happy.

'Were you in love with him?' Miranda asked. There seemed no other reason to keep such a devastating secret.

Spud returned her attention to her guest with a jolt, as though she had forgotten she was there. 'Yes, of course. But not in the way you young people are now, with your revenge porn and your acid throwing. I adored him, but it wasn't sexual. He had no attraction to me, except as a friend, but I was used to that. I finally got used to the idea I wasn't sexy in my forties.' She shrugged. 'My sister, she's the sexy one! She's always in and out of relationships.' She snorted. 'But in the end, we both let my mother down.'

Miranda frowned. 'How so?'

Spud had been drifting off again, but she said, 'Oh! No children. My mother wanted grandchildren. In theory, my sister could—she's fifteen years younger than me—but she won't. Always chooses the wrong men. She likes the nutters!'

Miranda said nothing, uncertain what to say.

CHAPTER 18
QUESTIONS AND ANSWERS

Next morning, after braving the Password Queen and making it to the office, Miranda found Stevie making coffee and filled her in on the details of the interview.

'Honestly, Stevie,' said Miranda, 'I don't know what to make of it. Neil kills someone, tells the maths teacher, who by all accounts was in love with him, and then buggers off to live another life.'

'Why did he tell her?'

'What?'

'Well,' said Stevie, 'it happened when they were working together and he kept it a secret, and then he tells her when he has left teaching and is working as a pilot. Years later. Why tell her? Especially as she said he wasn't in love with her. It would open him to blackmail for a start.'

'Good point.'

'And why did she tell you about it? There she was, going on about how she didn't do revenge porn or throw acid like the current generation, and she is telling you something that never need be told. Why?'

'Another good point.'

'And how did she know he was dead? I agree it would be easy to find out, but it isn't on the internet. Although,' said Stevie, suddenly stopping in thought, 'I suppose it might be now. If his dad has buried him, it could be on one of the funeral sites. But that would necessitate her looking for him.'

'I suppose a mutual friend might have told her. Or perhaps a ghost.' Miranda giggled.

Stevie stared at the computer. 'Unlikely. I'll look up the dead girl, see what I can find out about her. What was her name?'

'Spud couldn't remember. I wasn't sure how seriously she took it; she seemed more animated when she was talking about Neil himself. By the way, how was your trip to the nightclub?'

'Good,' said Stevie, 'but Victoria can't have murdered anyone. She's in a wheelchair and has been for years.'

For some reason she couldn't explain to herself, she didn't tell Miranda that Victoria was the woman with the stolen Yaris.

'Ha,' said Miranda, 'there speaks someone too young to remember *Ironside*.'

Stevie frowned. 'Re the car crash: I'll ask a few of my police friends or your sister, but I doubt anyone will remember a car accident in March 1988, although there will be records; deaths are always recorded. Did Spud think the dead girl was a stranger to Neil or a friend?'

'I thought a stranger, why?'

'Well, since Spud said they were celebrating her job it would make it unusual. In the eighties, there were very few female commercial pilots. It would certainly give someone a motive to kill Neil, say if they saw their friend drive off with him, and then the next day she was dead.'

Miranda nodded.

'Incidentally,' said Stevie, struck by a sudden memory. 'Victoria said it was her therapist who suggested she moved to Owly Vale. He seemed to know about the house.'

'Oh,' said Miranda away in her head and missing the question. 'Do you think someone in the village found out about Neil's crime and decided to do him in? At least that would make the location understandable.'

Stevie shook her head. 'But what would be the connection with the house, Wild Garlic? Unless it was just coincidence. Someone who was living there. Or perhaps Neil wanted to rent it.'

Miranda nodded. 'OK, so it's back to the house lists. Who was living there in 1988?'

Stevie leant forward. 'Actually, Clive Creamer.'

'Well,' said Miranda thoughtfully, 'he is nutty as a fruitcake. Could it be a front, and really he's a steely cold deadly killer? Perhaps he just liked the idea of killing someone. Or maybe this relates to his ancestor.'

She danced around the room, still talking. 'How about that Neil is a descendant of the chap in the tower, and Clive got revenge for his forebear by luring him to Wild Garlic and killing him? As motives go, it might be a hard one to prove.'

She stopped and hovered over the doughnut thoughtfully. Pulling her hand away regretfully, she said, 'We should interview him. You want to do it?'

Stevie pulled in her chin and shook her head. 'No way. Right out my league. Pilots are hard enough but crazy freeholders. Uh, uh. No thanks.'

Miranda twisted her nose. 'Since he speaks English, we

don't need the multilingual Cat to do it. I guess I'll do it myself. When a thing needs doing…'

Miranda started singing.

Stevie grabbed her headset and turned back to the computer. Why did everyone around her keep bursting into song?

'Good luck,' she mouthed at Miranda, before turning up the volume in her headset.

CHAPTER 19

SWITZERLAND IN WEST SUSSEX

S tevie was working on the computer when her phone rang. It was scheduling and she heard with a sinking heart that yet again her flying had been cancelled. 'We've put you on another flight in two days' time, love,' said the voice. 'All right?'

Stevie felt like saying she was not her 'love' and, no, it was not at all 'all right' and this was at least the third time her schedule had been changed, but instead she said, 'Yes, fine, thanks,' hoping they heard the exasperation in her voice.

She hadn't got back into her work when the phone rang again. Honestly, could they be going to pull that flight too? It was so annoying. She looked at the legend. No caller ID.

It could be from the scheduler's own phone, in which case let her try again. Tiresome people. So irritating.

Or perhaps it was spam. She didn't like the phone much at the best of times, and she certainly didn't want a salesman pushing her to buy something she didn't want. It went to answerphone and a moment later the phone pinged with a text message.

The message said: Victoria at Spinners. Call me back, please.

Stevie moved the phone from hand to hand uncertainly. At least it said please, although it did sound like a command.

Why would Victoria call her? Had she left something behind? Was there something she wanted to tell her? What could be the reason?

While she dithered, Victoria rang again.

Stevie stared at the machine. It must be important if she was ringing again immediately. Perhaps there was an emergency, or perhaps she had found the therapist's details to give her. This time she made the choice to answer.

'Hello?'

'Hi, Stevie, it's Victoria, from Spinners. Sorry to call you, but I wondered if you could help me with something. It's a bit strange but I couldn't think of anyone else I could trust to help me. Usually I use the boys, but this is something where only a woman can help.'

Stevie's mind boggled. What could Victoria need that could only be done by a woman? And one she hardly knew.

'Are you very busy,' asked Victoria, 'or would you mind coming over? I'm not far away. I'm not in Clerkenwell but staying in a hotel near Goodwood. Can you help me?'

Stevie hesitated. Uncertain. She didn't do things on the spur of the moment. She was a planner. A planner on the edge of an adventure? Scary! She could say no, she was busy. She would have been busy. But, thanks to scheduling, she wasn't. She dithered.

'Hello, Stevie,' said Victoria. 'Are you still there? Have I caught you at a bad time? I'm so sorry, it's just...' and her voice trembled slightly. 'It's just I didn't have anyone else to turn to.'

'Yes, of course,' said Stevie, feeling guilty. Here was the poor woman asking for a bit of help and she was dithering. How silly she was. 'Of course, what would you like me to do?'

Victoria's sigh of relief spun out of the phone like a congratulatory telegram.

'Thank you. Can you come over, and I'll explain.'

'OK, I could be there in half an hour. Would that work for you? Where exactly are you?'

'Thank you so much.' Again, Victoria's voice was a mixture of joy and relief, and Stevie felt the power of her gratitude. She smiled to herself feeling a spurt of joy knowing that she could help another human being with a problem

'That would be perfect. I'm at the Hotel du Lac. Ask for me at the reception and they'll tell you how to get to my room.'

* * *

The Hotel du Lac was in a well-developed park with an avenue of trees that had probably seen the Conquest. It led to the building, itself an inspiring neo-gothic edifice with a sweeping staircase and two large turrets on either side of the facade. There was no evidence of a lake unless it was behind the house. Stevie had had time to look it up before leaving home, and although she thought the name a bit pretentious her investigation had shown why. The Hotel du Lac was half hotel and half sanitorium, based on a Swiss Alpine model, something that reflected the wishes of its benefactors.

She asked for Victoria at reception and was greeted with a wide smile and a sing song voice. 'Miss Victory is in her room. I'm Heide. If you follow me, I'll show you where it is.'

Stevie followed the receptionist down a rabbit warren with wide corridors: someone had considered wheelchairs when they built this place. Heide told her the hotel spa was started by Second World War Jewish refugees from Romania, who had escaped first to Switzerland and later to the UK. Their experience in Switzerland had left them with an everlasting feeling of gratitude to the Swiss clinic in which they had been hidden, hence they had decided to create this place, which was half clinic and half hotel.

'Here we are,' Heide said, knocking on a wide door. It swung open automatically. Victoria was sitting in an armchair framed by large windows, which gave out to a hilly, though not mountainous, view. Stevie's stomach gave a strange leap; the woman looked so vulnerable and beautiful sitting there. Backlit as she was, Stevie could imagine what she must have looked like before injury riveted her face with lines of pain.

'So, Miss Victory,' said Heide, walking in and automatically tiding a few things in the room, 'now your friend is with you, I'll be gone.'

Stevie went over to the window and sat down opposite Victoria. She noted absently that both chairs had controls to lift you forward if necessary and started investigating how they worked.

'Hello,' said Victoria. 'I'm over here.'

Stevie jumped and forced her attention away from the controls of the chair.

'Sorry. I was just seeing how it worked.'

Victoria spat a laugh. 'Ever the pilot! Or perhaps that should be the engineer. I know plenty of pilots who hardly know how their planes fly.'

Stevie grimaced and hastily returned to a safer subject. 'Why do they call you Miss Victory?'

Victoria snorted. 'It's from a song, "Miss Victory Overcomes". Listen.'

She took a deep breath and, raising her head, slowly eased into the song in an elegant, alto voice. Stevie bit her lip; it sounded so sad and yet so lyrical. The words, too, had resonance as the story of a young woman who overcomes every challenge she is set until the last impossible task when she perishes. Stevie saw there were tears in Victoria's eyes, and she longed to put her hand on the woman's arm, the way she knew Miranda would have done, to comfort her. But Stevie did not dare.

'That's so lovely,' she said. 'I've never heard it before.'

'Thank you,' said Victoria, 'I wrote it myself. Before my accident I used to sing in a folk band, and I often wrote the lyrics and the music. It was rather too perspicacious!'

'And now?'

'No. With the club it was too much commitment, but it means I can interview all the singers for the nightclub and really enjoy and evaluate them. You sing?'

Stevie shook her head. 'What was it you wanted me to do?'

'Help me go swimming,' said Victoria, smiling. 'I've had terrific backache recently.' As Stevie looked sympathetic, Victoria shook her head. 'It's very common if you live in a wheelchair, all the wrong muscles wasting and wearing away. Anyway, the physios suggested lots of swimming. I can do most of it myself, but it's difficult to get in and out of the pool and to get changed. Even in the pool it helps to have someone there. I don't want to waste the physios' time, but I find it almost impossible to do unaided. You on?'

'Yes, of course, but if you need me to swim too, I'll have to go home to get my costume.'

Victoria shook her head. 'It's OK, I bought one in your size. I had to guess, but I'm quite good at sizes. I'm used to buying clothes for the nightclub staff.'

Stevie looked at her, hoping desperately Victoria hadn't bought her a bikini. She'd much rather wear a burkini than that. 'OK,' she said, her heart beating rather faster than normal. This adventure was really testing her courage.

'It's in the bathroom. Do you want to change and then come and help me do the same.'

Stevie followed her pointing finger and found a big room with large hoist over the bath. Whey did her mind jump to the inquisition? To lowering sinners into boiling oil. She bit her lower lip. She really was awfully strange. Did other people also think like that?

On a chair with a cork seat was a one-piece swimsuit and a beach dress. She put them on.

'Thank you,' she said, walking back into Victoria's room. 'They're perfect. Exactly what I would have chosen myself.'

Victoria smiled. 'My gift to you for helping me. I realize you must have thought my phone call a bit strange, but I don't know anyone else down here. When I lived in Owly Vale I wasn't in the mood to make friends.'

Stevie nodded. 'I so understand. I'm not someone who makes friends easily, either, not like Miranda, who only has to be introduced to someone to become best buddies.'

Victoria laughed. 'I'd like to meet your colleagues one day; they sound fun.'

Stevie nodded, wondering why she hadn't told her colleagues that she was meeting Victoria. She shook herself. She couldn't tell Miranda and Cat every detail of her life.

'Yes,' she said in a positive voice, 'they are. OK, where do we start?'

'OK,' said Victoria, 'I can undress myself—obviously—but if you help me, it will be quicker. Then I need you to help me put the swimming suit over my feet, I'll stand and you can drag it up the rest of the way. Is that OK for you?'

Stevie felt slightly dizzy, but she nodded. 'Yes, sure. I'll try and be gentle. I do occasionally have to help my mother dress and undress, but she complains I'm rough.'

Victoria made a gesture. 'I don't believe it.'

Stevie helped Victoria take off her clothes, but as the girl stood up, pushing from the arms of her chair in a strong, swift movement, and Stevie removed her trousers, she couldn't help feeling a strange sensation in her stomach. She'd never seen a beautiful woman completely naked, and Victoria, despite being so thin, was a marvellous piece of human architecture: a Greek marble goddess with long, elegant bones and lean muscles. Her skin shone smoothly between the scars, which glared out like red tattoos. Stevie tried not to stare at her body and concentrated hard on helping her into the swimsuit.

When they were ready, Victoria said, 'OK, in the bathroom there's a towelling robe, I'll wear that until we arrive at the pool.' She spread her hands and grinned. 'Clothes that would be normal at the club would be embarrassing here.'

As Stevie walked back into the bathroom, she noticed there was a shower at the far end of the room and a plastic chair flipped down, so someone could shower sitting. The shower itself was huge enough to drive in a wheelchair and the controls were at waist height.

She forced herself to stop thinking about the equipment and picked up the towelling robe. Back in the bedroom, Victoria, leaning on the wheelchair arms, was already standing. Stevie was a little surprised how well she was standing, given she couldn't walk. *Shows how little I know about the human machine*, she thought.

Victoria noticed Stevie's gaze and said, 'It helps to stand a bit. Stretch. Cramps. Pains that travel from one side to the other, that's my fate from now on.' Her smile was ruefully twisted. 'OK, put the robe on, one arm at a time. Yes, just like that. Brilliant, thanks.'

She sat down again, and Stevie looked down at the chair, analysing it. She saw there were basic brakes and bent down to push them off in the quick movement.

Victoria laughed. 'Nice. You'd be amazed how many people try and push against the brakes. You obviously have a technical mind.'

Stevie shrugged. 'I do, but sometimes it seems like an impediment, rather than a blessing. I just don't think the way other people do.'

'Ha,' said Victoria, 'welcome to the world of the few.'

Stevie pushed the chair out into the corridor to the lift that took them down to the pool. On the lift there were two sets of buttons, one set lower than the other. Stevie pursed her lips. There was so much here she had never considered before. When the lift doors opened, Stevie saw the space inside was huge, easily room enough for several wheelchair users and their attendants. A couple of physiotherapists and a nurse were helping a man with cerebral palsy.

'Hi, Miss Victory,' said one of the physios. 'Off swimming?'

'Yes, you too?'

'Yes, it's so good. Swimming does wonders for us all.' She paused and smiled. 'Are you still in touch with Anthony? I'd like to get in contact with him if I could. I've got a patient who would benefit.'

Victoria grimaced. 'No, sorry, not anymore.'

'Never mind.'

The lift ended at the far side of the swimming pool, and Stevie pushed Victoria over towards the steps.

'Who was Anthony?' asked Stevie.

'My therapist,' said Victoria in a dismissive voice.

'Oh. Of course. I forgot.'

'OK,' said Victoria, before they reached the steps, 'if you take off your dress and my robe and hang them over there, then roll the chair to the edge of the pool where the railings are, I'll stand up while you take away the chair and then you can help me walk into the water.'

Stevie did as instructed, putting Victoria's arm around her shoulder to help her into the water.

'You are a lot taller than I thought,' said Stevie, as the girl towered above her slight frame.

Victoria snorted. 'Yes, I was tall before, but I lost height in the accident. Of course, when you only see people sitting down you don't realize how tall they are.'

Stevie hoped she hadn't insulted her and looked anxiously at the woman, but Victoria was still smiling in her rather tense manner.

'You don't weigh anything,' said Stevie, helping her into the water and floating her on her back. 'I feel as though I could knock you over with one finger.'

Victoria laughed. 'You'd be surprised. My upper half is all muscle. I could lift you up, or indeed a full-sized man, provided I was seated when I did it. OK, so if you just support my legs and I'll swim with my arms.'

Stevie balanced her arms under Victoria's legs. Her legs were discoloured but not entirely, as though the circulation only moved through sluggishly, and thin as though the muscles had wasted away from disuse. *Were bodies like machines?* Stevie wondered. Was there some way you could inhibit the engine of the body, presumably the heart, so, like an unused aircraft engine, it would be perfect when it restarted?

As they swam up and down in unison, Victoria said, 'Lots of similarities between the freedom of swimming and that of flying in the air. Maybe one day we could go wild swimming together. That would be just like taking the Cub to unknown areas.'

'I'd love to,' said Stevie sincerely. 'I've never been wild swimming, but I love taking my Tiger Moth to strips or unknown places.'

Victoria gasped and nearly sank. She coughed. 'You've got a Tiger Moth? Wow! How wild. I'd love to see that.'

Stevie smiled. 'You can, of course. I'd be happy to take you flying.'

Victoria balanced her head back on the water and said nothing. Stevie hoped she hadn't upset her: it was hard for pilots to be just passengers.

After an hour Victoria said she felt much, much better.

'You'll have to help me get out—it's hard, I'm afraid.' Her smiled was twisted as though an apology. 'But my arms are strong, and I can help you.'

Stevie brought the chair to the edge of the pool, by the steps. Victoria swam to the base of the steps and with a quick flick of her strong arm and shoulder muscles transferred onto the third step. She reached her hands into the water and pulled her limp feet on the second step.

'OK, put the brakes on, then I'm going to push up on my hands and balance with my feet, and you can push the chair under my bottom.'

Stevie could hardly believe it was possible. It seemed much more likely that she would end up flipping Victoria back into the water headfirst. She didn't argue but did as she was told, and to her joy, Victoria's bottom ended up on the seat.

'Brilliant!' said Victoria. 'Well done, Stevie. Not everyone manages so well first time. I've been tipped, knocked, bruised and occasionally nearly drowned. But you are a natural. Thank you.'

Stevie blushed. 'It was nothing,' she murmured.

As she wheeled Victoria back to her room, the feeling grew in Stevie that she actually had done something amazing today, totally helped another human being in a way she never had before.

'OK,' said Victoria, 'can you wheel me into the bathroom? I've got a chair in the shower and if you can just help me off with my swimsuit and then push the chair close to the stool, I can transfer.'

Victoria stood, shaking slightly from the exertion, while Stevie helped her off with her swimsuit, again trying to avert her eyes from the woman's beautiful body. She imagined Victoria would have married if she was not injured. Perhaps it was harder to find boyfriends if you used a wheelchair.

'OK, Stevie,' said Victoria, 'if you don't mind helping me out, when I've finished you can have a shower after me.' She paused. 'Unless you'd like to shower with me, but I don't want to embarrass you.' She smiled gently. 'I don't want to use you, but if you stay you can help me wash the chlorine off my back. But *definitely* don't feel forced. I don't want to make you uncomfortable.'

Stevie had been about to leave the room, but hearing Victoria's bashful voice she paused. She'd seen every detail of Victoria's body, and it seemed almost childishly arrogant to be so shy about her own. Nobody had ever seen her naked since she'd grown up. But perhaps she was being silly.

Perhaps Victoria meant her to enter the shower still wearing her swimsuit. She stood anxiously vacillating.

'Of course,' said Victoria, and her voice sounded slightly harsh to Stevie's ears, 'doctors, therapists, nurses, they all find it perfectly normal that I am stripped naked in front of them. But I never see anything of their bodies. I am the ultimate survivor of *Le Déjeuner sur l'herbe*: the naked Dalit amongst clothed Brahmins. Even while they do me good, they lord over me.'

'Oh,' said Stevie, her heart beating hard with sympathy. 'No, of course I'll help you.'

Taking a deep breath, she slipped off her costume and joined Victoria in the shower.

'Thank you, Stevie,' said Victoria, her voice full of emotion. 'You are so kind and sensitive. Few people understand how much like a piece of meat it is possible to feel, when everything is done for me, and I can do so little for myself.'

Stevie turned on the water and tried to close her mind to her nakedness so close to another human being. However, Victoria remained so matter of fact that Stevie started to relax and washed the girl's back, staring curiously at the rib bones which protruded sharply from the skin and muscles. Even so, she felt relieved when Victoria said that was enough, and even when Victoria turned on her seat and brushed Stevie's body, she realised it must be an accident.

Stevie turned off the water, and leapt out of the shower, getting the towel, draping it over the chair as instructed by Victoria's pointing hand.

'OK, push the chair in here and I'll do a transfer.'

Stevie did as she was told, although really, she wanted to grab her own robe and put it on. But poor Victoria! So hard always to be the person who was helped and being unable to do anything in return. How must that feel? At least she, Stevie, had a choice.

'If I stand up,' Victoria was saying, cutting into Stevie's thoughts, 'then can you help dry me? Obviously, I can't reach anywhere below the waist and if the skin isn't properly dried it can get quite sore.'

'Yes, of course,' said Stevie, doing as instructed. It was just like helping her mother, wasn't it?

'Thanks, and if you push me into the bedroom, you'll find some cream on the dressing table. Yes, that's it, if you could just rub that on my bottom ... Ah, thanks, prevents sores, which is so important. When you're able-bodied, you have no idea how many things are difficult for someone wheelchair-bound.'

Once they were both dry and dressed, Stevie thought it was probably time to go home. She imagined this type of therapy must be quite tiring for Victoria. However, before she could say anything, Victoria said, 'Thank you so much, Stevie. Let me buy you dinner before you go home. When are you next flying? Have we got time?'

'Oh, yes, thank you,' said Stevie, hearing her stomach rumble at the thought of food and smiling in embarrassment. 'I'm starving. I've got two days, and then I'm off to South America. Unless scheduling change it again.'

Victoria frowned sympathetically.

The dining room had been designed with the same ethos as the hotel. It was a canteen with everything at a lower level than normal and with inlets into the serving area. Between the chairs at the table were large spaces, and the floor was flat and even. For the first time ever, Stevie realised that most canteens did not usually cater for disabled people: to access most of the food you had to be accompanied by a friend or ask the servers for help. *Wow,* she thought, *it never crossed my mind before, how narrowly I think.*

Although the choice of food was limited, the quality was excellent. Stevie had a steak sandwich and salad, while Victoria had a veal and mushroom ragout.

'I like coming here,' said Victoria, 'even though the food at Spinners is much better, and they don't serve alcohol here.' She looked at Stevie and smiled. 'Not, I suppose that you care about that.'

Stevie shook her head. Again, feeling like that church mouse.

'Tell me about the Tiger Moth. How did you get it? A present from a devoted lover? You must have had lots of those.'

Stevie blushed and shook her head. 'I was on my way home from school, on my bike, and I saw a Tiger Moth had landed in a nearby field. I ran up in case the pilot wanted help. When the pilot's helmet came off I saw it was an old woman. She told me her name was Claire and that she had been taught to fly by Douglas Bader. She offered me a flight. I couldn't believe it. I sat at the controls while she hand-swung the propeller. And then, as soon as we lifted off from the ground, I knew I wanted to do this forever.

Every weekend she took me flying—she wouldn't let me miss school, although I'd have been happy to. Soon, I was the pilot and she was the passenger. When she died, only two years later, she left me the Tiger in her will.'

Stevie looked out of the window at the growing darkness. 'She was one of the kindest women I've ever met.'

Victoria laughed. 'So, you learnt to fly on the Tiger? Nice. Wheeled and soared and swung / High in the sunlit silence...'

She paused and Stevie continued, grinning. 'Hov'ring

there, I've chased the shouting wind along, and flung my eager craft through footless halls of air.'

'Lovely,' said Victoria. 'Not many people can finish that quote for me.'

The girls both laughed and Stevie felt an odd surge in her heart.

'There were several Tigers at White Waltham,' said Victoria. 'I used to swap rides with the Cub; it was brilliant. One day we will fly together, but now I guess I'd better get to bed, and you need to go home.'

Stevie looked at her watch and realised, shocked, it was already ten p.m.

'I'll walk you to your car,' said Victoria and then laughed. 'You know, after all these years I still say that. It doesn't sound the same to say *I'll wheel you to your car,* although that's what I'm doing.'

As they moved through the car park Victoria looked up at the starlit sky.

'Do you ever navigate by the stars?'

'What?'

'Don't you fly the Tiger at night?'

'Well, no, not usually. I don't have any lights on the strip.'

'But you have friends.'

'What?'

'And they have cars, with car headlights!'

'Yes, of course.'

Victoria laughed happily. 'You have no idea what I'm talking about, do you? We used to do it all the time. Place the cars around the strip, lights on full beam. It's perfect. It's like a full lighting system, even better if you fly in a full moon. We'll have to do it together sometime. You got any reliable friends with cars?'

'Oh, yes. Well, that is my colleagues, Cat and Miranda,

would love it. Or Cat would. Miranda isn't one for planes, but she loves a laugh, a bit of fun. She'd be on for it!'

They arrived at the car and Victoria smiled seeing the Triumph Spitfire dwarfed by the Audis and BMWs around it.

'It's like you,' she said, laughing gently.

Stevie pouted. 'How so?'

'It's a classic, bit old-fashioned and everyone would love to have one, if they could afford to run it.'

Stevie laughed. 'Thank you.'

Victoria smiled at her, held out her hand. 'Thank *you*, Stevie. This was such an amazing day. I couldn't have done without your help.'

Stevie blushed. 'Oh, it was nothing. How much longer are you down here? Do you need any more help?'

'Sadly, I must go back to London tomorrow. I find that if I'm away too long standards in the club start slipping and I really don't want that. One of the unique things about Spinners is its attention to detail. But, Stevie, I hope you'll come and visit me again at the nightclub. I need to buy you a big drink for all your help.'

'Oh, yes of course,' said Stevie, suddenly filled with a crashing sense of abandonment. She had had the most intimate moment of her life, but perhaps to Victoria it was just another day, another helper.

Victoria waved her goodbye and wheeled herself back into the hotel without looking back. Stevie lifted her hand in response before climbing into the car. Once in the Spitfire, she flopped back not even noticing the softness of the seats in her daze. A moment ago, she was the closest she had ever come to another human being, and she had done something special. Now what?

On the other hand, she could already see Victoria had

mood swings. Did she even like her? She wasn't sure. She couldn't explain the conflicting feelings in her body and was so glad that she was going flying in a couple of days and would be away for a couple of weeks. Only flying could help her here.

CHAPTER 20
CLIVE CREAMER'S DREAMS

Clive Creamer lived in a small hamlet close to Owly Vale. It was up a steep hill and for a moment Miranda considered taking her e-bike, but, after another glance at the hill, she got into the open-top Mazda Phillip had found cheap on the internet.

Clive was waiting for her, standing outside, leaning on a stick, and he waved his free arm when he saw the Mazda. 'Great little cars. Remind me of Noddy, remember that?'

'I know what you mean,' said Miranda. She had the vague idea that Noddy was some cartoon from the 1950s.

'Odd woman, that Enid Blyton,' said Clive, putting both hands on the stick and leaning forward. 'Came to talk to us once at school. When it came to questions, she took everyone's except mine. So unfair. I kept my hand up the whole time, even when she was talking, so it wasn't that she hadn't seen me.'

'Oh.'

'Yes, never forgave her. Wouldn't have those Noddy books in the house. They got banned anyway, didn't they? Can't call someone Big Ears these days, can you?'

'No.'

'So, how are you getting on with my house? Found out why the blighter won't sell? Honestly, one moment they're telling you that post-COVID village houses are like hot cakes steaming out the oven, then they're saying no one wants to live in villages as they would have to use their cars and they're all eco babies, so they don't have independent transport. Well, the government should have thought about that before they pulled up all the train lines and dis-enfranchised the buses, shouldn't they?'

He glared at Miranda as though it were her fault. She almost expected him to lift his stick and wave it at her.

'All right? Well, I suppose you want coffee, do you? Women always want coffee. It's as though they have some kind of underachieving vessel in their bodies that needs constant regeneration. You don't find men meeting for a coffee, do you? We go out for a beer in the pub. Honestly, women! Don't understand jokes, get the punchline wrong every time and drink coffee and tea instead of beer. What was God thinking of, eh?'

Miranda guessed that he might be joking, but she wasn't sure.

'What did you want to talk to me about, anyway, if you haven't found out why it wouldn't sell? Come on in. We'll go into the kitchen while I make that coffee you insisted on. Got a machine, you know. You'll like the coffee. Really good. Could be in Tuscany. When I get rid of that doghouse that's what I'm going to do, get a house in Tuscany. They don't have wild garlic in Tuscany. Once I reckoned that was why the blooming place wouldn't sell: the smell. Even when I tried to dig the damn things up, they all came back the following year. It's a curse, I tell you!'

He stopped to open the door and ushered Miranda into

the sort of farmhouse kitchen that had never been used by a farmer.

He continued talking as he limped along behind her. Miranda wondered what had happened to him that he needed the stick.

'By then, the Queen should have granted my grace-and-favour house. You know about my poor ancestor, don't you? They should have given me compensation years ago. But bureaucracy takes forever, don't it, eh? I keep writing to the Queen and I know she's very sympathetic, the first letter said so, but now all her so-called ladies-in-waiting—although I can't imagine what they are waiting for, unless they want a grace-and-favour house too, then they'll wait for ever!' He reached out to slap her on the shoulder but missed and ended up stoking her arm and almost over-balancing himself. 'Funny, eh? But as I said, all those ladies-in-waiting now block the letters, so the Queen never gets to see a leaf. And I have written quite a few leaves over these last few years.'

He stopped talking to put a coffee in front of Miranda, and she hastily started the interview before he started again.

'Can we talk about when you lived in Wild Garlic, please?' said Miranda.

Clive sat down heavily on a stool, balancing the stick on his knees. 'Hmm, yes. I lived there back in the late eighties and early nineties, seems like a hundred years ago now, doesn't it? Things were good then. I had a lovely girl then, Phylida was her name, gorgeous girl, full of life and fun. Such a shame.'

'Shame? Why? What happened?'

'She was killed in a road traffic accident. Some hit-and-run driver, bastard. Not far from here. Poor love. Devastating it was.'

He was silent, while Miranda battled with her detective self. Presumably this was the same ghostly Phylida who had haunted the Haydons. Was this more of his eccentricity or had she really been killed in a hit-and-run accident?

'I'm sorry,' said Miranda, keeping her face serious, her detective side winning the battle. 'Did you ever find out who did it?'

Clive stared at her as though he hadn't heard the question. Eventually he said, 'No.'

He hit his stick on the ground fiercely.

'So, what happened. How did she come to get killed? And when?'

'March 1988. She was picking flowers along the verge and some drunken git driving far too fast went out of control, car spun, and she was knocked right off the road and into the field. Drunk, of course. Pubs are open far too long these days. They should bring back licencing hours, those stopped people getting drunk, but everything has changed since my youth. And not for the better. He was so drunk he drove off in the opposite direction. Not even realising the car had done one-eighty degrees. Can you believe it?'

'How do you know?'

'What?'

'Well, there weren't any cameras or anything in those days. If you don't know who did it, how do you know he drove off in the opposite direction?'

Clive stared at her, his face changing from amused to angry. 'You think you can trick me, don't you, silly bitch? Well, ha! Bad luck! It was from the skid marks in the road. What? You think then that I tracked him down and murdered him. You think he might be the body in the house? That's a laugh! As though I'd do that to my own house. You detectives, you think of everything, don't you? Well, you put that out of your mind and find out why my house won't sell. I'm paying you lot enough. Got any clues yet why no one wants my house? Bloody useless freeloaders, you lot are.'

Never again, Miranda told her detective alias. Why didn't she get the interviews in the bar?

* * *

'Honestly, Cat,' said Miranda later, 'he's mad as a hatter. Pretty much accused me of thinking he was a murderer. He is a weirdo, all right. He might just have done it!'

Cat gave an ironic laugh. 'There would be a sort of circular craziness of employing us to find out why the house wouldn't sell, when it was owing to a murder he himself committed. Nice! Ah well, better go. Frank's got a gig tonight and I'm probably going to be his only audience.'

'Oh! OK,' said Miranda, 'have fun.'

She watched Cat leave, humming to herself, and felt left out. Cat could have asked her to go too; they could have been an audience of two watching Frank's weirdly unfunny comedy.

Of course, Cat had been miserable herself after her husband, Charlie, died, but after recovering from a suicide attempt—something, Miranda reminded herself silently, she only failed to do thanks to Miranda's intervention—she got herself a translator's job and travelled the world. There she met Frank; the only Liverpudlian comic in Seville.

Miranda snorted. If Cat could do it, so could she. She walked to the fridge and was about to pour herself a drink when she thought about Neil. That was not what she wanted; talking was what she needed.

Miranda's mother, who brought up three daughters on her own after her husband committed suicide, said to her eldest daughter, 'When I feel too down, I put on my best clothes and go out to tea somewhere lovely. It makes me feel better.'

'OK, Mother,' said Miranda putting the bottle back in the fridge. 'I'll do that. But, it won't be a cup of tea. Stevie isn't the only one who can visit a nightclub!'

CHAPTER 21
WALKING ON THE WILD SIDE

Jenny was excited; she was trembling so much she could hardly open the car door, and her dress shook around her like a swan's wings in a tornado.

In social life, as in work, preparation is everything. In the bath Jenny'd shaved her legs, already dreaming of the beautiful dress she would slip on, how sexy she would look, the glances of admiration she would get as she walked into the bar, her high heels clicking on the wooden floors.

How she loved the anticipation of it all.

She often went to Spinners nightclub, but tonight was a bit special. Her spouse, a pilot, was away flying, and she had taken the opportunity to meet an old girlfriend; someone who understood her in the way her lovely but unidirectional spouse never would. Jenny loved Spinners because it was a safe space, full of pilots and their partners, free from hassle but with the knowledge you could make new friends, dance with anyone there and nothing would be expected from you. The owner was a pilot, and all the staff were briefed to keep a close eye on anyone hassling the clients. You had only to flash a look at the barman for him to come over and protect you; especially that sexpot with the muscles and tantalising scar: Jenny's favourite.

Spinners had an underground car park so Jenny could drive. Again the owner had thought about protection from inquisitive taxi drivers and from the possibility of attack when leaving the club. There was even a little bed upstairs for dire emergencies, although Jenny had never used it. Clients were encouraged, if they thought they were over the limit, to leave their cars behind and return in the morning to pick them up, for no extra charge; 'Prior Planning Prevents Piss-ups,' said Jenny to herself and smiled: many a pilot had repeated that to him or herself, but whether they acted on it or simply had another piss-up, that was another matter.

The climb up from the car park to the bar above was short, and there was a lift and a ramp. Victoria parked her own car here. It was unique that car: Victoria had had it specially designed inside so it accommodated all her needs. Something, Jenny thought, that would baffle any joyrider attempting to steal it; not that they'd dare, Victoria was far too powerful and her reach too wide.

Jenny walked into the club like an actress arriving at a gala: swirling in, bestowing her favours widely.

'Here I am!'

But no one noticed. The place was half empty and none of the clients even glanced up, in admiration or otherwise, too busy with their own entertainment to give a middle-aged woman a second glance. Jenny bit her lip in frustration.

Her friend was already at the bar and smiled in her direction.

'Jenny.'

'Trixie.'

They kissed carefully, making sure not to disturb the make-up that had taken so long in the creation.

Trixie waved her hand at a woman sitting next to her. 'Miranda'. Jenny smiled at Miranda. 'Hello.'

Miranda, rather rudely, Jenny thought, stared at her and her mouth dropped open.

'Oh, hello,' she said. 'Trixie here has been talking about you, but I never thought ... didn't realise you'd be so ... well, beautiful.'

Jenny felt a mixture of joy and relief. 'Thank you, thank you,' she said, fluttering her long eye lashes and swanning out her dress. 'I aim to please.'

Miranda laughed but Jenny heard admiration, not cynicism, and she saw this was a girl she could trust.

'You fly?' she asked.

Miranda shook her head and reached for her glass. 'I have a colleague who does. A Tiger Moth.'

'Oh bliss. My father flew those when he was training, during the war. Lovely planes. They say if you can fly a Tiger, you can fly anything.'

Miranda laughed. It took a moment before Jenny realized why. 'Oh! I suppose it does sound funny. But it's true. They are squirrelly little devils, tail skid and on tarmac ... well, there's been some damage done there all right and not only to the runway lights.'

Miranda laughed some more. 'Flying Tigers, Squirrels and Devils in the sky. If I'd known you as a child, I might have enjoyed flying.'

Jenny echoed her laugh, then stopped as another girl joined them, a small thin girl, her pose angular almost to the point of aggression. Jenny recognized the girl from the last time she'd visited Spinners.

'Are you following me?' were the new girl's opening words, which made Jenny jump and exchange glances with Trixie. But the comment came without heat, and it seemed it was a literal question addressed to Miranda, who answered, 'not exactly, but I thought I'd come and help. How is Victoria?'

'Fine. We saw you from above.'

Jenny wondered if this was some kind of religious reference, but in fact the girl was indicating the mirror in the wall above a picture of Spitfires and Hurricanes.

The girl, whose name, Jenny now remembered, was Stevie, had apparently only come down to fetch some tonic and soon returned upstairs. Miranda, however, had no desire to leave Trixie and Jenny, but instead was keen to buy them both drinks and chatter away.

Jenny and Trixie exchanged glances. 'She seems very at home here,' said Trixie, 'your friend.'

Miranda glanced up at the mirror, her forehead furrowed with worry lines. 'You think? Tell me about the owner, Miss Victoria Bell.'

Jenny patted her perfect hair, checking everything was in place before saying, 'I don't know much about her, really. She is a bit of a mysterious figure, up there in her ivory tower, watching from her variable mirror. I wonder if she was once a spy and having retired keeps her hand in by watching the clients. What do you think, Trix?'

Trixie laughed and her deep voice contrasted with Jenny's light contralto when she said, 'I think you have a marvellous imagination, my sweet Jenny. Outside literature, how many spies work in wheelchairs?'

'Perfect cover!'

They all laughed then, but Miranda stopped first. 'I

wonder,' she said, 'did you ever meet a man called Neil O'Banyon here?'

Jenny paused for a moment, thinking. 'Yes, I did. I heard recently he died, sad that. I remember him as being rather a fun, lively man, always willing to have a dance or a drink, rather too many drinks if I remember rightly!'

'Was he a friend of Miss Bell?'

'Now you're asking,' said Jenny, 'can you remember, Trix? Did she unexpectedly emerge from her chrysalis like a beautiful butterfly and entertain us when he was here? Or did he just come here because it's a great space for pilots?'

Trixie shook her head. 'No idea, darling, you were the one on the prowl if I remember rightly. I am always the chaperone!'

'Hark at her!' said Jenny. 'Always the bridesmaid, never the bride!'

They both laughed but Miranda continued inquisitively, 'So, did Neil try and seduce you? I've been told he was very keen on women pilots.'

Trixie and Jenny exchanged glances. 'My darling,' said Jenny, 'everyone I meet tries to seduce me: I'm that kind of girl.'

'That is her misfortune,' said Trixie. 'Mine is that I am not.' And they both giggled.

'Oh,' said Miranda, aware she was being mocked but not quite sure why. 'Oh.'

'So,' said Jenny, 'now I'm worried. Darling, why haven't you tried to seduce me? Don't you find me attractive?'

Miranda laughed. 'But I told you how beautiful you were.'

Jenny fluttered her eyelashes. '*That* is a big put-down! I ask you if you find me attractive, and you tell me a past compliment.'

'Sssh, Jenny,' said Trixie, 'leave poor Miranda alone. She doesn't need your games.'

Miranda took a gulp of her wine and pressed on. 'So, did Miss Victoria meet Neil here? Any idea? Trixie says you come here a lot.'

'Work, work, work,' fluttered Jenny provocatively. 'Since you insist on knowing all the sordid details ... She's a good woman, Miss Victoria. Oscar, the sexiest barman, tells me she found Neil drunk in a ditch, cleaned him up and brought him here to sober up.'

Miranda frowned. 'She brought him to a nightclub to sober up? Isn't that rather like taking a pheasant to a clay pigeon shoot?'

'Interesting analogy,' said Trixie, while Jenny added, 'With a similar result, I suppose.'

'Which was?'

'Well, he stayed off the booze when he was up in her den, but once he was allowed down on the floor with us reprobates, he went back to his usual pattern. Once a drunk, always a drunk. Then when BA threw him out, well, he no longer had the money for a nightclub. Miss Victory had given up on him and before long he was back on the streets. I guess you know the rest of the story, or you wouldn't be asking. Was he a friend of yours?'

'In a manner of speaking,' said Miranda, thinking the SeeMs detective agency probably knew more about him than anyone else alive, apart, that was, from Miss Victory. She hoped Stevie was here to ask more questions but found it hard to convince herself. How much had Victoria told Stevie about Neil? Did Stevie even know there was a connection? There had been a sort of dreamy look on Stevie's face when asked about Victoria that made Miranda feel nervous. Why was the girl here?

CHAPTER 22

THE BEST LITTLE AIRFIELD IN TOWN

When Stevie returned with the tonic Victoria was looking at the map, her fingers running up and down the London heli routes as though she were flying them. Her hand moved on to an airfield just outside the London zone. Stevie stared down curiously, reading the name.

'White Waltham.'

'Indeed. You ever been there?'

Stevie shook her head.

Victoria smiled. 'It's a dream of a place, or it was then, in the eighties. I've no idea what it's like now but then it had six grass runways—fantastic, you could always take off into wind or close enough. It was the perfect place for a Tiger Moth, a Cub or any taildragger really. And the people were so much fun, so relaxed, they'd let you do anything, and we did: low level flying across the airfield, buzzing the tower, even wing-walking.'

She stopped and grinned at Stevie. 'I was the first person to fly with my mother standing on the wing. We used a friend's Tiger Moth: the first mother-daughter wingwalk in the world. My sister didn't even think of it.'

She sat up tall. 'I practically grew up there. It was my favourite place in all the world.'

'Sounds great,' said Stevie smiling. And, she thought, so different from her own life battling to be a pilot, to not live her prescribed life of wife and mother. But then Victoria's wonderful life had come to a stupendously painful end, while Stevie was still living the life she wanted, even though the battle was sometimes hard.

'We did so much flying around, my sister and I, that sometimes guys at the airfield would ask me to deliver things for them,' said Victoria, moving in her chair. 'One Saturday, just as I was about to push out the Cub and go flying, this funny old boy I knew quite well from the airfield approached me. He asked if I could fly a propeller to the engineer who lived near Sandy? I looked at the prop and realised straight away it would never fit in the Cub. "Oh," he said, "you can take my Mousquetaire. It will fit in that. You flown one before?" I hadn't, of course, but I reckoned if I could fly the Cub, I could fly anything so I said "yes". Well, of course, it was a doddle, so I took up his propeller and he gave me instructions on where to find the engineer. Pointing at the map he said, "See this mast here?' He indicated a radio communication mast. "You'll see it from the air perfectly; it's on the edge of his strip. Just land there, he'll come out and take the prop and you can come back here."

Of course, I thought it would be great. What could go wrong!'

'Did your sister go with you?' asked Stevie, wondering what it would be like to have a sister to fly with.

'No,' said Victoria, 'we weren't getting on very well at that point. Basically, I thought she had farmer's hands, and she thought I took too many risks. You know how it is with siblings.'

Stevie shook her head. Victoria continued, barely glancing at her friend.

'Yeah! Must be a family thing, my mother cut off her sister completely years before, when she made a couple of small mistakes—haven't spoken since forever. At least my sister and I talk, although her voice has a nasty rasp.'

Victoria laughed and Stevie echoed her. An only child, she would've loved to have a sister, she would have taught her to make things, to fix them when they were broken and how to fly. She shook her head, how super it must be to share all your dreams with such a close friend, they would have laughed together, perhaps built their own flying machine. Stevie imagined the craft, a slender two seater somewhere between a Tiger Moth and a helicopter, what engine would they...

'Well,' said Victoria loudly, snapping into Stevie's dreams, 'I found the mast all right and sussed out the strip. Rather short in length. I was a bit surprised there weren't any other planes sitting around there, but I thought, well, hell, perhaps he's such a good engineer that things go through in record time.' She laughed loudly again, making sure she had Stevie's full attention.

'So, I lined up on finals and went in. Landing, I noticed there was a hidden ditch that I had just cleared.'

Stevie put her hand to her cheek; sharing Victoria's story. 'And you said it was already short without that, and I don't think the Mousquetaire has brakes, has it?"

'Spot on. Luckily the grass was quite long, so the drag was like a brake itself, but I did wonder if I would be able to get off easily. Still, the engineer must have had this problem before. Anyway, as I taxied in the "engineer" came out wearing nothing but a pair of shorts.'

'Oh?'

'Yup. And his first words were, "Oh! Are you my fairy godmother?" Instead of being at the engineer's place I was at the local greyhound racing track.'

'Greyhound racing track!' Stevie bit her lip. 'But was that legal? You could've been done. Lost your licence and it wasn't your fau—'

Victoria snorted, shaking her head. 'It wasn't like that then. Times were completely different. No one with a mobile phone to grass you up. You did what you wanted. We were completely free.'

'Oh,' said Stevie, wishing she had lived in such a golden age for aviation. 'So, what happened?'

'Oh, the man in shorts was a great guy. The Mousquetaire wouldn't have been able to take off with the weight of the propeller, so he looked up the engineer's address in his phone book. He had a caravan at the site with a telephone.'

'A phone book,' echoed Stevie. 'I do remember them.'

Victoria pursed her lips but continued.

'He drove me and the prop' over to the engineer's place. You should have seen the engineer's face when I arrived with this almost-naked man in his truck. It was hilarious.'

'But weren't you scared?' asked Stevie. 'All alone with a strange man?'

Victoria looked at her and shrugged. 'No, I suppose I might have been now. But then it never crossed my mind. Times were different.'

Stevie nodded. 'How did you get back?'

Victoria's eyes shone. 'When we got back to the caravan, the naked one called his brother, and the two men held the Mousquetaire's wings while I revved up to full power and did a short take-off. I made it over the ditch, but it was a bit touch and go.'

'Ha,' said Stevie. 'Wow. You really had such an amazing life.'

'Yes,' said Victoria, and suddenly her voice had lost its excitement and become bitter.

CHAPTER 23
VIEW FROM THE REAR WINDOW

'Your sister sent over this piece from her training course,' said Stevie, when Miranda and Cat arrived at the office next morning, having passed Blinkey's password test. 'She wasn't sure if it would be any good but it's from Owly Vale and in 2008, so she thought there was a chance.'

'Great,' said Cat, getting the doughnuts out of an enormous red and black handbag. 'I'll put the coffee on, and we can watch a film with the nibbles.'

Miranda stared at her enemy, the doughnut. 'I'm on a diet. I'll have half.'

Stevie put the film on the biggest screen and armed with coffee and doughnuts, or bits of them, the girls sat down to watch.

'I've already looked it through, and I'm pretty sure it's the back gate of Wild Garlic we're looking at.'

Titled: *Owly Vale 2008* Agata had added, *possibly March or April judging by the flowers.*

. . .

The back gate was closed, and the only action was the gentle swaying of the garlic between the door and the house. As they stared at the soothing movement, a car drew up and stopped. The driver sat inside, and they could see him fidgeting about, possibly listening for something or waiting. It was hard to tell. Unexpectedly, there was one short toot on the horn. Then silence. There was no response from the house, which remained dark and unresponsive, and in fact no response from elsewhere in the village.

Miranda thought that if they were in London there would already be people there, looking into the car and making comments.

Eventually, the driver got out of the car. Despite a security light between the camera and the house, it was too dark to see what he was wearing, and, backlit by the light, he appeared like a moving shadow. He opened the gate. Walked slowly up the drive, limping slightly, using a stick. At one moment he stopped and waved the stick at the pulsating garlic. He staggered slightly, rebalanced, and moved on, pulling out some keys from a trouser pocket. In front of the door, he fumbled around with the keys as though looking for the correct one but eventually he walked up to the door and, after a bit of pulling and pushing, managed to get it open and walk inside.

It was impossible to see what was happening inside as he didn't put on any lights and for a long time nothing happened at all. No one went past the house, and the back door remained solidly shut.

Miranda sighed and shrugged. 'Is anything going to happen? Looks like it's all over. Perhaps he lives there?'

Stevie shook her head. 'Wait! Remember I've already

seen it; something does happen. Get yourself a coffee and come back.'

As she spoke, the back door opened again and what appeared to be the same person came out. He stopped and locked the door and walked down the drive. He appeared to be dragging some sort of bag which he pulled along to the car, where he stopped, opened the door on the passenger side and heaved it in. It took a couple of attempts but eventually he succeeded in squishing the bag onto the seat and hobbled around the front, got into the car and drove away.

'What did we just see?' asked Cat. 'Shall we watch it again?'

The other two stared at the final picture on the screen. They were now staring at the back gate of Wild Garlic. It hadn't been shut properly and it moved back and forth occasionally, alerting the film.

'How did Agata get this information?' asked Miranda. 'Don't tell me she's on a training course. I mean, where did it come from? We already know there aren't any cameras at the back of the house from when the Yaris crashed there.'

Stevie nodded. 'Yeah, OK. Agata said that the people in the opposite house got nervy with the place being empty so much and the constant change of tenants. So, they decided to put in a security camera, but then they looked at the price and it was too expensive, and they put in a security light instead, but, as we saw, it isn't very effective.

'The fourteen-year-old son of the family saw the light flash on and went to the window to investigate. He'd been given a camera for his birthday and he thought this might be something exciting to video. And, when he saw the car drawing up, he probably saw himself as a future detective.

'But, as we saw, nothing exciting happened, especially

nothing to excite a fourteen-year-old boy. So, instead, he used it as a school project on making CDs, so that's where it ended up, along with a whole load of family photos.

Eleven years later, he didn't have a birthday present for his youngest sister, so he pulled out this CD as a present.'

'Huh!' said Miranda. 'Not a very generous present.'

Cat shrugged. 'She might like the family photos.'

Stevie frowned at them. 'Anyway! The sister was looking through the family photos, and saw the video. They were doing a school project on surveillance, and she used the video short as a piece. The observant teacher asked about its provenance. She might not have thought anything about it at all except... and this just shows how the world moves in circles... Miranda had just been to visit the teacher's sister in Essex: Marianne de Langley.

'Of course, this kid and family still live in Owly Vale, and the older people remembered the death of the homeless man eleven years before, so she took it to the police. They, on the other hand, didn't think anything of it at all, but put it in their "to be used for training" file, which is where your sister found it.'

'Wow,' said Cat, 'Agata is going to make a good detective. She has a nose.'

Miranda laughed, but she felt that slightly conflicting jealousy of a girl whose much-loved sister has done well in her own field. Of course, she wanted her sister to do well, and it was very useful having her in the police, but ... but...

Cat looked at her thoughtfully: perhaps she understood. She too battled with family relationships. The older woman put her hand on Miranda's arm and stroked it silently. Sometimes Miranda remembered why they were such good friends.

'You notice the man has a limp,' said Stevie.

Cat turned back to the screen. 'What man?'

'The driver.'

'Why do you think it was a man? Could be a woman.'

Stevie shook her head. 'Looks like a man,' she said stubbornly. 'He had a walking stick. How many women have walking sticks?'

Miranda started to say something, but Cat intervened, smiling slightly. 'Play it again, Sam.'

They watched the video again and this time Cat also noticed the driver was limping slightly. 'If it is a man, he was quite slight.'

'But tall,' said Miranda, now focusing on the screen. 'When he opens the gate, he is tall compared to me, almost Cat's height. In fact, like Clive Creamer.'

'Clive Creamer?' said Cat. 'You think it's him?'

'Not necessarily, but he does have keys, he is slight, he has a limp and uses a walking stick, I think he said he's waiting for a hip op.'

'Maybe, but this was in 2008. Was he waiting for a hip op then? Eleven years ago?'

'Not impossible,' said Stevie dryly. 'Think how long my mother had to wait for the memory clinic to get her on their books.'

'Maybe,' said Miranda, waggling her head. 'I certainly don't think we should jump to the conclusion it's him or anyone else, until we're sure.'

'No,' said Stevie, 'not even Amy who was the owner of the lease at the time. And I think I noticed that she had a limp, probably the result of being in a car crash with Neil.'

They all nodded sagely but two of them wondered a little about their colleague.

CHAPTER 24
SPINNERS IN HEAVEN

J enny and Trixie were sitting at a small table away from the bar. By choice, Jenny would be in the heat of the action, usually dominating the conversation at the bar, but tonight Victoria was doing a special deal with the local hospital and partially wounded people were filling every available table and bar stool. They'd been lucky to get a seat at all.

There was another reason, too. Trixie had had a bad day at work and wanted to complain about her employees. Jenny listened with half an ear. She had plenty of problems with her own employees and really wasn't interested in Trixie's ins and outs, more so since Trixie leant forward, arms on the table, and enumerated each challenge on her fat fingers, pointing at Jenny in between. And her nail varnish was cracked: it was a thoroughly unpleasant experience.

'So,' said Trixie, 'as though that wasn't enough, my secretary then upped and left without even working out her notice, and I was left in chaos...'

Blah, blah, thought Jenny. She knew very well Trixie was the CEO of a large company that had an HR department for most of these problems, and she could afford an agency secretary if hers just *up and left*. It wasn't like Jenny's business, which was always on the edge of bankruptcy and was now finding it problematic to get suitably qualified staff. She stifled a yawn and looked around the room discreetly.

Coming towards them was a tall woman with long, blonde hair and symmetrical facial features to die for. Her eyes were darting around the club as though she was lost or looking for a friend. Perhaps, thought Jenny, she was just looking for somewhere to sit in this fashionable crush.

'Hello,' she said, rising, smiling her sweetest smile. 'Would you like to sit with us? The place is heaving tonight; it's not usually so busy.'

The girl looked at her almost vaguely, then at the wicker chair she had pulled out and sat down suddenly with a sigh. 'Thank you.' She continued to look around. 'I was hoping ... I wanted to meet ... but it's hard to see...'

'And then,' said Trixie, striking her fist on the table, so involved in her complaints she hadn't noticed they had been joined by a stranger. 'I gave him the third written warning and HR complained it hadn't been properly written!'

The new girl jumped in her seat. 'Oh!' She breathed nervously, staring at Trixie as though she was a frightening wild animal. 'Is she ... she ... is she OK?'

Jenny laughed, sitting down beside the girl. 'She's wound up, work, you know how it is. Can I buy you a drink? I'm sorry, I don't know your name. It's such a bunfight up there I don't think you'd get one without my strong arms.'

'It's ... er ... El,' said the girl, her eyes still darting around the room. 'Er yes, thank you, tomato juice or, if they have it, a hot chocolate would be lovely.'

Jenny said nothing, considering what response she would get asking for a hot chocolate. Spinners was an unusually benign nightclub, but even so it was hard to imagine the barman kept a store of Ovaltine or Bournville. She had known people ask for milk, but that was usually to make a point.

'Let's start with tomato juice, shall we,' she said smiling in a motherly way. 'Do you like it spicy or not?'

'Oh, yes, please, yes, spicy would be ... er ... lovely.' The girl's eyes flashed quickly over Trixie again.

Jenny had her own ways of getting quick service and soon returned to the table with the tomato juice and a bar of chocolate. She gave it to El, saying lightly, 'Oscar, the super sexy barman, was sorry, no hot chocolate but he has this.' She handed over a bar of chocolate. 'It's seventy percent. I hope you like your chocolate dark and strong like your men.'

'What?' said El, leaping out of her chair. 'What do you mean?'

Jenny smiled warily. 'It was a joke. Sorry. I'm old school. I sometimes forget you youngsters...'

'Oh,' said El, sinking back into her chair with a relieved sigh, 'yes, like my mother. That's just the sort of joke she makes.'

Jenny's smile was rather tighter than before, and she wondered how old El's mother might be. El herself could be anything from twenty to thirty-ish. Jenny didn't like the idea of being compared to an older woman.

'I think I'd like your mother,' she said, giving El a sloe-eyed look.

El stared vaguely at her. 'You do? I preferred my dad, though he was a chauvinist, but at least you knew where you were with him. Mum's forever changing. You know, until my dad died my mum was a housewife, never did anything and agreed with every word Dad spoke, made my sister furious. Then, after he died, she upped and, dressed in tiger prints and short skirts, went vamping around looking for young men. It was sooo embarrassing. Honestly, she went into pubs trying to pick up young men! Can you believe it!'

Jenny roared with laughter. 'I would definitely like your mother,' she said. 'Are you meeting someone?' *Your mother perhaps,* she thought hopefully. 'You seem to be looking for someone.'

'Yes, no, that is...' El made a noise, but couldn't meet Jenny's eyes. 'I was sort of hoping someone would be here, but we haven't got an appointment.'

Jenny raised an eyebrow, but her face showed no further emotion. Odd term for a nightclub, an *appointment*, she thought. There was something rather odd about El. Jenny had been employing men and now women for nearly thirty years and she'd got used to judging character quickly. There was something fey about El, something that indicated she was not only unhappy with her life, but that she was the type of person who acted without thinking of the consequences. Jenny would not have employed her; she seemed to be the type who would pick up a knife and lash out. In Jenny's world, unplanned consequences could be fatal.

'Does he know you are coming?' she asked gently, getting out her mirror and checking her hair with her left hand.

'She,' said El, her glance still wandering around the room, refusing to meet Jenny's eyes. 'She's the owner.'

'Ah,' said Jenny, 'then she will no doubt be here somewhere. She's here most nights.'

This time El's eyes did meet Jenny's and Jenny felt

nervous about what she saw: darting pinpoints, enlarged white areas, all signs of fear.

'Do you know her?' asked El, and the chocolate paper trembled in her hands.

'By sight,' said Jenny. 'Don't you?'

El sucked her lower lip like a child. 'Well, no. But I know she uses a wheelchair.'

Jenny snorted and tilted her head over at a table on the other side of the room, where three bridge players sat in wheelchairs, deep into a game.

'There are lots of wheelchair owners here. Victoria encourages them to come and access here is fabulous; you'd get any type of wheelchair in, speedy or slow.'

'Oh,' said El.

She dropped her chin into her hand and stared out into space. Her tomato juice remained untouched, but she had chomped her way through half the chocolate already without apparently being aware she was eating it.

'... so,' Trixie ended, sitting up sharply and staring unseeingly at the other two occupants of the table, 'what should I do about that?'

Both El and Jenny jumped and stared at Trixie. Jenny was about to say, *for gawd's sake go home* when Oscar, Jenny's favourite barman, approached their table. He addressed El although it was obvious he didn't know her name.

'Miss. Would you like to go up to the observation room? Miss Victory invites you.'

El stared at him for a moment. Then she said, 'Oh, yes. Miss Victory. Is that Victoria Bell? Yes, thank you. Where is it?'

Oscar swept a hand in front of himself. 'Let me show you. This way.'

El got up to follow, then stopped. 'Thank you, er, Jenny, isn't it? Thank you for the drink and the chocolate.'

She looked at the wrapper in her hands, realised she'd finished it and dropped it on the table. Jenny wondered if she had any idea of what she was doing. El turned and followed the barman towards the stairs.

What a mystery, thought Jenny. Something was going on. She looked at Trixie, who was still waiting for an answer to her question.

'So,' said Trixie, 'what would you do with such a useless employee?'

Jenny patted her hair. 'Bring him here, darling. I'm sure we can educate him in the ways of the world.'

Trixie sighed. 'Pearls before swine,' she muttered.

CHAPTER 25
ABSOLUTION IN SUBURBIA

Donald O'Banyon and his friend Hugh lived in neighbouring houses in a Victorian suburb south of London. Their identical houses nestled in a short, terraced row with collapsing fences, peeling paint and flowerless gardens. Cat had been instructed to knock on Hugh's door first as Donald refused to see the detective alone. As she was Cat, not Miranda, she did as instructed, but she imagined that Miranda would have sneaked around the back and peered in at Donald before entering with Hugh.

Hugh was waiting for her, and as soon as she knocked he came out, pulling on his coat even though they were only going into the next-door house.

'Bright an' early; on time as I'd expect,' were his greeting words.

Cat suspected Miranda would have insisted on going in for a pee, so she could examine the house, but Cat herself just meekly waited while he shut the door and followed her down his own garden path and up the identical one next door.

'You don't like flowers?' asked Cat, herself a fanatical gardener.

Hugh looked around as though wondering what she was talking about and said, 'Vegetables. We used to grow them in the war. My mother was an excellent woman, totally dedicated to the art of bringing up children and making them eat properly. Marvellous what you could do for so little in those days. Now it's all plastic and throw-aways. Not then: my mother saved everything. Marvellous woman.'

As they had reached Donald's door, Cat leaned forward to press the bell. Hugh shook his head. 'Don't work. Hasn't done since Mrs O'Banyon died. She was a marvellous woman too. Fixed and mended. Wonderful. Don says he doesn't want anyone to visit so he ain't fixing the bell, but really, he ain't a fixer. It was his old woman who did everything.'

Cat smiled but couldn't think of anything to say. Hugh opened the door, which wasn't locked, and walked in yelling, 'Don, we're in. Got any tea?' To Cat he said, 'In there. Sit in the lounge. I'll get Don and make some tea.'

A strong smell of burnt kippers wafted up the hall, and Cat stood for a moment wondering if this was the house in which Neil grew up. A short staircase shot steeply up from where she was standing, a stairlift positioned at the bottom. A small table with a couple of hearing aids on it abutted the whitewashed wall and a framed photograph of a middle-aged woman hung above it. Cat moved nearer; the woman looked rather nice. Kindly. She looked back at Cat with cheerful but thoughtful eyes.

'You still here?' said Hugh, pushing Donald past her into the lounge. He almost made it in one sweep but hit the door frame and had to reverse, narrowly missing the small table.

'Eh, Hugh, almost had the downfall of hearing there, eh?'

He chuckled and rammed the wheelchair on, into the lounge. Cat followed.

She sat down on a wide armchair while Hugh, sweeping up a plate from the back of the wheelchair in a flamboyant manner, offered her a sandwich. A choice of peanut butter or honey. The bread turned up at the edges, so it was possible to see the innards were slightly coalesced; Cat wondered if he used the same knife for both.

Hugh fumbled around under Donald's blanket. 'Keeping both warm at once,' said Hugh, bringing out the teapot with such a flourish Cat thought the fluid might fly across the room and land in her cup like a conjurer. He backed the wheelchair around so Donald could see Cat and poured some dark brown tea into a mug. Cat took it politely and put it beside her, leaning the uneaten sandwich on the cup.

'So, Mrs Detective,' said Donald, 'now you've got your tea, what do you want?'

Cat leant forward in her chair so he could hear her; his hearing aids were still out in the hall. 'As you know, we are trying to find out who killed your son, and I thought it might relate to the time before he ended up on the streets.'

'Don't look at me that way,' Donald broke in, his bushy eyebrows streaming up his face angrily. 'It wasn't my fault he ended up there. I hadn't seen him since his mother died. He was a pilot then, proud of himself too, didn't want to associate with his common old dad, sniffling round those posh women. I met one once. What was her name, Hugh?'

'Amy,' said Hugh. 'Blonde girl, very pretty.'

'Yes. Well, *pretty is as pretty does*, as my mother used to say. She pretty much used my fool of a boy, simpering Miss. Was it her you wanted to ask about?'

He turned his eyes sharply towards Cat, and she was surprised to see them full of rheumy tears. He pulled a handkerchief out from the chair and wiped his eyes. 'Yes, full of airs and graces that one.' He sighed. 'What was the first one called, Hugh?'

Hugh muttered silently then said, 'Showgirl name, something like Bell or Beauty ... Bella, that's it. Bella. It made me think of those girls in the Follies Bergère. Not that I'm old enough, you understand,' he said, looking at Cat as though she might think he was fibbing. 'But my dad had been there. Wartime, you know, different times. People did things then they wouldn't now. Anyroad, she was like that: very tall, long limbs and pixie cut hair. Athletic.'

Donald moved in his chair. 'There, so you see how it was. Always chasing the posh birds. That's what got him on the streets, stupid bugger.'

Cat wondered if Bella could be short for Marianne, but the descriptions didn't sound very similar. She thought she'd risk it anyway.

'Was she a maths teacher?'

'No,' said Hugh. 'I think she was still at school. She drooled over him and kept touching him like he was a dog. She was very young. Of course, they all look young now, but I was younger then, myself. When was that? Twenty years ago, maybe more.'

'Listen to the old fool,' Donald shouted over his shoulder. 'He thinks he's still in his sixties. Must have been forty years ago. When did my wife die again?'

'In 2001,' said Hugh. 'Just after the Twin Towers came down; not that it's related, just a way of dating things. I find it helpful to refer to the dead dying as a way of remem...'

His voice petered off, and for a moment Cat thought he might have remembered that he'd told them that already, on the phone, but in fact his voice puttered out because he saw the front door opening and someone coming in.

They all sat transfixed, as though Neil's ghost had suddenly come to join them, then a voice said, 'Postie! Leave it here for you shall I, Mr Banyon? Got Mr Hugh with you? Shall I leave your post too?'

Hugh jumped up and took the mail, thanking him.

'Another nice day. See you tomorrow.'

Cat saw neither Donald nor Hugh had touched their tea and wondered if they'd made it just for her, or if every day they made tea and sat with undrunk mugs, passing the time until it was OK to have a beer.

'So,' she said, 'returning to my questions. The only thing you can think of that might have caused Neil to end up on the streets was love of women, is that right?'

Donald coughed. He looked around for his cigarettes before Hugh reminded him he'd given up smoking. 'Oh yes, doctors want me to stay alive until I'm a hundred,' he said, coughing again. 'Women, yes, that and the drinking.'

'Did your son drink a lot?'

Donald raised his hands to his head and shot backwards, just missing the sofa. Hugh hastily leant down and put on the brakes.

'Are you crazy? Women, honestly, not a straight one amongst them. He was a fucking alcoholic, and you ask if he drank a lot. Of course, he fucking drunk a lot! What do you think an alcoholic is, a teetotal in disguise? Silly cow!'

Cat let his fury wash over her. 'I meant, did he drink a lot before he became an alcoholic,' she said, 'when he still lived at home?'

Donald gave a catarrh-filled laugh.

'Ha! When did he live at home, Hugh, can you remember? Can't say I can. All I know is when I came back from the Navy, he was eighteen and he was already gone. Came back to see his mother, but he was living away from home as soon as he could. Silly bugger, couldn't stand living in this tight little box, could he? Not with his snotty friends. Nah. He went and good riddance. I said it then, and I say it now. Any other fool questions or can Hugh and I go down the pub?'

Cat drove home thinking about what she had learnt, apart from not to use the same knife for honey and peanut butter. That Neil was ashamed of his background? Or he never really got to know his dad. Both things were common when she was growing up. Dads were away a lot, especially if they were military, and as salaries got higher and people got richer, children did sometimes wish they had higher status parents. It wasn't usually enough to lead someone into a life of drinking and homelessness. So, was it this time? Or was there something else? Something more fundamental?

There certainly must be something in Neil's life that had led to his tragic death, alone in a small cottage in a remote village.

CHAPTER 26
RUNWAYS TO HEAVEN

S tevie was driving down the M4, having finished at Heathrow for the day, when junction 8/9 jumped up and shouted at her like a lost friend yelling *here is an airfield you will love*. What had Victoria said? 'White Waltham, the best airfield in the 1980s.'

A sign indicated the way to the Airfield Industrial Park, and she followed it, longing to see the place where Victoria had been her happiest. A time before her mood swings. A time when she was a young, enthusiastic girl in love with flying.

Stevie turned off the motorway and followed the directions, past the industrial estate to the airfield. As she parked, it struck her that the cars appeared to have been dropped and left, without any thought to where anyone else would park, no lines or posts like most airports. She walked through a little white picket fence, following the path around to double doors and, once inside, turned left up to the control room. Except there was no control here as such, just a radio room with a couple of boys chatting about their last flight.

'Hello,' she said quietly.

The boys stopped talking and one looked towards her.

'Hello to you? Come for a flight?'

'Er no, I wanted to talk to the manager.'

'She's not here,' said the nearest boy.

'Oh, when will she be back?'

He shrugged. 'She doesn't tell me her movements,' he said, smiling in a way that made Stevie wonder if he was being deliberately unhelpful, or if he had a problem with the manager.

'Is there anyone here who would have flown here in the eighties?' she asked.

The boy smirked at her. 'The *nineteen*-eighties?' he asked in a sarcastic voice. 'Doubt it.'

However, the other boy broke in. 'Yes, there is. Lots of people still here used to fly in the eighties. What about Malci or Bob: they were all here then, weren't they?'

'The *eighties*?' said the first boy, still behaving as though that was an era before flight. 'Well maybe.'

The second boy smiled encouragingly at Stevie. He stuck out a hand to indicate the passage she had just come up.

'Go to the end. In the bar. If an older guy is in there, ask him. He knows everyone.' He smiled. 'They always do, the old guys.'

Stevie walked down to the bar. It was an inviting place with lots of little tables for chatting or flight planning. It looked so comforting and familiar. So familiar! An electric shock pulsed down her body. It was indeed familiar: Victoria's nightclub was modelled on this room. Even down to the wicker chairs at each table.

There was a bar on the left-hand side of the room. She walked up and asked for a coffee, noting that above the bar were a replica Cub and a Tiger Moth, and, on the wall, a Curtiss Jenny propeller that had a clock in its spinner. The barista made Stevie a latte asking, 'You come for a trial lesson?'

Stevie shook her head. 'No, I wanted to talk to someone about people who flew here in the 1980s.'

The girl, who looked as though she was born after 2000, smiled. 'You need Bob, he's been here since the place opened.'

'Really?' Stevie had done enough research about the place to know it had been running in WW2, so Bob must be very old.

'OK,' said the girl, 'well maybe not since it opened, but for decades.'

'OK. If he comes in, will you let me know?'

'Sure.'

Bob did come in, shortly after. He walked to the bar and had a little joke with the girl making his sandwich and then, as instructed, came over to Stevie's table. She looked up to see a man somewhat past sixty years old hovering next to one of the chairs.

'Er, um,' he said, 'Clare said ... that is the girl at the bar ... Clare, that is ... said ... er um ... she said you wanted to know about someone who flew here in the eighties.'

The last part of the sentence was said so quickly that if Stevie hadn't known what was coming, she would have missed it all.

'Yes,' she said. 'Would you like to sit down?'

He gave a deep sigh as though that was what he had wanted all his life and collapsed into a chair. 'Woof,' he said. 'Sorry, been doing aero; does you in sometimes.'

Stevie looked interested. 'In what?'

'Oh, in a ... I say ... do you fly?'

Stevie nodded. 'For BA, but I've got a Tiger Moth, I do aeros too, but only low G, nothing special. What were you flying?'

'The Cap Ten, crazy machine. I love it but sometimes when you are teaching ... well, you know ... Did you do the self-improver route?'

'Yes, but I didn't teach. Someone lent me some money. I worked in a factory, did deals with flying schools. You know, others did it that way too.'

Bob's face became a miasma of smiles. 'Wonderful,' he said. 'I loved teaching, but sometimes I wish I'd missed that bit out. I used to fly for BA too. Retired last year, more's the pity.'

Stevie looked sympathetic. She couldn't imagine how awful it must be to retire. She hoped to fly until she died.

'But you still fly?'

'Yes, I went back to teaching. Not just aeros, mostly straight and level.' He grinned. 'Mind if I eat my sandwich?' he murmured, staring at it ravenously.

She waved her hand, nodding, and he started eating.

'I wonder,' she said, 'did you ever meet, or perhaps teach, a man called Neil O'Banyon?'

Bob's face seemed to crumple into the sandwich and the following sigh came from a deep cavern within. 'Poor old Neil! He was a nice man. Such a shame.'

'What?'

'Oh, sorry. I heard he died, drunk himself to death.'

'Yes,' said Stevie uninformatively.

'Never could keep off the booze. Was why he got kicked out from BA. Silly fucker! That was over a girl, too.'

'What?'

'Oh, yes, he used to fall for these girls. He'd do anything for them. You just had to be a female pilot and he'd be all over you like a rash. He'd give them anything for free. Free lessons. Free aeros. That Blonde Bint took him completely for a ride. Got most of her training from him for free. Then dropped him like a hot potato. Silly fucker!'

'Amy?' said Stevie.

Bob's face drained of blood and his eyes appeared to grow. 'Oh, shit! Do you know her? Should have realised. Small industry for women. Oh shit, shit! ... oh, my goodness, sorry. Sheeser ... You won't tell her...?'

'I don't know her,' said Stevie, 'only, I've been looking for people who knew Neil and she contacted me. Said they were engaged.'

Bob snorted. 'Yes, twice. You'd think he'd be once bitten, twice shy, but not that silly fucker. I bet he'd have married her, given her everything and then she'd have walked away with everything except the whisky bottle. Silly fucker!' He appeared to realise he'd been swearing again and said, 'Oh!' looking remorseful. 'Ah, sorry, one does get wound up, sometimes, er sorry.'

'I wonder,' said Stevie. 'Did you know a Victoria Bell? She used to fly here in the eighties, did some of her training here. Her parents flew here too, in two Piper Cubs.'

Bob frowned and licked some of the mayonnaise off his lips. 'Victoria Bell? Nope, never heard of her. There was a family who had two Piper Cubs, flew all over France and Spain, they did. What a blissful life. But they were called Chantry. He was an accountant, and she was a doctor. Two daughters, Rebecca and Isabella, I think.'

'Oh,' said Stevie. She rubbed the side of her head feeling confused. Victoria must have been here. She said she was. The Spinner's bar was almost a replica of this place. Perhaps he had got the names mixed up. Perhaps?

She was silent a long time before realising she had been

staring at Bob. He had been immersed in his sandwich but now he looked up, as though wondering if she was OK, but not liking to ask.

'Did the Chantry family know Neil O'Banyon?' Stevie asked slowly.

'Might have done because the flying world is very small, was even smaller then. He was already flying for BA when I met him. That was after one of the daughters was in a car accident.' He shook his head. 'Sad that. Whole family suffered. Sister went off to Hong Kong to work for Cathay. The parents moved to Australia to be near their daughter. Even had their planes shipped out.' He shook his head. 'Put them in the hold of one of the Cathay Flights. Amazing, eh.'

He shrugged. 'No one could ever tell me what happened to Isabella. I wondered if she'd died.'

CHAPTER 27
THE CHOCOLATE THIEF

C aroline's voice on the phone sounded uncertain, rather as it had when she was a child admitting a misdemeanour.

'Mum ... er ... I'm ... er ... look, I'm dropping by with something for you, OK?'

'Lovely,' said Cat, trying not to let her voice sound wary. 'That's nice. Are you replacing the chocolate?'

'Ha, ha,' said Caroline, adding to her mother's unease: normally a quip like that would have got a sharp response from her daughter. 'No, I've got something for your investigation, OK?'

'Great,' said Cat. 'I'll put the kettle on. When are you coming?'

'Now,' said Caroline, and this time Cat could hear relief in her voice; something was clearly happening. 'I'm entering the village now. See you in five.'

She rang off, and in less than five minutes had joined her mother in the kitchen holding out a CD case in front of her, as though it were a tray bearing a peace offering.

'Do you know how to play these, Mum?'

Cat frowned. 'Yes, of course, I'm not a hundred!'

'No? Anyway, Anthony was given it in 2008. He told me to give it to you as it's relevant to your investigation.'

Cat raised her eyebrows. 'How does he know about our investigation?'

Caroline shrugged. 'It's not exactly a secret that you are investigating the death of the homeless man in Owly Vale. He and I discussed it. I do remember it now, but I'd forgotten about it. I was in London when it happened, and it seemed rather unimportant. He asked why you hadn't known about it, but of course that was just after Dad died, when you dressed like a cougar and went off whoring…'

'Caroline! I did not dress as a cougar and go off whoring. I dressed to please myself, which may not have been the way your father would have liked, but since he was dead that was irrelevant. And far from going off whoring, I merely got a job and had a few boyfriends. I was finding myself. OK?'

Caroline shrugged. 'Whatever.'

'Besides,' said Cat, still feeling this irresistible need to justify herself, 'if I hadn't gone travelling, I would not have met Frank, and that would have been awful.'

Caroline shrugged again. 'Yeah, well, I did tell Vanessa his jokes were getting better, although they aren't really. But he's OK.'

Cat refused to rise to the bait and took the CD. 'So, you've seen it?'

'Of course, Mum. I didn't want you to see anything that might shock you. But it is weird, right! You'd better watch it with Miranda; she's a bit more streetwise than you. Oh, and Anthony said there was a second one, explaining the first. Only he hasn't seen it. OK?'

'Thanks, darling!' said Cat, rolling her eyes like Miranda.

Caroline laughed. 'Nice. I'm going now, but have you got

any more chocolate? By the way, don't buy the dark stuff. I only really like the milk and the one with just nuts, not the raisins. They are yucky.'

Cat sighed. 'You are the best reason I know for people not being teetotal. If only you'd drink alcohol, you'd leave my chocolate alone. OK, help yourself, but don't take it all.'

'Thanks, Mum.' She dived into the larder, coming out a few moments later laden with chocolate. 'Oh, by the way, I almost forgot. I had a message for you from Victor.'

'Victor?' repeated Cat.

'Yes,' said her daughter cheekily, 'had you forgotten you had a son as well as your lovely daughters?' She dropped the chocolate into her bag and started rummaging in there for something else. 'Ah, here it is. Victor got his accountant to look at Spinner's accounts. He's printed out a crib sheet, which he says you should be able to understand.'

'Thanks,' said Cat.

Caroline narrowed her eyes. 'You're not surprised!'

'No.'

'Did you ask him to do it?'

'Yes. I did.'

Caroline bit her lip. 'OK, Mum, back to your old tricks of divide and conquer.'

'Caroline! Honestly, all my children are equal.'

'Hmm, but some more equal than others. You could have asked Rupert to do it. He trained as an accountant.'

Cat said nothing, and mother and daughter looked at each other silently. They both knew Rupert hadn't passed the exams and never worked as an accountant. Cat wondered how much she was being punished for Caroline's deferred pain at her problems with her husband and said nothing.

Caroline made an animal noise.

'Never mind, Mum. You've just driven me to an emergency therapy session, but nothing to worry about. You just go on with your hobby; don't worry about my pain.'

She swept out the room and rushed to her car in tears, getting Anthony's number up on speed dial.

Thank God, thought Cat, for Anthony and his therapy. She got her handbag and left for the office.

CHAPTER 28
TIGER MOTH TAILS

'W here's Stevie?' asked Miranda, breezing in, closely followed by her dog. 'Taking her mother to the clinic?'

'No, Blinkey's asleep in the library. Stevie went off flying as soon as I arrived. She called me in a panic: Blinkey's carer is on her two-hour break and Stevie desperately wanted cover so she could take the Moth out. I think she needed to think.'

'Oh dear,' said Miranda, filling the dog's water bowl, 'what do you think is on her mind that she can't tell us about?'

Cat wrinkled her nose. 'Do you think she goes flying to think or to keep her mind away from thoughts?'

The two women looked at each other silently. 'She has been spending a lot of time with Victoria,' said Miranda, 'and we can't yet rule her out as a suspect.'

Cat nodded. 'You realize neither of us have met Victoria, don't you? It just feels like we have because we know her through Stevie. What did she say when you told her Jenny's story, that Victoria had met Neil and tried to stop him drinking?'

Miranda wrinkled her nose. 'She said, "Oh yes, Victory told me about that."'

'She calls her Victory?'

'Apparently, Victoria wrote a song called "Miss Victory Always Overcomes, Until She Doesn't". It's a madrigal, like they sing in church, but the lyrics were hers. And she changed the music slightly for her alto voice.'

'How do you know?' asked Cat. 'Did Stevie tell you this?'

'No, Jenny. She seems to know quite a lot about Victoria, even though at first, she wasn't very forthcoming.'

'So, you think Victoria hadn't mentioned she knew Neil, and Stevie was shocked by it and went flying to try and explain it to herself.'

'Looks like it.'

'Well, she's going to like this even less.'

'What?'

'Two things. One, I asked Victor to look at Spinner's accounts and see how they are doing.'

'You did? Why?'

'Habit. Perhaps it is the result of having been married to a business man. You tend to be suspicious.'

'And?'

'"It was successful when it was first set up. Made lots of profit, but that all stopped about ten years ago. Since then, it's been deeply in debt.'

'Ooh,' said Miranda, pursing her lips. 'And the second thing?'

'Do you remember Anthony, my daughter's therapist?'

'Oh, yes, the black guy.'

'Yes, white woman, that one.'

Miranda waggled her head. 'OK, beanpole. Go on.'

'Well, Caroline told him all about the case we are on.'

'Discreet. How come she knew about it? Was Mummy leaking a bit?'

'No, obviously she knows about the dead man in Owly Vale and that we're investigating it. I may have mentioned his name was Neil when we were talking about why she doesn't drink, but it never occurred to me she'd go discussing it with her therapist.'

Miranda made a face. 'Sounds like one of those moving conversations. How about you get straight to the point!'

'OK! Anyway, Anthony offers pro bono therapy for any homeless people who need it. He's an amazing guy, big heart. So, in Caroline's last session he gave her a CD. It's of Neil O' Banyon when he was trying to dry out. Neil gave it to Anthony at the end of one of his sessions, to show that someone was helping him with his treatment, and Anthony looked at it and thought it was far from helpful, indeed destructive. But then Neil disappeared, so he was never able to give the tape back or even discuss it with him.'

Miranda frowned. 'Are therapists allowed to share their client's material? This has a whiff of dodgy to me.'

Cat looked vaguely surprised. 'Oh, I don't know, but he helped us before with a case, don't you remember?'

Miranda rubbed her nose thoughtfully. 'I wonder.'

'What?'

'How old is Caroline now? Twenty-six?'

'She's over thirty!'

'And he's been her social worker and then therapist since she was fourteen years old. How did they swing that?'

'What do you mean?'

'Well, when my younger sister had therapy, after my father killed himself, they were very careful that she didn't become dependent on a father figure.'

Cat blew air through her lips. 'Yes, I see. Twenty or so years. Longer than she's known Rupert.'

'Who, to be honest,' said Miranda, 'is a deadbeat.'

Cat shook her head, frowning defensively. 'Caroline likes him.'

'Come on, Cat! He hasn't worked for years. She pays for everything with her illustrations, and her work as a book-keeper; you're going to pay the school fees for Lagertha. All he does is go out shooting and fishing with friends and drink and drink and drink. She should get rid of him.'

Cat sighed. 'Maybe, but it's not my business. Back to the matter in hand, we now have this CD, which I think you should watch.'

'OK. Have you already seen it?'

'Yup. Caroline thought it would shock me, but I don't know why. We deal with murder. Why would a bit … anyway, let's look at it again. I'll be interested to hear what you think.'

Cat opened her laptop.

There on the screen was the homeless man, Neil O'Banyon, but a cleaned-up version. Someone had cut his hair and trimmed his beard. His eyes were still bloodshot, and as he moved his hands shook, but his voice, when he spoke, was clear. Although he stumbled slightly over the words, which made Miranda wonder if he was reading them from some autocue. He enunciated slowly and clearly through the whole piece, only occasionally stopping to glance away from the screen. The room behind him was bare but tiled like a bathroom.

'I am Neil O'Banyon. I have been engaged three times. Twice to Amy Earhardt, and once to Bella Chantry. I let them both down. I drove drunk with both of them, and I killed Bella Chantry. Bella didn't recognise me when we met, even though we'd been engaged. I was angry with her, so I drove too fast and then they went into a ditch, and she was hurt. It was an accident.'

He stopped and a quiet voice said, 'Go on. Tell the truth.'

He nodded and pulled at his beard. 'On both occasions I left the scene of the crime. Amy came after me, she broke off the engagement there and then on the Billington corner on which we crashed.

'Bella could not escape. She was drowned. If I had called someone she could have been saved. It was my fault and I should be punished.

'I have been bad since I was born. I stole from my parents to pay for my flying lessons and to give women money. I'm even cheating Anthony who is giving me free therapy and who has never had any of my advantages. I'm a thoroughly bad person.'

He stopped again and looked at someone off screen. Then he mumbled, 'And I don't deserve to live. I am a murderer.'

The video stopped and Cat looked at Miranda. 'What do you think?'

'Weird,' Miranda said. 'Presumably this Bella Chantry he mentions was the drunk girl Spud told me about. But why would anyone make a video like this, what for?'

Cat shook her head. 'Caroline said there was a second video, but Anthony never saw it.'

'Ah yes, Anthony,' said Miranda, 'presumably he is the same person who was treating Victoria.'

Cat nodded. 'Seems likely. Did you notice the room they were in?'

Miranda wrinkled her brow. 'It did look like a bath-room, I thought. Are you going to tell me you recognise it?'

Cat gave a spurt of noise. 'Yes, in that I saw it in more detail than you. From the ground up!'

Miranda frowned. 'Are you saying he, or rather they, made this video in the upstairs bathroom at Wild Garlic?'

'Yup.'

'So, either just before he died, or at some time before that when he visited the house.'

'Looks that way,' said Cat. 'And remember Amy was living in the house in 2008.'

Miranda frowned. 'But ... she said she hadn't seen him again after he left BA, but this was sometime later, when he'd been on the streets for a while.'

Cat moued.

'And,' said Miranda, 'there was that quiet voice in the background...?'

Cat nodded. 'Yes. Did you think that was a man or a woman?'

'I thought a woman, but it was hardly more than a whisper, so it could be a man. It could even have been Anthony.'

'Anthony?' said Cat shocked. 'Are you suggesting Anthony made this tape?'

'Well, he was the one who gave it to us. He said it came from Neil, but maybe it really came from him.'

'But why?' asked Cat incredulously. 'Indeed why would anyone want to make a tape like this?'

Miranda pinched her chin. 'Well, I'm guessing whoever made it knew Bella Chantry and wanted to show Neil was a murderer, before then killing him. They also wanted to stress the Wild Garlic connection. Or maybe this was made by someone else, who wanted to lead us to a killer.'

Cat inclined her head. 'Of which one? Bella Chantry or Neil?'

Miranda sucked her upper lip. 'Let's say a third person

made this tape, for example a therapist like Anthony who couldn't voice his suspicions or even what he knew. Neil may have told Anthony he killed Bella Chantry and Anthony knew someone who would want revenge on her killer.'

Cat rubbed her own nose. 'Interesting. OK. Good idea. And we know that Anthony was treating Neil, because he told Caroline, and Victoria mentioned that she had a therapist called Anthony who knew all about Owly Vale and the empty house at Wild Garlic. So! Do you think we should go and visit a nightclub?'

Miranda laughed delightedly. 'That's what I've been saying since day one. If you'd listened to me then Stevie wouldn't be getting all conflicted.'

Cat shrugged. 'She's a young girl. At some point she'll have to face her own sexuality and make decisions. Now is as good a time as any.'

'Well, yes, apart from the fact she has chosen a suspect in the case she's working on!'

Cat shrugged. 'Can you get childcare for tonight?'

Miranda nodded. 'Phillip will be there, asleep on the sofa as usual.'

'OK, I'll drive then you can enjoy yourself!'

'Love you too!'

CHAPTER 29
FLY ON, YOU CRAZY PILOT

W hen Cat and Miranda arrived at the Spinners, they discovered that Victoria was not there.

'Sorry, my loves,' said Johnny, the barman of the night. 'She rushed off around five-thirty saying she had forgotten an appointment and to close up without her. She said she might not come back until tomorrow.'

Cat sighed and offered Miranda a drink. Miranda looked around the club. 'Just my luck, I get to go to a nightclub and the only action is my mother.'

'Ha, ha,' said Cat. 'I would of course love to be your mother but I'm not sure if you wouldn't be even more trouble than my children's throuple and Caroline put together. At least all the members of the throuple have good jobs.'

'Ha! As opposed to being detectives, you mean?'

Cat sneered at her, but at that moment Miranda spotted Jenny arriving from the car park area and gave a flamboyant wave nearly knocking over a man trying to reach the bar.

'Now I'm going to introduce you to someone else who

will enlarge your horizons,' she said, skipping happily over to offer Jenny a drink.

Jenny was on her own tonight and delighted to have company. She hadn't forgotten Miranda was a fan.

'Darling Miranda,' she said, sitting down at their table with her Negroni, 'you have a wistful little look on your face, as though you were longing to ask me all sorts of secrets, whereas I like them to slide out during the night, perhaps in a moment of passion. So much more stimulating, don't you think? Why don't you start by introducing me to your tall friend? Who, interestingly, I think I have met before or perhaps it was someone related to her.' She grinned at Cat. 'Or is it because you are one of the very few women as tall as me? Even my darling-darling is nothing like as tall as you.'

Cat nodded. She had a feeling Jenny was trying to wind her up. 'Nice to meet you, Jenny,' she said. She took Jenny's hand and was amazed by its size and strength. She looked at the girl a little more closely and Jenny, seeing her look, batted her eyelashes seductively.

'Well, darling Miranda, I can see your tall friend is already falling under my spell. Is she another detective like you?'

Cat frowned at Miranda: with her usual discretion it seemed that everyone knew she was a detective and probably even the details of the case they were working on.

'Look, Jenny,' she said, 'I want to ask you something, but don't take it personally.'

Jenny laughed wickedly, playing her long nails over Cat's bare arm. 'Oh, my darling Dicky—since the lovely Miranda won't tell me your name, I'll call you Dicky. Darling Dicky, did no one ever tell you that when you ask a question with a prefix it becomes a barrier to a correct answer? Rather like saying *with all respect*, when clearly respect is nowhere in the picture.'

'It does?' said Cat. 'Yes, I guess it does. I never thought of it that way. And my name is Cat.'

'Ooh,' said Jenny, 'how lovely. Jennyanydots cat, which is soooo much nicer than grumble cat. Jellicat, Practical Cat. I bet that one is you.'

'Oh no,' said Miranda. 'Her children call her Cougar Cat because—'

Jenny gave the most unladylike guffaw of laughter. 'Cougar Cat, of course, I should have realised. I can just see her in short skirts on the prowl. Which is the best field for naughty, naughty mice, darling Cat?'

Cat frowned. Unlike Miranda, who was loving this banter, she was feeling very uncomfortable. 'Now my question—'

Jenny batted her eyelashes again and smiled deeply. 'Tell me: what would you like to ask? My inner soul is yours for the taking, anything you desire...'

Cat was so far out of her comfort zone she was tempted to say she had forgotten, but she had started, so she had to finish.

'I just wondered. Are you? Are you—?'

Jenny sighed and looked disappointed. 'Am I naturally blonde? No, I must admit it is a wig. My natural, lovely curls are dark and luxuriant but tucked away under the beautiful disguise of love.'

Cat slowly laughed, but Miranda said, 'Ah well, I suppose there is no alternative but to ask you to come for a slow, smoochy dance and see what we discover.'

Jenny roared with laughter, again throwing back her head like a donkey braying. 'Miss Cat, I love your friend. She is so *fabulousa*!'

When Miranda and Jenny returned from their dance, Miranda was panting slightly as Jenny had shown her a lot of unexpected moves, most of which involved far more exercise than she was used to. Cat offered her another drink.

'You girls,' said Jenny, winking at Trixie, who had arrived with the late crowd, 'are trying to get me drunk and incapable, aren't you? I'll have a another Negroni.'

'Nice,' said Miranda. 'Make that two.'

Trixie widened her eyes to show she would join the Negroni party.

Cat ordered, buying herself a tonic water. She had a rule that when driving she didn't drink at all.

'You are quite a dancer,' said Miranda, still fighting to get her breath back. 'Do you dance a lot?'

Jenny laughed excitedly. 'Thank you. When we first dated, Amy and I used to do competitions. She would wear black tie and we would leave the judges so confused. We loved it.'

Cat passed around the drinks. 'Amy?' she asked casually. 'Is she a pilot with BA? Amy Earhardt?'

Jenny smiled. 'Yes, do you know her?'

Cat nodded. 'I think my colleague might have met her. She an old friend?'

Jenny laughed again. 'I had worried that tonight might not be a good evening, but I was so, so wrong. I think we are going to have a ball tonight, don't you, Trixie?'

Trixie tilted her head.

'Amy is my darling wife.'

'Oh,' said Cat, while Miranda giggled.

Jenny looked gently at Cat. 'I suspect, my darling Cougar Cat, knowing me will be quite educational for you.'

CHAPTER 30
DANCE UNTIL DEATH

Stevie knocked on the door of the old cottage. Nothing happened although she knew Victoria was there and wouldn't have forgotten. Only today she'd got the text:

How do you fancy seeing my getaway house?

Xxx

Come around 6.30.

Stevie had sent back an immediate reply saying she'd love to, so she was expected. However, she was a bit early, as usual. She peered in through the window. Inside she saw Victoria slowly manoeuvring herself into her wheelchair.

Stevie almost hit herself on the head. Of course, Victoria didn't, couldn't, move quickly. She felt the red heat of guilt on her face and hoped Victoria hadn't seen her at the window. She sneaked back to the door.

A few moments later the door swung open, and she could see Victoria in her chair by the table. There was music playing low in the background.

'Hi. Come in and close the door. These gadgets are great at opening the door, but not so good at closing them properly. I suppose the makers thought since you were opening the door for a TAP, they'd be able to close it themselves.'

Stevie said nothing and walked in.

'Before me, you hadn't really thought about the difficulties of being disabled,' said Victoria, blowing out her cheeks, 'had you?'

'No,' said Stevie, and then as Victoria clearly expected more, 'sorry.'

Victoria compressed her lips. 'I saw you at the window, wondering why I took so long opening the door. It takes time when you are one of the wounded! Before all this happened, and I was a TAP too, I could jump around. No longer! Now I must plan ahead, always be thinking how I can manage a situation. Mind you, as good pilots we always did that anyway!'

'PPPP,' said Stevie reflexively. 'Prior Planning Prevents Piss-ups.'

'Precisely!' Victoria smiled. 'And to celebrate all future piss-ups let's have a drink. I certainly planned that part.'

The drinks were on a low table and a quick look through the doorway showed Stevie that all the cooking equipment in the kitchen beyond was also low level.

'You'll like this wine,' said Victoria. 'It comes from an English vineyard and is highly decorated. They are one of the few British vineyards that beat the French at their own game. Do you know how rare that is?'

Stevie wasn't really listening. She was thinking, *I must ask Victoria about White Waltham immediately, before I lose my nerve*, but how to bring it into a conversation about wine? She hesitated, then she saw Victoria was looking at her deeply.

'What is it, Stevie? You're looking so troubled. Has something happened? Is your mother OK?'

Stevie smiled. 'Thank you. You're very kind. She is fine. It's just ... it's ....' She paused again. 'Look, I went to White Waltham. I wanted to see where you had been happy.'

Stevie looked up at the ceiling. She noticed absently Victoria had a pulley there. This was so hard.

Victoria looked at her compassionately. She put her hand gently on Stevie's knee. 'And what happened? Didn't that beautiful airfield live up to expectation?' She gave a twisted smile. 'Perhaps I praised it too highly.' Her eyes laughed gently.

'No,' said Stevie, 'it looked lovely. It's just ... I met a man called Bob.'

Victoria raised her eyebrows. 'A man? Are you saying it was love at first sight?'

'What? No, of course not.' Stevie found herself blushing. What was Victoria talking about. Clearly, she was putting this very badly. 'No. I mean I talked to this old guy called Bob.'

'Phew,' said Victoria, laughing gently and swaying slightly to the music, 'you had me worried there. What did Bob say that upset you?'

'He said, he said ... He said he didn't know you,' said Stevie, and heard the ridiculousness of what she was saying. 'I mean ... he said the only family at the airfield who had a Cub and the life you described yourself as having were called Chantry, not Bell.'

'Ah,' said Victoria. 'So, my secret is out?'

Stevie stared at her. 'What? Bob said that the daughter was hurt in an accident.'

Victoria gave a snorty laugh. 'And so, because I was the only other paralysed person you knew, you assumed we must be friends.'

'What? No! I only meant...'

Victoria shrugged. 'It's OK, Stevie, you're not unusual. It's like meeting someone from another country, and you immediately ask if they know the only other person from that nation that you know.'

Stevie blushed deeply. 'No, I didn't, I mean...' She wondered if Victoria was right. Was that why she had mentioned it? How awful! And she hadn't even seen her own motivation.

'But,' continued Victoria, 'in fact you're right. I am a Chantry, but not Bella. That was my sister. My sister was killed, as I think I told you, in a car accident with a drunken driver. We had both been accepted by Cathay and we would have been fantastic, even though she did have farmer's hands. We would have been the brilliant Chantry sisters, the first women in the airline, the first two sisters to qualify together in the world. All swept away in one awful drunken night.'

'Killed?' said Stevie, missing most of the conversation after that. 'Bob said he thought she might have died.'

There was a strange look on Victoria's face, which Stevie put down to sorrow. 'Yes,' she said, 'she died, and I lived, but injured. How ironic is that? How the mighty fell. I changed my surname for her. That's why I'm Victoria Bell, not Chantry.'

'Oh,' said Stevie, but...'

'What?'

'Well, Bob said another sister, Rebecca he called her, got the job at Cathay.'

'Phrr, shows how rumours start. No, poor Bella, she's dead as they come. The woman they got instead is called Rebecca Finlater, not Chantry. And she may be OK at her job, but she is definitely not as great as we would have been!'

'Oh,' said Stevie, nodding, although her stomach was still churning restlessly. 'So you are in contact with her?'

'No, but Spinners is a nightclub for pilots. One hears things. I hear that Finlater is only so-so at the job, not like Bella would have been. But the more important fact is that Bella was killed in a car crash ... and you know who was driving.'

Stevie shook her head. Wild ideas filled her mind. Could it be Clive Creamer? Or Bob from the airfield. 'No. Who?'

'Your Neil O'Banyon.'

'Neil O'Banyon? How do you...? But why—' she started to say, but Victoria was still talking.

'Bella was going to work as a pilot for Cathay; she would have been one of the very first women to work in that job. A job so coveted by men that no one could say women only get the dregs that men leave behind. She was in a straight competition, man to woman, woman to man, man to man, and she was one of the few to succeed. What a girl she was!' She sighed and was clearly so filled by emotion it was a few moments before she could go on.

Stevie stared at her. 'What? So, Bella was the girl celebrating? The one Spud told Miranda about? The drunk one whom he tried to save by not letting her drive ... but actually ended up accidentally killing?'

'Bastard!' said Victoria, hitting her hand on the chair. 'Is that what he claimed?' Her face contorted with fury. 'He claimed it was her fault she was killed? Well, that is gaslighting if ever I heard it. What cheek. He offered to drive her, and yet he was drunk as a lord. Not sober as a judge but drunk as a lord!'

Stevie hadn't heard her sound so angry before, cynically cutting yes, but never this straight rage. She stared at her silently, wishing for nothing more than to run away right now, fly away, escape into the purity of the air.

Victoria sighed, she breathed deeply to control herself and took a few moments. Then she seemed to have made a decision.

'Look. I didn't want to do this but I'm going to have to show you a tape Anthony gave me. He made it with Neil as part of their therapy. Neil admits he murdered Bella.'

Stevie gasped. 'Anthony showed you another patient's video? That can't be ethical. Or even legal.'

Victoria looked at Stevie, raising her eyebrows. 'He was good, Anthony, at the beginning, but he started...'

Stevie frowned. 'Did something happen with Anthony?'

Victoria sighed. She filled up Stevie's glass and took a deep draught of her own. 'Yes. It did. I try to put it out of my mind. I trusted him completely but then he ... Look, you're not interested in this. It's nothing to do with the case.'

Stevie gulped. 'But, yes, of course I am, Vic. I'm interested in anything to do with you ... everything. And, if Anthony upset you, well, then...'

Victoria had another drink. 'Look, it's not simple. You're going to hear things you won't like.'

Stevie shook her head quickly like a dog shaking a blanket. 'Go on. We're friends. We can tell each other everything. I'm completely behind you.'

Victoria drank deeply. 'OK. Well then, I think he started to have feelings for me.'

'Amorous?' said Stevie, then thinking that sounded rather pompous. 'I mean...'

'Well, I'd say lust rather than love,' said Victoria.

'What?' said Stevie. 'What? He forced you?'

A strange look came into Victoria's face, and her eyes darkened. 'Yes. Yes. I hate to talk about it, but ... yes. Right from the beginning, he insisted on having the door closed in sessions. I didn't think much about it. He was very touchy-feely. Often stroking my arm or touching my head. But then, I was often crying, so it seemed natural that he cuddled me.'

She took another gulp of wine, and Stevie made a sympathetic movement towards her but restrained herself.

'Then,' said Victoria slowly, 'in one session he suggested that next time we have our therapy somewhere else. Why not, he said, in one of our homes. We would feel more relaxed there. He said he still felt I was holding things back from our sessions and if I was more relaxed, I would open up better. Of course, I agreed. He was the therapist. I trusted him completely, so I invited him here.'

She paused and gave Stevie some more to drink. Stevie raised the glass, but put it down without drinking, while Victoria took another gulp of her own.

'Here?' asked Stevie, confused. 'He wanted to come here? Is that allowed under therapy rules?'

'I've no idea. I trusted him.'

'Oh, wow,' said Stevie, leaning even closer to Victoria as though to protect her from any memory to come. 'Are you OK? You don't have to tell me about this if it hurts.'

Victoria's eyes softened. 'Oh Stevie, I want to tell you about it. I want you to know and understand.'

Stevie breathed deeply. How could she have ever mistrusted this gentle and hurt woman? She had a sip of her drink. 'Go ahead. Tell me.'

'Well,' said Victoria, manoeuvring her chair so she was closer to Stevie, 'when he arrived, he brought a bottle of wine. He said it was better if we both relaxed, and then I could tell him everything about my relationship with my parents and how I did that dangerous flying after Bella was killed. Almost trying to join her in death. And succeeding too well.'

'So, he knew by then how much you admired your sister? And that she had been killed?'

'Yes, you know what it is having an older sibling. Well, you don't because you didn't, but even though you see their faults you admire them. Even though she wasn't as good a pilot as me, she was a trailblazer.'

Stevie felt bemused. 'I thought you said she was your younger sister.'

Victoria smiled lovingly at her. 'Oh, you remember what I said. How lovely you are. Most people forget things I tell them.'

She raised her glass to Stevie, her eyes soft.

'But don't be the detective now, darling. I was telling you about Anthony as a friend.'

'Oh, I'm so sorry,' said Stevie, feeling a rush of anxious adrenaline in her veins. 'I ... er...'

Both women took a deep drink. Stevie felt slightly woozy.

'He sat where you are sitting now,' said Victoria, putting down her glass. 'He was talking to me in a low voice. He took my hand like this.' She took Stevie's hand. 'And he held it very gently, unthreateningly. Just talking. Then he took my other hand. Like this. Even as he was asking me about my accident, he slipped slightly forward.'

A lock of Stevie's hair slipped into her eyes as she leant forward. Victoria put up her hand and slipped the hair behind Stevie's ear.

'He was like that,' she said, her voice lyrical and sonorous, 'gentle, kind but resolute. I slipped into his fantasy. As I fell under his spell, I pulled back. I was frightened, but he was insistent. Then he leant back and I found myself destabilised.'

Gently, Victoria swayed backwards while moving forward so that she was on the edge of the chair. It seemed she was about to fall. Stevie moved her hands up Victoria's arms to prevent her falling, and the woman collapsed into her as though Stevie had pulled her.

'Kiss me!' said Victoria.

Stevie wasn't sure if that was what Anthony had done or if this was what Victoria wanted? She lifted her eyes and saw Victoria looking at her, her pupils enlarged, wistful, longing. For the first time in Stevie's life, she was not acting to plan. Life was zipping around her, completely out of control. The music, the alcohol: her mind buzzed. She heard Victoria's voice, soft, compelling: 'Just go with me. If you help me re-enact this, it will save me. Now lift me up and carry me to the bed. Ignore me if I struggle, remember we are re-enacting a scene and I need your help. You are the only person who can help me.'

And Stevie followed Victoria's lead.

When Stevie's mind focused again they were lying, gently cuddled together, on the bed and Victoria was telling her all about her time in hospital after the accident.

'I woke up,' she said, 'behind bars. At first, I thought I had been kidnapped and put in a cage. Then I realised I was in a hospital bed and the metal arms were up. I was wearing a brace. I couldn't move. I was trapped. The most painful loss was my identity. Who was I? I had been a pilot, one of the best, an aspiring leader. I was going to rule the world ... and now what? Now I was a derelict, not even a has-been but a never-made-it-at-all. A dream destroyed and a life made ordinary. Do you understand, Stevie?'

'Yes,' said Stevie, stroking her cheek lovingly, 'I do.'

'Do you?' said Victoria. 'Perhaps you do? People came to see me. Friends. They tried to take me out of myself.'

She put on a deep voice. "Oh, don't you worry, V, you'll soon be up and running. Why I had a friend knocked over by a bull; we all thought he was a goner, then three weeks later he made a full recovery and started training as a bull-fighter! That made me laugh, but you know what Proverbs says, Stevie?'

'No.'

'Laughter can conceal a heavy heart, but when the laughter ends, the grief remains.'

Stevie stroked Victoria's arm sympathetically.

'Yes, I made people believe I would be OK. I didn't want their pity. But I wanted what I had before, a perfectly healthy body and a job in flying.'

Stevie stroked her cheek. There was no more talk about Anthony, and although Stevie was interested in what he'd done next, and how he was able to remain a therapist after such behaviour, she said nothing. She didn't want to upset her friend ... even ... she blushed thinking it, her lover.

Victoria reached behind her and switched off the light.

'Oh,' said Stevie, 'clever gadget.'

'Yes, and rather necessary if I don't want to transfer in the dark, don't you think?'

Stevie nodded, biting her lower lip. Something else that she had not considered.

After a while, Victoria fell asleep. Stevie heard her rhythmic breathing and finally had time to think through what had happened. It was all so new. So different. She wasn't even sure she did know what had happened.

Just before she too fell asleep it occurred to her that Victoria had neither finished the story of Anthony's abuse, nor shown her the tape. Nor had she completely explained the Bella Chantry confusion. Why was that? Perhaps, she stopped her talking. Still, no doubt it would all be explained in the morning.

And she looked over at Victoria, who had now rolled away from her in her sleep. Stevie moved gently over and put her knees into the bend of Victoria's and hooked her arm around her stomach, lightly placing her arm over the sleeping body beside her. She gently stroked her. How beautiful she was.

CHAPTER 31
DRINKING IN THE DARK

'Well,' said Miranda, trying not to slur her words, as Cat drove home. 'That was a zurprise, wasn't it?'

'It was,' said Cat. 'More for me than you, I guess. But it does mean another interview for you, and with a pilot. Luckily, we have no idea where Stevie is, or she might get cross if you interview Amy, but it must be done.'

Miranda laughed. 'Ha. I see you are not offering, despite your expertise with throuples and the like.'

'No,' said Cat, taking her eyes off the road to stick her tongue out at her friend, 'but I'll be your getaway car if you like.'

'Thanks. I'll cope.'

Miranda looked at her phone. Midnight. Probably too late to ring a normal person but Amy, like Stevie, was an airline pilot, and that meant she might be anywhere in the world and in any time zone. She sent her a text:

Hi Amy, Stevie's colleague Miranda here. Any chance you are in the UK and fancy a coffee tomorrow? It is about Neil O'Banyon.

To her delight Amy came straight back:

I'll be landing at Heathrow 7am tomorrow. Could meet you in the café in One Tree Books, Petersfield, 9.30.

Miranda texted back: *C U there.*

'OK,' she said to Cat, who was falling asleep over the wheel. 'Wake up! I've got an interview with Amy at nine-thirty tomorrow. Do you think she knows about Jenny?'

Cat thought about it. 'I would say with a character like Amy's, chances are she would be totally behind Jenny or totally against. Your only difficulty is to find out which!'

'Thanks,' muttered Miranda. 'Very supportive.'

CHAPTER 32
HOT ASHES FOR WINGS

I n the morning, Stevie awoke with a sense of happiness. She had a couple of days before she had to go back to work, and perhaps she could spend them with Victoria, getting to know each other. Victoria still had lots of things to show her, including the Neil O'Banyon tape she talked about, and they had so much to discuss.

She smiled and looked across the bed, only to find it empty. Victoria had gone. At first, Stevie thought she might be in the kitchen, but then another thought crossed her mind. How did she get there? The wheelchair had been in the middle of the room—a quick glance showed Stevie it too had gone—but did she drag herself across the room into it? Quietly, so as not to wake Stevie. She must have been in a hurry. Why? And where was she?

Stevie got up and walked into the kitchen. There was a note under the butter dish. Pulling it out, she saw Victoria's handwriting for the first time and was vaguely disquieted. Stevie didn't know much about graphology, but even she could see this script with its spikes and hard lines where someone else might have had spirals and soft swirls, was angry and driven. It was like a terse reply to a well-intended question, and yet the message itself said simply:

Sorry, darling, trouble at Spinners. Had to go. I'll call you ASAP.

Xx V

Stevie wondered what sort of trouble could have occurred at Spinners and why Victoria hadn't woken her. She could have helped. Could there have been a fire? She had read somewhere that nightclubs were prone to that sort of thing. Or had a fight broken out and things got smashed? Stevie sighed and stopped speculating. She would find out soon, she supposed.

She put her hand in her pocket to check her phone, and discovered it was not there. She didn't remember taking it out of her pocket, but then in some ways last night was just a blaze of colour and excitement. She looked around and eventually found it on the floor near the chair where she had been sitting. It must have slipped out. She opened it and saw there were messages from Cat and Miranda.

Cat's simply said: *Where are you?*

Miranda's, sent at 4.30p.m. last night said: *Off to Spinners. If u there, come 2 bar.*

There was another one from Miranda, clearly sent later that night, which said: *Call me ASAP, loads to discuss. Xx*

For the first time in her life, Stevie felt no inclination to call either of her friends. What had happened to her last night needed a lot of thinking through, and they could not possibly help. She was going to drive straight to the airstrip and go flying. Later they could talk.

CHAPTER 33
AMY WONDERFUL AMY

The café in One Tree Books was set back off the street and did a good line in breakfast things. Miranda ordered a couple of large croissants and a latte trying to avoid counting the calories in them. Amy asked for a long black coffee.

'Good flight?' asked Miranda.

Amy nodded. Her tired eyes viewed Miranda expectantly. Miranda wondered how to breach the subject tactfully.

'Did you get an email from Stevie, about the time Neil was killed? You were leasing Wild Garlic at the time. I wondered if you knew about it.'

Amy nodded. 'Yes, but not that it was Neil, of course. I had no idea he was on the streets. As I remember it, and it was a long time ago, a policeman rang me and told me there'd been a break-in at my house and a homeless man was dead. He asked if there was anyone nearby – I was away at the time in Australia—who could come and verify what was missing and so forth. Well, by then Graham and I had got back together, and I was living back home, so he went over and did all the paperwork and so forth, and I never heard any more about it.'

Miranda nodded. 'Could you tell me a bit more about your second engagement to Neil?'

Amy frowned and twisted her hand in her long blonde hair. 'You said you had some information to give me. I thought you were going to tell me the killer had been identified.'

Miranda looked at her. Amy had been up all night; she was probably longing for bed and fed up with questions. 'We are pretty close, but there is just someone I want to eliminate from my investigation.' She liked that, sounded rather official. 'I want to ask you about a friend of yours, Jenny.'

Miranda was watching closely and saw Amy stiffen momentarily before saying, 'Jenny who? I know lots of Jennies.'

Bother, thought Miranda, she hadn't thought to ask for a surname. Would Jenny even have one? She wasn't sufficiently versed in the ways of Jenny to know.

'OK,' said Miranda. 'Can I ask you a different question? Why did you and Graham split up?'

Amy shrugged. 'Why? What does it matter to you? These things happen, OK?'

Miranda looked at her silently. This was going nowhere. Either she was being particularly poor with her interviewing technique today or Amy was blocking her. She decided to be more direct. 'I went to Spinners last night.'

Amy shrugged again. She glanced at her watch.

'There was a fun girl there; I met her with Stevie.'

'Victoria?'

'No, one of the clients. A slim, attractive, but very tall pilot called Jenny.'

Amy frowned; she dropped her hair. 'What is this about, Miranda? For God's sake, you're not even a proper detective, are you? You and your lot find lost dogs. You just happened to get lucky on a couple of other cases, otherwise you're just a lower-class snoop!'

'Thanks.'

Amy stood up. 'I don't have to stay for this. I agreed to meet you freely because I thought I could help find Neil's killer and now you start on some rubbish about Graham.'

'Graham? Or Jenny?'

Amy stopped, balanced on one foot. She looked at Miranda calculatingly. 'What did Jenny say? Did she say she and I share the lovely Graham? That she is Graham's mistress and I'm just the wife, who of course does not understand him as much as his mistress?'

She cocked her head, watching Miranda.

'No,' said Miranda, 'she said you did dance competitions together when you first met, and often won. She said you enjoyed putting on full tails.'

Amy sat down again and smirked. 'We did. It was funny. The judges got so confused. But there's no law against a man and a woman swapping roles in a dance competition. And we were just so much better than the other contestants.' She shook her head, grinning widely.

Miranda smiled silently.

'So, little Miranda. Did you get all confused?' Amy wound her hair around her hand again. 'Did you say to yourself: so, are they a couple of lesbos? Pilot lesbos. Male pilots love thinking women pilots are lesbians. I think it turns them on. They like the idea of reforming us! Or did your instincts kick in and you said to yourself: is this a man dressed as a woman? There is no other woman in Jenny's life, only his wife? Which was it, Miranda?'

Miranda drank her coffee and smiled at the woman. She seemed so strong. So totally in control but this appeared to be her weak spot. Know their weak spot and you know the woman. She smiled at Amy. 'It came out by chance. Jenny and I had a dance, and I just couldn't keep up.'

Amy laughed, she leant forward and put her arms on the table relaxing. 'But he could! OK. No. I can see that.' She drank her coffee.

'There are some things,' said Miranda modestly, 'even a brilliant dancer cannot keep from his partner.'

Amy roared with laughter this time, throwing back her shoulders. 'OK. I get it. But you must admit he is brilliant. There's many a time he and I have been to parties, and no one has any idea that I'm the girl and he's the man. Sometimes we get propositions from the most amazing combinations.'

'Still,' said Miranda, 'it does seem odd, that you know your husband's a cross-dresser and didn't mention it to Stevie.'

Miranda was starting to think it wasn't worth letting Stevie out of the office. So far, not one of her interviews had revealed anything even when there were very clear points to be revealed. And worse, interviewing seemed to be getting her into serious emotional trouble.

Amy frowned. 'Why would I? Do you talk about your husband's other lives when meeting people at a party?'

Miranda looked blank. Distracted for a moment, she thought about the workaholic Phillip; what would his *weakness* be? Even when they were having a break before they got married, he only used the time to do night school and improve his working potential. Miranda thought if he started wearing her clothes, she'd be rather pleased. They could buy more expensive things and share them. She brought her mind back to the interview.

'But given how much he must have hated Neil, and given that Neil was dead, you don't think it might have helped us? Allowed us to rule him out of our enquiry?'

'No,' said Amy, 'much more likely to make you suspicious. Of course,' she said, her voice hard with sarcasm, 'you dog detectives are completely unbiased in every way, but even you woofas—'

'But what?' said Miranda, irritated. 'But what?'

'But most investigators aren't so broad-minded. Haven't you heard of the Broken Windows policy implemented by the mayor of New York, William Bratton, Giuliani's, first police commissioner? They arrested people for small offences like jumping turnstiles, arguing that tolerating low-level crime and disorder would encourage more serious crimes?'

'Yes,' said Miranda, although she hadn't, but she did understand that Amy was suggesting if the police saw Graham was a cross-dresser, it was a natural step to think he might be a murderer.

'OK, since you're asking, I can tell you Graham/Jenny is not a killer and most especially Jenny/Jenny is not a killer. Although maybe if pushed by an extremely tiresome trainee, Graham might kill.'

She stopped and looked at Miranda through narrowed eyes. 'That was a joke by the way!'

She pushed her hair out in a wave. 'But Jenny is his gentle, caring side, his jokey, flirty side, and *that* side would allow someone to kill her before she killed them. Trust me. There's not a lot I don't know about Jenny or transvestites. Yes, you were right, that was originally why we split. I had loved the cross-dressed dancing, but I didn't think that was more than a bit of a laugh. Slowly, I realised how serious about wearing women's clothes Graham was, how often we were going to do this, and I worried about what it would do to my career. Airlines and airline pilots are not the most liberal thinkers, and I started to long for the normal. For the relationship I had had with Neil.

'Then, as I told you, I met Neil again. He seemed so much more fun than he had been, and always wanting to do what I wanted, unlike Graham and his selfish cross-dressing. I'd had enough. So, Q.E.D., I left.'

'And?'

Amy shrugged. 'Well, I told you this bit before. Neil began drinking again and I started to think more deeply about it. Graham was the man I loved. Shouldn't I get to know him and his ... his interests better?' She slipped her hair around her hand and dropped it. She smiled at Miranda in a brazen way, as though she felt she had bared her soul and it was enough. 'So, I went back to him.'

No, thought Miranda watching the way Amy stared at her, trying to force her to believe with the strength of her personality, *you are hiding something. There is something more and I need to know what it is.*

'Tell me the truth,' said Miranda, staring directly back at her. 'It wasn't like that, was it?'

Amy blew her lips into a gale; she stroked the ends of her hair. 'As though I haven't exposed more than I ever have before, you mean.'

Miranda moved in her chair. Was Amy just covering or was she really finding it difficult to speak about this? Amy was unlike anyone Miranda had ever met before: she seemed so cool, so totally in charge of her own destiny, and yet ... perhaps under that steely front there was an unhappy little girl.

'So,' Miranda said, 'the truth is you had another break, but from Neil, and he met Jenny in a bar, and he tried to seduce her, didn't he? We hear again and again how obsessed he was by women pilots. And Jenny said most men can't resist her. It seems that she has all the best bits of a man and a woman. They went off to Wild Garlic. Graham knew you were away and that the house was empty. But once there Neil discovered *she was a he*. He freaked, and Jenny had to kill him before he killed her. Was that it?'

Amy separated her hair into two halves, bringing them down under her chin and stroking them mechanically. 'You are a tiresome woman, Miranda. And, quite stupid and, of course, as I would expect, you've got it all wrong. You think just because Graham is a cross-dresser, he is in some way inhuman, kinky, odd. You've been watching too many biased movies. Deep down you, like your police friends, think *it's the weirdo what done it*! If you don't obey society's norms, then you must be a big deviant and capable of killing.'

She stopped and looked down at the dog, who had accompanied Miranda as a better backup than Cat and was sitting quietly under the table. 'Like your dog,' she said in a tense voice. 'You think the killer instinct is always there, hovering at the edge of a deviant.'

Miranda said nothing. Waiting.

Amy put her hands under her hair and threw it out, so it billowed up into a wave behind her. 'OK, I suppose I didn't really know much about transvestitism before I knew Graham, either. I also had biases. But...' She grabbed a lock of hair and secured it behind her ear. 'Yes, OK, Neil was interested. You already know how Neil wanted to inspire women to be pilots. And you know, now, that I went off with Neil when Graham and I were having a break, but you may not realise that Graham knew all about Neil. He'd hired a detective as soon as I left. Didn't take rocket science.'

Miranda nodded. The fact Amy was rambling was probably a good thing in someone usually so in control.

'Well, Graham considered using the detective to seduce Neil and then show me the photos, but then ... Look,' she picked up her hair again, 'you clearly don't know much about this subject, but OK. Lots of transvestites just like wearing women's clothes, OK? They aren't gay, and they aren't planning for the chop. You got that?'

She stopped, looked at her persecutor furiously and Miranda nodded obediently.

'Well, Graham was like that, but, although I didn't know it then, he liked to fantasize about having sex with men. Some of them do. God knows, I've even had fantasies about having sex with women, although I'm not a bit gay. It's just fantasy. Right?'

Miranda nodded again. She realised she was holding her breath and tried breathing out slowly, hoping Amy didn't notice.

'So, since I was away, he goes into Spinners with the intention of seducing a man, to try it out but maybe not go all the way. Now I don't know if he was already focused on Neil, or if some other chap would have done but, he arrived at Spinners and, lo and behold, there is Neil. God knows why Neil was there, although the owner was a pilot, and it is a really good hangout for pilots, but he was, anyway.

'Anyway, Neil doesn't recognise Graham. Why would he? Sometimes I hardly recognise him myself when he's wearing the full kit, and I know him well, whereas Neil had only seen him a couple of times and both times as a man.

'So, Graham/Jenny sees Neil at the bar, talking to the barman, and he takes a stool next to him. Smiles and then offers him a drink. Neil accepts. Well, then Jenny starts the full seduction. You know: "Oh you're a pilot. That's so fantastic, I've always wanted to be a pilot!" That sort of thing. Honestly, you've seen him, and you know that Jenny is a good-looking woman. She thinks Neil is falling for it, but then suddenly he hops up and says he must go. Perhaps his instinct warned him, or perhaps he thought of me. Well, by now Jenny has her teeth into the game so she says, "One more for the road, handsome? Don't leave a lady lonely." Neil accepts, and Jenny spikes his drink with GHB.'

'Date rape?'

'Don't sound so shocked. It isn't only women who get abused, you know.' Amy stroked her hair and Miranda thought she was learning more than she expected.

'Go on.'

'Well, Neil says he's feeling hot—temperature, that is— and Jenny helps escort him outside. She has to be careful to avoid the barman because Victoria has them all well trained to check any sign of abusive behaviour and Jenny doesn't want to be thrown out. As I say, it's a great hangout for pilots of all types.

'So, they get outside, and Neil is losing it; he can't stand upright, and his eyes are starting to lose focus. Jenny calls a cab. She takes him back to our home. Our shared home. Not Wild Garlic.' She sneered slightly.

'Wow, why?' asked Miranda.

'Well, for one thing it's much closer but rather more because,' Amy's eyes shone, 'what greater revenge is there on your wife and her lover than to have sex with the lover in the wife's own bed? Clever old Graham, eh?'

'Err,' said Miranda, her heart beating uncertainly. 'Go on.'

'Well, Graham may be slight but he's tough and strong.

Neil is unconscious by then, so Jenny gets him into the house by a combination of lifting and dragging. She strips him naked, puts him in our bed and takes off most of her own clothes, just leaving on the padded bra and suspenders, stockings and high heels. Then she lies down beside him. Jenny gets her selfie stick, takes a load of selfies and puts them on WhatsApp to me, with the legend: "You can come and get your lover now; I've finished with him. I hope he isn't broken." That, incidentally, is a quote from Tommy Sopwith; no idea if it's a true quote, but it was a shared family joke.'

Miranda looked up at Amy and to her surprise saw Amy was laughing. 'And then you ask, why did I leave Neil and go back to Graham? Well, who wouldn't?'

Me, thought Miranda, but she didn't say anything.

Amy stared at her, her look turning slowly from triumphant to cynical. She put her hand back in her hair. 'Well, my little Miranda, I do believe you are shocked. What a little parochial you are.'

Miranda shook her head. 'So, what happened?'

'I went over to the house, and by the time I arrived Neil was awake. He was so embarrassed; I can't tell you. He kept saying he didn't do anything, and he didn't know how it happened and so forth. Well, I had started to guess a bit by then. I'm not a fool, as you may have noticed. So, I screamed at him and told him to get out and never darken my door again.'

'He left?'

'He did. And Jenny and I had the best sex ever and I agreed to come home. Graham started to understand that Amy was, as he put it, jealous of Jenny, but we would try and work it out. Pretty cool, eh? How many husbands would do that to get their wife back!'

Miranda laughed but only because she was trying and failing to imagine the same scenario between her and Phillip. 'Not many, certainly.'

'But, Miranda, my child,' said Amy, 'Neil was most definitely alive when he left us, and neither of us killed him then or any other time. OK?'

CHAPTER 34
SETTING BOUNDARIES

When Stevie landed the Tiger Moth and went into the house, the office was full of dogs. To Stevie, who preferred dogs outside, it seemed as though all the carpets had got up and started giving their opinions; the office reverberated with howls and yowls.

'What's going on?' she yelled at Cat, taking off her helmet and dropping it on the table, trying to be heard over the noise.

'Police raided an encampment and found all these girls; looks like a puppy farm and the dogs seem overjoyed at their release.'

One dog grabbed Stevie's helmet and dashed across the room with her prize.

'There are some puppies amongst them,' added Cat.

'So, I see,' said Stevie testily, retrieving her helmet before the puppy destroyed it. 'Where is Miranda? Looking after dogs is usually her remit.'

'She's having breakfast with a friend,' said Cat guardedly, not wanting to tell Stevie Miranda was interviewing Amy.

Stevie threw up her hands in disgust. 'And meanwhile? What are we supposed to do with all these creatures?'

As she spoke people started arriving at the house, rushing in, dazed with the joy of being restored to their pets, briefly confused by Blinkey's demand for a password, and finally laughing and cuddling their dogs.

Within ten minutes the place was clear again.

'Wow,' said Stevie, 'it's a form of magic!'

'Yes,' said Cat vaguely, guilty about having lied to Stevie, something she had never done before: they were one for all and all for one, right? But Stevie's friendship with Victoria had changed that. Then, before she got the chance, Stevie spoke.

'Cat, I've discovered something odd.'

'What?'

'You remember Clive Creamer told Miranda his girl-friend Phylida had been killed by a hit-and-run driver.'

'Oh yes,' said Cat. 'Why?'

'Well, interestingly, I was just surfing, and I found out two things about Phylida. One is that her surname is de Laney, like Spud. And the other is that yes, she was hit by a hit-and-run driver, but not killed. It did have catastrophic effects, and she has had terrible epilepsy since, but she's alive and she still works as a teacher, although in a limited fashion. Recently, though, she had a very bad attack and has gone to live with Spud.'

Cat frowned. 'How do you know? That she went to live with Spud? Surely the internet doesn't carry people's private lives on it.'

Stevie snorted. 'Oh no? People post, and what do they post about? Private lives, of course. It was on Facebook, on Spud's site. She said her sister Phylida had come to live with her. I looked up Phylida and there she was. A quick search of her friends and up comes Clive Creamer; she hadn't even bothered to block him.'

Whatever that means, thought Cat, shaking her head. Sometimes she thought she was too old for the current generation of life but felt better remembering her father had also thought so, and he died long before the internet.

'Oh,' said Cat, 'I wonder why Clive lied about her being dead. Do you think he was embarrassed she left him?'

'Could be,' said Stevie, 'but with that and the sighting of him going back into Wild Garlic after Neil's death, it all makes him look rather suspicious.'

Cat felt an odd shiver in her spine. 'We don't really think that was him, do we?' she said.

Stevie shrugged and wouldn't meet her eyes.

'Even if it was him in the video,' continued Cat, helping herself to another doughnut, 'all it does is confirm what a nutter he is; it doesn't go further than that. We'll have to ask Miranda what she thinks when she gets back from interviewing Amy.'

'What?' Stevie was making some coffee, but she turned suddenly towards Cat, spilling beans all over the floor. 'What? Miranda's interviewing Amy? Who? Amy the pilot? Wasn't my interview enough?'

'Oh, yes, it was fine, but we found out some more information.'

Stevie dropped down to pick up the beans, still frowning in thought. 'What? What information?'

'Oh,' said Cat, 'look, I know you like to interview the pilots.'

Stevie stared at her. 'Well, yes, I do, but I guess this was important and so Miranda had to do it while I was still flying. So, what did you find out?'

Cat looked at Stevie. The girl was giving her a way out.

She wanted to leave it like that, but to tell her about Jenny and what they'd discovered at Spinners would be to emphasise they had also intended to interview Victoria without her. She didn't know how to continue.

Stevie put her own construction on Cat's silence. 'You didn't want to tell me because you thought Miranda might get more out of Amy than I did, is that right? In fact, you think I'm a useless interviewer?'

'Oh, no,' said Cat, 'that's not it. It's just you have got yourself involved with Victoria, and we are still viewing her as a suspect and—'

'Victoria? Victoria? What has this got to do with Victoria?'

Stevie left the beans where they were and moved towards Cat holding the plastic measurer like a weapon. 'What has this to do with Victoria? Does she even know Amy? Just because they're pilots, you think—'

'No,' said Cat, worried at Stevie's cold anger. She was usually so logical, so quiet; any kind of emotion was rare from Stevie. 'No, look we went to Spinners—'

'You went to Spinners, without me? Why?'

'We needed to talk to Victoria, but she wasn't there.'

'You needed to talk to Victoria?' Stevie was staring at Cat fiercely. 'You think she's using me to find out what's going on in the investigation, and you went behind my back because you can't trust me anymore. Is that it?'

'No,' said Cat, 'it's just that we were worried—' She broke off because Stevie was grabbing her Tiger Moth helmet again.

'Basically,' shouted Stevie, 'you think I'm a liability, no use, a lousy detective and probably sleeping with the enemy. Thanks. I'm going flying.'

She ran out of the room, nearly bumping into Miranda

on the way.

'Hello, Stevie, don't go. I've got news.'

'Oh yeah!' said Stevie. 'I don't suppose you can share it with me. I'm a leaky vessel, a liability, a sex fiend...'

And she ran down to the strip.

Miranda turned to Cat in surprise. 'Now what happened there? Did I say something or did you?'

Cat sighed. 'Me, and don't say "no wonder I'm always falling out with my children." I think I spoke a bit rashly about Stevie's relationship with Victoria.'

Miranda sighed and sat down on the sofa. 'I thought you were going to wait for me. Never mind. I'll talk to her when she gets back. Meanwhile, I've got some interesting news about Amy and Jenny, and you were quite right, when Amy likes something, she *really* likes it!'

Cat laughed as Miranda told her story and in return related what Stevie had said about Clive Creamer's ex-girl-friend Phylida being Spud's sister.

'Ah,' said Miranda, 'that explains it then.'

'Explains what?'

'I always wondered how Spud knew about Neil's death. I knew she hadn't seen it on the internet. So, if her sister was living with Clive Creamer at the time, they would have known about it then. Bit odd she lied, though. Not that I'd want to admit to having a sister mad enough to live with that lunatic.'

'It also,' said Cat thoughtfully, 'potentially gives Clive an alibi for the night in March 2008 when Neil was killed. Perhaps we should go and visit Phylida; have a chat.'

'OK,' said Miranda, 'but before then we need to see Victoria, and since we know that Stevie is flying to Caracas tomorrow night...'

Oh dear, thought Cat, now they were planning to deceive their colleague. How awful life could be.

CHAPTER 35

TRADING GHOSTS FOR PILOTS

This time, when Cat and Miranda arrived at Spinners, it was heaving. Stevie had left for her flight to Caracas without talking to her colleagues again. She had managed to avoid them by going out shortly after landing the Tiger Moth. When Miranda, who was trying to be peacemaker, asked where she was going, Stevie replied, 'To see a friend.'

Miranda didn't want to speculate but they all knew Stevie had very few friends.

'OK, sweetheart,' said Miranda, 'we'll let you know how everything goes while you're away.'

Stevie turned away, but not before Miranda saw something she had never seen before: tears in Stevie's eyes.

'Wow!' said Miranda, as they arrived at the nightclub. 'Much busier than last time we were here.'

'Perhaps they've got some special night, you know like Quiz Night at the pub, which always makes it much fuller.'

Miranda rolled her eyes. 'Hopefully more exotic,' she said, wondering if Cat had ever been to a nightclub before this job. Perhaps there was a reason she and Stevie liked each other despite the age difference: both *innocents abroad*.

It seemed there was a dance competition halfway through. There were tall feathers on display and real peacocks strutting around the stage. The girls could see, through breaks in the crowds, a tall, muscular woman with long fingernails stroking the peacock's train which fanned out behind her. Many of the drinkers were lifting phones and even the barman's attention seemed to be on the stage rather than the bar. The detectives exchanged glances.

'Shall we just pop up the back stairs?'

Cat nodded. 'Is it a form of trespass, do you think?'

Miranda shrugged and led the way up the spiral staircase she had seen Stevie using on previous visits.

At the top, they quietly opened the door into the observation room. Victoria's back was turned to them as she watched the floor through her two-way mirror. She was wearing a headset and listening to the conversations in the bar. They watched her silently, seeing her absorption in the games playing out below.

'Nice,' whispered Miranda, while Cat nodded in silent agreement.

Victoria must have sensed their presence like a threatened animal because she turned so quickly her wheels stuttered on the boards. Her eyes opened wide, and she whipped off the headset, stared at them for a moment, glancing behind at the shut door. Then she seemed to relax.

'Oh well, it's Cat Ballou and her dog!' she said, her voice lilting in mockery. 'I see you've come without Air Hawk, then.'

'Stevie's flying,' said Cat, not even pretending to misunderstand. 'She should be over the Atlantic right now.'

She glanced at Miranda wondering if she too realised that they had seen a picture of this woman. She was the owner of the Yaris, and Stevie had not mentioned it: definitely bad news.

'When the cat's away,' said Victoria, and then laughed, 'but of course you aren't the mice, are you, Cat? Is this delegation because I told Stevie I'd love to meet you, or are you slipping in without her knowledge? Were you hoping for a quick libation with the boss, hoping to check out the new girlfriend?'

Miranda stood completely still, but Cat knew her colleague well enough to know it was the stiffness of anger.

'We wanted to ask you about Neil O'Banyon,' said Cat, 'and a tape he made.'

Victoria nodded. 'Oh, yes, the one Anthony gave me. What of it?'

For a moment the women were silent. Then Cat continued, 'When did Anthony give it to you?'

Victoria frowned. She spoke slowly, thinking. 'Must have been just after I saved Neil from the Billington ditch. Probably when I tried to clean him up for the first time.'

'Which was when?'

She blew out her lips. 'I'm thinking a few years after I started Spinners in the 90s. Let's see, maybe around 2006 but he may have given me the tape as late as 2008. You know, I suppose, that Anthony was also treating Neil, much good it did him.'

'Why did you try and clean Neil up?'

Victoria sighed. 'Hello, here comes the inquisition. Don't you trust Stevie to interview me? Is she a little too kind to be a real tough Marlowe? Or are you frightened she's getting too close to me? Might ruin your throuple!'

Miranda took a chair from the table and sat down. Cat leant against the table. Neither spoke.

'Oh, look,' said Victoria. 'It's bad cop, bad cop! Well, I'm not one for repetition and I've already told your *untrusted* colleague, but if I must ... Look around you.'

Victoria waved her hand around the room.

'You can see I used to fly. So did my sister, but she was killed, and this is a memorial to her; everything, the night-club, the room, everything.'

She stared back at them.

'So, what else do you need to know? That I miss flying? Well, there's a surprise. That I miss my sister? Ditto. None of that is a crime, you know, not even for you *thought police*.'

She sighed and moving her wheels slightly, glanced back at the floor and the dance competition. Jenny and Trixie had just taken to the stage and Jenny was giving deep curtseys. Miranda wondered if they would win the competition. Victoria turned back to the detectives.

'So, you might be surprised to know my sister was engaged to Neil O'Banyon, and then she kicked him out. Drinking. It was always his weakness. She didn't tell many people and I was honoured to have been the recipient of her secrets. I liked him myself, but he was never interested in me. I guess he thought I was too young. Later, I discovered I preferred girls, anyway. But when I saw him drunk on the side of the road, I remembered those glorious days of our youth back at White Waltham, and I thought I would try and save him, in memory of my sister, Bella Chantry.'

'What happened to Bella Chantry?' asked Cat.

Victoria made a face, pulling her lower lip above her upper. 'Neil killed her.'

Both girls frowned.

'What do you mean,' asked Cat, 'killed her? Are we talking metaphorically? He wanted her to die. When she jilted him?'

Victoria blew air from one side of her mouth. 'You've seen Anthony's tape, haven't you? Don't try and play games with me; I'm way ahead of you. Neil admitted he was angry with her for not having recognised him, so he drove too fast and then they went into a ditch, and she was hurt. He buggered off and she died. If he'd reported it, she might have been saved.'

'Did you make the tape?' asked Cat.

Victoria looked at her cynically, raising a lip. 'You dog detectives. On! On! On! I don't know who made the tape, but Anthony gave it to me. Since he was clearly breaking all norms of patient confidentiality you start to get a view of the man. You ask him about my sister; he knows all about her.'

Miranda felt a cold flash in her stomach, and she saw that Cat was wrinkling her brow. 'You told Stevie you weren't in contact with Anthony any longer.'

At the mention of Stevie's name, Victoria glanced at Cat severely. She seemed to be thinking about something and then she relaxed. 'I'm not. As I said, I've had the tape a long time. I didn't think about showing it to anybody but now I hear Anthony's been throwing it around like confetti. Do dog detectives like confetti? Presumably only if it's choco-late! Woof, woof, woof, woof.' She laughed, grinning at the detectives.

Neither Cat nor Miranda spoke.

Victoria continued. 'I suppose you want the whole sad story. Well then! I was at one of the trade shows; I some-times go to them for old times' sake, and a former colleague approached me. "You remember Neil O'Banyon?" he asked. I said I did.

'"I'm sure I saw him the other day," he said, "on the streets, drinking from a brown bag. He was filthy and had a huge, long beard and his hair hadn't been cut for who knows how long, but I was sure it was him. I called his name but he ignored me ... he turned away, so I left it. But I thought you'd be interested, since you were friends."

'Well, after that I had to find him. I drove my car up and down the streets where my colleague had seen Neil. And finally, I found him, in Billington of all places, as though he had returned to be near the scene of the crime. He was sitting, his back against a long brick wall of the pub, a brown paper bag in his hand ... drinking ... drinking ... and I suddenly knew what he had become and why.

'I stopped the car and got out. He looked up. His eyes were bloodshot, but he was still on this planet. He knew who I was, and he started to cry. To apologise. Then. Apologise then, way too late. When he had had the chance of a career in aviation. And blown it. Blown it for the booze that took away Bella's chance. Why couldn't he have been the damaged one? Why did Bella have to suffer?

'I took him home with me, I helped him dry out. I gave him a plan of survival. I took him to the club. But I couldn't look after him twenty-four-seven, so one evening I left him to his own devices. And you know what?'

Cat shook her head, but Miranda remained perfectly still. Victoria eyed her up and then continued. 'That very evening he was seduced by Jenny. Left the club with her. No doubt to have a threesome with the lovely, lithe Amy!'

She shook her head and blew out strongly making her cheeks shake as though in support.

'Disgusting people! They didn't care about him. They

just wanted their sex lives enhanced. He was back on the streets within a week. And you know why? Amy, that's why! Problem was he couldn't stay away from that bitch. That's what killed him. That bitch! No wonder he needed intensive therapy.'

CHAPTER 36

FLYING THROUGH THE
WATER GLOBE

A s they drove home, Miranda said, 'What to believe, eh?'

Cat shook her head. 'Might be true about the night Neil met Jenny. You can see she watches everything that goes on, and she would have seen the seduction. She might even have known that Jenny spiked Neil's drink. But I wonder about the rest. I get the feeling she is lying – almost as though lying is a way of life for her. And she clearly hates Amy.'

'Yes, jealous. I read somewhere that if a woman kills a man, ninety percent of the time another woman is involved. Although I think ninety percent might be too high.'

'And,' Cat continued, 'certainly regarding Anthony, she's lying. It's not just that I know Anthony too well to think he would make a tape and use one of his clients but he doesn't have any motive. Why would he kill Neil?'

Miranda shook her head. 'Honestly, Cat, I think you are as much in love with Anthony as your daughter!'

Cat drove off the A3 at Petersfield and was silent until she was on the Midhurst Road, then she said, 'Character!'

'Come again?'

'Character. Even if Anthony did give her the tape, which I doubt, Anthony doesn't have a killer character, especially not something that would involve leading a client to destruction. He just wouldn't do it.'

Miranda sighed. 'We've had this conversation many times before; good people *do* do bad things … even good people turn bad if circumstances push them. You should have a chat with my sister about the things the police see.'

Cat was now passing through the sleeping villages on the way to Owly Vale. For a while she concentrated on sharp bends and occasional passing traffic, then she said, 'Yes, I'm not saying bad things don't happen or that surprising people don't commit them. I'm saying that Anthony has had a difficult battle to become what he is today, and you don't get to his level without a great deal of integrity and ability. He not only doesn't have weakness in his character to deceive, but he wouldn't jeopardise the career he has spent so long building up by killing a homeless man. I mean, why would he? It just doesn't make sense.'

'And yet,' said Miranda, 'those very things make him vulnerable to blackmail.'

Cat drove into her drive and stopped, turning to look at Miranda. 'Blackmail? Where does that come in? Is anyone suggesting Neil was blackmailing someone?'

'No,' said Miranda, now unsure how to articulate something her instinct was telling her was true. 'I'm not sure where that thought came from, but listening to you it struck me that the kind of character you are describing is vulnerable to blackmail because he is so straight; he won't see the perverse angles that blackmailers fasten on to immediately.'

'Ah,' said Cat, somewhat dismissively, 'it's that detective instinct again.' And she reached into the back of the car to get her things. 'Although I'm not sure if you are right about that, but we do need to talk to Anthony and I'm not going to ask Caroline to do it.'

Miranda collected her own things from the footwell. 'Well, Stevie won't be an unbiased interviewer, will she? Besides, was it strictly moral or even legal to give Caroline that tape? And, if it was made ages ago, why give it to us now? Especially if, as Victoria claims, he gave it to *her* long ago.'

Cat shut the door and locked the car. As they walked to the house, she said, 'So, you do believe that? That Anthony gave her the tape? Even though she had broken with him. Sounds completely incredible to me.'

Miranda shrugged. 'Well, they both have the tape. Someone made it.'

Cat opened the door to the house and waved at Frank, who was putting the dogs out in the garden. She inclined her head towards him, her voice deep with emotion, 'Never sleeps, that man!'

Miranda, about to walk round to her house stopped and laughed. 'Opposite of Phillip, then. Only awake to work, that's his motto.'

She blew them both a kiss and turned to walk the short distance home.

'OK,' yelled Cat after her, 'I'll interview Anthony tomorrow. I think he might open up to me more, even though, or perhaps because, I'm Caroline's mother.'

Miranda sighed, staring at her colleague thoughtfully. 'OK, go ahead. But don't say I didn't warn you if you hear things you don't want to tell your daughter.'

As she was walking away, Miranda stopped and turned around and came back to Cat's door, just in time to see Frank and Cat giving each other a loving welcome.

'OK, break it up! I've just had a thought, Cat.'

'Umm,' said Frank, 'certainly wouldn't want to waste that.'

'Ha, ha, Frank. Cat, Victoria claimed that Bella was her older sister, but haven't we heard somewhere Bella was the younger sister? Wasn't there a Rebecca somewhere in our investigation?'

'Rebecca Finlater?' asked Frank.

'What?' Both detectives stared at him.

'The woman whose car crashed into Wild Garlic. The police asked about a Rebecca Finlater, and the hijacked woman said that was her sister. That it was her sister's car.'

'Interesting,' said Cat, 'but if Rebecca Finlater is her sister, then who is Victoria Bell? And who was killed in the car crash? Could there be three sisters?'

CHAPTER 37

PAIN COMES IN MANY COLOURS

A couple of days later, Stevie returned to Heathrow early in the morning. The flight to Caracas had been cancelled the previous night and the dispatchers had asked her to fill in on another flight, which had brought her home earlier. She'd agreed, even though she knew her body clock would feel the difference.

She checked her messages. Nothing from the carer, which meant no problems with Blinkey. That was a relief. She thought for a moment of going to see Victoria at Spinners, but she might be at her hideaway. Should she just go home, get some rest? She longed to see Victoria, but she was so tired. It was after midnight. Perhaps she should go home: it wasn't much fun when a friend arrived unexpectedly and then fell asleep. She didn't want Victoria to think she was boring.

She was about to turn for home when her phone rang. Victoria's voice was soft and held a hint of longing.

'Hello, darling. I just wondered where you were. It seems ages...'

Stevie laughed in delight. 'I'd love to come over, but will

you mind if I crash almost immediately? I didn't get much sleep in the last few days.'

'Doesn't matter at all. I can watch you sleep. I'm in the hideaway. See you soon.'

This time Stevie was more cautious about looking through the window. She went to the door and tried it; it opened just as Victoria was getting out of her chair. Stevie noticed there were harnesses either side of the chair and Victoria was bringing out walking sticks with silver engraved heads. She'd never seen that before.

As Stevie walked through the doorway, Victoria leaned forward, one hand holding the crutches, the other pushing up from the arm of her chair, her upper body swaying slightly. Stevie dropped her bag and hurried over.

'Let me help.'

'No! I'm used to it.'

Victoria pushed up and was on the sticks in a single lithe movement. She moved forward, undulating slightly like someone riding a damaged bicycle.

Stevie looked in surprise. 'I didn't know...'

Victoria tilted her head impatiently. 'Yup. You've busted me again. I can walk, a little. It's just I tire easily, so I use the chair for any distance. Didn't you notice my legs are not completely wasted?'

'Yes,' said Stevie, going back to retrieve her bag. 'Sort of. I don't have any medical experience, outside my mother that is. You didn't tell me...'

She tried not to feel deflated by this strange welcome. It was as though Victoria was demonstrating how clever she was, as though their love wasn't enough. Why hadn't Victoria mentioned that she could walk with sticks? That wasn't a small thing, and it did explain how she had been able to leave the other morning without waking her. Stevie stared at the woman trying to quell a strangely dull pain in her stomach.

Victoria sat down on the first chair she came to with a whump. She apparently hadn't noticed her girlfriend's consternation and began singing about chairs far away from the cold night air.

She looked up and smiled at Stevie with such love in her eyes that Stevie forgot all her doubts and hurried to her side for a kiss, the pain in her stomach denied; dulled but refusing to go away.

Her body clock totally out of sync, Stevie woke up early next morning and checked her messages. Victoria was asleep beside her. Stevie, looking into her face, noticed with sympathy that she was looking haggard; her chin drooped slightly, and she had wrinkles around her eyes. Stevie suddenly wondered about her age. If Bella Chantry was old enough to work for Cathay in 1988, then she must have been twenty or twenty-one. Assuming her sister was only a little younger, that probably still meant that she was born in the mid-1960s. So, now she would be in her fifties. Some twenty-plus years older than Stevie.

She shook away the thoughts and checked her messages. There was one from Cat: the carer called me last night, said you didn't come home from Heathrow. Where are you?

Honestly, Cat sometimes thought she was her mother, just because she was the same age as Cat's children.

Miranda's message, also sent last night, said: Fun at Spinners and R young Amy, and getting clozer. Cat interview Anthony tomorrow. Miaow.

Honestly, thought Stevie, did Miranda ever read her messages before she sent them, or were they just sent off with illiterate enthusiasm? Was it sensible to let Cat go and interview Anthony? Now she realised that Caroline's therapist Anthony was the same as Victoria's Anthony, it worried her. Anthony and Caroline had such a bond it was hard to think that Cat, Caroline's mother, could be objective in her interview. What if Anthony *had* killed Neil? How would Caroline get over that, plus the lack of trust from her therapist? Much better and more likely that Clive Creamer had killed Neil in a manic phase and forgotten all about it.

She sighed. She had left them too quickly and angrily, and now she felt bad about it. She needed to get back and check they were all OK. Without her presence there would be hardly any internet interaction and who knows what they might have missed? She shouldn't have got cross with Cat the other day. Of course, Cat was worried about her, that was her caring personality, and they didn't know that Victoria was a darling and would never hurt anyone. She needed to see them and explain.

She started to slide gently out of bed, not wanting to wake Victoria at such an early hour.

As Stevie put her hands down to push herself up, Victoria suddenly rolled towards her in a sleepy manner, knocking the phone out of her hand. It bounced across the bed and Victoria, now totally awake, picked it up and started reading Stevie's message from Miranda.

'What does this mean?' she said crossly. 'We had some fun at Spinners and with young—huh, old I'd say—Amy. Getting closer? To what? What's going on, Stevie? Are you spying on me? Pretending to care for me and then leading me on?'

Stevie turned to her in amazement. 'No, I ... of course

not! The opposite. I almost fell out with my friends over you.'

Victoria was suddenly all contrition. 'Sorry, Stevie.' Her eyes filled with tears. 'I'm just upset. Your colleagues came to see me while you were away and made it horribly clear they think I killed Neil. Just because I tried to help him. They find that suspicious. Odd. My kind heart is suddenly being judged as peculiar. That and the fact I'm a lesbian. I bet that Cat has all sorts of hang-ups about lesbians. She's probably like my grandmother who used to call them Lebanese!'

Stevie said nothing. Her emotions were gambling across her body. She wasn't up to this level of conversation, again she longed for the safety of the sky.

'Honestly,' said Victoria, 'just because I had the tape of Neil that Anthony made, they are super suspicious.'

'Did Anthony make that tape?' asked Stevie, surprised. She still hadn't seen it. Perhaps Victoria would finally show it to her today.

'Frightening,' said Victoria, leaning back on the pillows, 'to think Anthony was a killer. I was lucky. I recognised the bathroom in Wild Garlic where he made that tape. Proves he did it, really.'

Stevie looked up puzzled. 'But the bathroom was upstairs. How did you get there? Even with the sticks it must have been hard.'

Victoria was silent for a moment, then she said, 'Oh, back in detective mode, are we? OK, Neil and I did meet at Wild Garlic occasionally, when I was helping him get his life back together. He used to carry me up to the bathroom. Anthony knew that. He must have made the tape there to incriminate me.'

Stevie stared at her. 'But ... but, how? Why?'

Victoria snorted. 'They both lusted after me, that's why. Even when Neil was engaged to Bella, he really wanted me. I was the one he took to meet his father. He just knew I was too young, but it wasn't Bella he wanted. It was me. Then, he killed Bella, and disappeared off to the USA without even a word. Didn't even contact me again until I found him in a ditch.'

'What?' Stevie's heart took a big leap. This was all so odd. 'But...' She struggled to get out of the bed, but suddenly the sheets seem to have a grip on her, preventing her moving. Victoria continued staring at a picture on the wall, she seemed to be reliving her life.

'I was very young. I didn't know what I liked. He seemed terribly glamorous, and he was so admiring of me as a pilot: for most people I was just a gofer. You know. *Bella needs something—Victoria will go for it. Thanks, Victoria, you're such a love. Bye!*

It was because of *me* Neil learnt to fly. It was thanks to *me* that he embarked on his aviation career. Everyone thinks it was my sister, but it was me.

'He was a physics teacher and on the point of marrying my sister. I saved him from all that, just as I later saved him from a life on the streets. But then he met Amy, the silly bitch, and he couldn't stay away from her, and that's what killed him.'

Stevie wanted to believe her, but she was troubled. Neil's father said he had met Bella and she was at school. That would make Victoria very young indeed. Did Neil like schoolchildren? That was suddenly making the whole thing rather creepy.

Still, she couldn't think about it now. She would reason through that later when she was up in the Tiger Moth. It must be Amy who had killed him, or perhaps Spud, in a fit of jealousy.

'Thank Heavens,' she said. 'I was so worried that you had done it by mistake. I thought he might have made a pass at you like Anthony, and this time you fought him off. Although I really couldn't believe you would. You aren't a killer, I know, I can feel it.'

'Indeed,' said Victoria lovingly, and she rolled closer to Stevie, kissing her gently.

'Shall we have breakfast now or later...?'

After a late brunch and several unanswered calls from her colleagues, Stevie said she really must go home.

'I don't want to leave you, darling,' she said, stroking Victoria's cheek, 'but I need to hear what Cat and Miranda have discovered. They are useless on the internet without me,' said Stevie, laughing. 'They came on it too late. The things they drag up. The other day—'

'Be careful,' interrupted Victoria. 'They think I'm involved, and they'll try and poison your thoughts.'

Stevie leant over and kissed her reassuringly. 'They probably do think you were involved; after all, they don't know you the way I do. But when I explain the confusion over Neil being in love with *you*, not Bella, and that Anthony made the tape here, having lured Neil to Wild Garlic by pretending to be you ... they'll soon see I'm right. After all, wasn't it Anthony who suggested you rent Wild Garlic? And then he made the tape there, to make it look like you did it. Such a let-down for Cat and Caroline, to discover about him. I'm not sure how Caroline will get over it.'

'Oh, yes,' said Victoria. 'Caroline, Cat's daughter. She'd

slipped my mind for a moment. Did you know she was Anthony's lover?'

'What? No. She's got Rupert, who admittedly is a dead-beat, and their daughter Lagertha, she wouldn't...'

'Wouldn't she indeed? It might interest you to know she came to see me a few weeks ago, at Spinners.'

'She did? Why?'

Stevie knew Caroline was rather inclined to do unexpected things, but this seemed completely irrational. 'Does she know you?'

'She does now. I was watching the floor at Spinners. I saw her talking to Jenny and Trixie, and the barman that night told me she had been looking for the owner. Sure enough she was, and up she came to see me.'

'What did she want?'

'She told me to leave Anthony alone. She said she knew I was trying to seduce him, and I was to back off or she'd kill me.'

'She said that?'

Even when Caroline was at her most unstable, she had not threatened anyone. This seemed extraordinary.

'But ... you hadn't seen Anthony for years.'

Victoria shrugged. 'Yeah, but that's what jealousy does to you. It eats you up. It puts irrational thoughts into your mind. But don't worry, I calmed her down. I explained you were my lover and that Anthony meant nothing to me.' Victoria laughed and stroked Stevie's face. 'She went away quite happy.'

'Oh,' said Stevie, *and then no doubt told her mother all about it*. No wonder Cat didn't trust her. She needed to go back and talk to her colleagues. Explain everything.

'I'd better go, Vic, there's so much talking Cat, Miranda

and I need to catch up on. We've got past the point of texting; I need to see them.'

Victoria kissed her shoulder.

Stevie got out of the bed and started to dress. Victoria rolled after her, pulling herself up on her sticks. She said, 'Wait just a moment. I have something else to show you. Something you need to see before you see your friends.'

Stevie smiled at her as she wavered across the floor in her determined manner. What a brave woman. However, she could see Victoria was rather jealous of the SeeMs girls and Amy too, but Victoria had to understand both her jobs were important to Stevie. Not just the flying, but also the detective work. She loved doing it and she was learning and getting better all the time. After all, even now she had information that the others didn't have and that she could share. She was the only one who knew about the love triangle with Neil, Bella and Victoria. She longed to tell them that she had got a piece of information first and by interviewing— well, sort of—not surfing. Perhaps then they would start to value her as a detective.

Victoria swayed back into the room holding a memory stick and her laptop. 'I think you need to see this before you go and chat to your friends,' she said, waving the memory stick, her smile twisted like a cross between pain and love.

She put the memory stick into her laptop. Got the video up on her screen and then turned on the TV. 'I thought we'd cast it, for greater effect.'

Stevie smiled happily. 'OK, sounds great. I'm sure I'll love whatever you are going to show me.'

Victoria's laugh sounded a bit strange. 'I'm sure you will,' she said. 'I do.'

And she started the video.

On the TV screen Stevie saw herself walking up and down, looking through the window outside the house.

'Quite a little voyeur, our Stevie,' said Victoria and her voice was gleeful with mockery.

Stevie stared at her, the dull pain in her stomach returning doubled. She felt a bit confused. She knew Victoria liked her little games, and they were all resolved in the end, but this seemed slightly frightening.

She turned her glance back to the film. The door swung open to reveal Victoria in her chair. The picture switched to a different camera and showed Stevie entering the house before focusing on Stevie and Victoria sitting and talking, which, since there was no sound, was predictably boring.

'But,' said Victoria, 'this bit is a little dull, isn't it, darling? I think we ought to get to the best bit, don't you? Pity about the sound, isn't it? I must have had it turned off.'

Stevie felt her body tremble. She wrapped her arms around herself hoping to get warm. The room wasn't cold, and she was now fully clothed, so why was her body shivering?

'I'll just fast forward a bit, shall I?' said Victoria, doing it. 'Let's get to the bit your mother and friends are going to enjoy.'

Stevie bit her lip. She thought about her mother watching this and realised she wouldn't understand a thing. She would probably focus on a flower arrangement on the table or one of the pictures. She almost laughed: that, at least, was an empty threat.

The film progressed to Stevie's bending over Victoria. Victoria put out her hands to push her away, but Stevie kept on coming relentlessly, forcing kisses on the clearly frightened woman. Putting her hands under her body despite Victoria's clear resistance and carrying her to the bed.

But, thought Stevie, *it wasn't like that. Why does it look as though I'm forcing myself on her? She was telling me to do it. We were re-enacting Anthony's* ... And suddenly she wondered, had Anthony done anything?

'But...' she said, 'this isn't how it was...' Her heart was palpitating, and her head shook violently.

'Nice, isn't it? You are so romantic,' said Victoria, 'and you made it look so exciting. Pity I didn't record the sound, but perhaps we can put some music in. Maybe "Rough Seduction"; that will make it so much more alluring, don't you think...? Or should I put some words in? Perhaps, *lie down and take it, bitch!* In that bit. Would that make it more fun, do you think? Oh,' she said, as Stevie, no longer able to watch what was on the screen, looked down at her feet. 'Oh, don't look away, darling, some of the best bits are coming.'

Stevie tried to look elsewhere but Victoria moved a little closer and lifting her walking stick to Stevie's chin, she forced her face back to the screen. She wanted to shut her eyes, but she needed to see what was happening. Her mind was blank. She wanted to go flying.

* * *

When it was all over and the screen women were lying side by side, the relentless camera continued to expose their nudity and Stevie's obvious enjoyment. Stevie thought sadly she had been totally entranced in that moment, quite unaware of anything outside, but clearly for Victoria this was just a vile power game: Victoria's words seemed to echo her thoughts.

'So, my darling. It seems you are now in my power, doesn't it? We will keep all these nice movies for us, for our own enjoyment, provided we remain friends, won't we? And we will, won't we?'

Stevie stared at her, unable to speak. 'Or should we share them with your colleagues? I'm sure Cat would be enchanted. Miranda might not be so judgemental but that Cat! Well, I got her measure all right. Old Cat!' She giggled.

'No,' said Stevie, with an effort, 'you're wrong. My colleagues will believe me. There's no problem there. They know and trust me.'

Victoria sneered. 'What? Even beyond the evidence of their eyes? I don't think so. In your naivety you may think you are "all for one and one for all" but I can tell you now the single woman—especially the lesbo—always draws the short straw. Men and women with families pull up the draw-bridge and we are left to fall in the moat!'

Just for a second, Stevie wondered if she was right. There had been moments when she thought Cat was rather severe with her own lesbian daughter, Vanessa, her girl-friend, Gloria, and their strange trio with Cat's son, Victor. Moments when she had refused to accept that her son lived with the other two in a throuple. There had been times when Caroline, the *normal* daughter, had appeared to be her mother's favourite. But then, Stevie made herself remember, that was not Cat's choice, but because Vanessa held both her parents at arm's length.

Stevie gave a deep sigh, which Victoria misinterpreted. 'Ah! So, I see you realise I am right. What shall we tell your nice friends, so they stop bothering me? Tell me your ideas now, Stevie. You are the detective; it should be easy for you to convince your little friends that I didn't do anything.'

Stevie frowned. 'What did you do? Exactly.'

Victoria laughed. 'You still don't know, do you, you little fool? Detective smaltz? I've got more detective ability in my broken spine than you have in your brain. Of course I am Bella Chantry and of course I killed Neil, and he bloody well deserved it. Not only did he take away my life, my future, but he didn't even make the best of his own.

And I did it brilliantly. Well executed, invisible death. Until your damn nosy colleagues started bothering themselves with my affairs. But even then, I was way cleverer than them. I thought of accusing Anthony. And I was clever enough to already have him in my power.

'You can make the Cat turn bad, too. Practical Cat becomes Rumpleteazer. Cat and Co will be so keen to protect Anthony, and Caroline, that we will have no problem with them. We can have a life of love and freedom and they will stop their *investigating* nonsense agency and go back to being wives, mothers and lovers, as they should.'

'No,' said Stevie.

'No, how no,' quoted Victoria automatically, 'nothing can come of nothing. Speak again.'

'Even if you do show this video to Cat and Miranda, they will only think I was a fool, no more. They are friends, and friends do not draw up the drawbridge when things go wrong. They stay and support you through everything.'

Victoria gave a short harsh laugh. 'So you say. We will see about that soon. But that is not the only place I will be posting the video, nor the only place where you will be seen as a seducer of innocent cripples.'

Stevie gasped.

'Yes, you didn't think of that, did you? When you were busy seducing me, all you thought of was your lust, not that I could not resist you because I was disabled. Ableism, isn't it? You don't even connect properly with the thoughts of the injured. You don't understand us at all!'

'But it wasn't like that,' said Stevie. 'You know it wasn't. I loved you. I thought you were the best thing that had ever happened to me. I'd never been so close to anyone and now ... now...'

'Now what?' said Victoria. 'You didn't trust me. You thought I would send that video to your friends. You didn't even suggest it was a joke, or that I might love you too much to do it, did you? You just believed the worst of me.'

'No ... I ... I...'

Stevie was so confused she couldn't think at all. She desperately wanted to go out flying.

'I've got to go, Victoria. I'll come back later, and we'll talk all this through.' She looked at her watch. 'But now I must go to the office and see the girls, talk to them, and have a check on the Tiger Moth.'

'The Tiger Moth,' mocked Victoria, 'always top in your thoughts, that little baby. You love it more than you ever loved me. But, young Stevie, you ain't going anywhere. If you do, I will post this all over social media as soon as you leave. Not only your detective colleagues, but all your flying colleagues will see you just as nature made you and doing things that—so we are told—nature did not intend! How long do you think it will be before BA gives you the chance to leave? They may not fire you for this; that would be politically naïve, but they will be looking for an excuse, and they'll find it. You'll be jobless. And don't tell me anyone else will employ you, not after this. Do you think the SeeMs Detective Agency will be able to get clients either? After seeing one of their operatives seducing an innocent? I don't think so. Which means you'll have to sell your precious Tiger Moth just to make ends meet. Oh dear, poor Stevie, she'll be just like ordinary people who have to work in dull jobs because they can't get anything else. Poor little girl. I'm weeping for her.'

Stevie got up.

'I don't care. Do your worst, Victoria. I will not be black-mailed by you. I'm leaving. You can do what you like but even though when I thought you were genuine, I was in your power through love; I will not be in your power through hate. I will not be party to your murder and deception. Goodbye!'

'I think not,' said Victoria, and as Stevie watched she put her hand into the pouch on her wheelchair and drew out a small pistol.

'Sit down, Stevie, I've got another movie to show you. This one you'll like very much; they even have a special name for the series of films like this one. Do you know what it is?'

Stevie had no idea what she was talking about. Was this another sex movie? Victoria making love to someone else, Neil perhaps, or another woman, which was supposed to make her jealous. All she felt now was sick.

'There is a name for these movies, isn't there?' repeated Victoria. 'I'm sure you know it. You've probably watched a few in your time.'

Stevie looked at her blankly.

'Snuff!' said Victoria. 'Isn't that a lovely name? And you must be expecting it, you wonderful detectives. After all, you saw me retrieving my equipment after the death, didn't you? Didn't you wonder why Neil was wet? Didn't you ask yourself who would hate him enough to throw water on a dead man?'

Stevie stared at her baffled. What was she talking about? And then, slowly, it occurred to her she was talking about the person leaving Wild Garlic by the back door in 2008. The person she had convinced herself was Clive Creamer, freeholder, with his mad ideas.

'No,' she said automatically, 'that wasn't you!'

'But it was, my gorgeous girl. Can't you recognise my limping walk? My sad shuffle? Something good enough to allow me to walk again, but not good enough to allow me to be employed as a pilot. No cripples here!'

She gave another hard laugh.

So, thought Stevie, Cat and Miranda had been right. She had refused to believe it, refused to doubt Victoria. She wondered if she would ever be able to trust anyone again or, she thought, suddenly remembering the gun, if she would be alive to do so.

'Is that really a gun?' Stevie asked, even knowing it was stupid. 'Do you know...' She faltered.

Victoria waggled her head. 'Do I know how to use it? Dear me, what a rude question! Yes, when your father is the sporty type and only has girls, guess what? He makes them learn all the things he would have taught his son. We became honorary boys. I can shoot, stationary and moving targets and even a man, if I must. My father believed in self-defence, as he called it. I can fish, shoot, look after myself in the wild. Or I could before my accident. I was much better than Rebecca, of course; I was better than her at everything. I had better hand-eye co-ordination and I was cleverer.

'But you don't want to hear that, do you, darling? You want to see the next video.'

Victoria's eyes glittered and Stevie watched her, her body no longer shivering. Now she was wary, thinking. She could easily overpower Victoria, but with a gun pointing at her possibly not before she was injured or killed. She waited; there would be opportunities and she would take them.

'All these lovely films,' said Victoria. 'I call them my insurance policy. Nice, eh?'

Victoria started the film. Stevie remained silent.

The film started in the bathroom at Wild Garlic. Neil entered the bathroom, looking around he began searching the shelves. He opened a cupboard door above the basin. And fell back, hitting his head on the edge of the porcelain and disappearing out of view.

A few moments later he climbed back into the picture and slumped over the basin with blood oozing from his head. His hand mopped at the blood, streaking it down his face. The camera showed a punchbag now, dangling on a spring. He reached into the cupboard and pulled out some pills. Turning, he left the room and the film stopped.

'Of course,' said Victoria, 'I never thought they'd still have kept the same locks on the house. When I discovered I had the key already, I laughed. I had made an appointment to look around Wild Garlic, planning to steal the key and make a copy, but when I saw my key still worked, I didn't need to. They were using the same one I'd used, except I had several copies. Their key even still had my tag on.'

'But the punchbag?' said Stevie, shrugging.

'Um, yes, I put it there earlier. Dragged myself up the stairs and then the silly fool hardly noticed it, did he? He was so smitten by me he could think of nothing but doing my bidding. Fool! He trusted me. Just like you, Stevie,' she said gleefully. 'He was in love with me too. You fools!'

When the video started again, Neil and Victoria were sitting at the kitchen table drinking champagne.

Stevie watched, her mind empty as Victoria brought out an e-cigarette and they passed it between them like a shared joint. Little shivers ran up and down her spine as they drank bottle after bottle. Her head reflexively tried to turn and watch the beautiful fluffy clouds passing across the windows, but Victoria relentlessly forced her face back to the screen.

Stevie looked at Victoria in despair. 'I don't understand,' she said. 'What is this? Why did you get him drinking again? You said you wanted to save him. Did he attack you or something?'

Victoria sighed. 'In spite of our shared love of flying, young Stevie, I don't think we would have made a good couple. You are too stupid!'

Stevie said nothing. She felt numb.

'I killed Neil because he killed me. As you recognised, I was too young to be engaged to Neil. He was indeed engaged to my elder sister, Rebecca, but she cared nothing for him. He was just a stepping stone for her.

'I, on the other hand, idolised him as a child and how did he repay that loyalty?

How? By taking away my beautiful future as an airline pilot and wasting his own chance just because I didn't recognise him. He did it on purpose. He walked away. He could have saved me.

'I am Bella Chantry. Did you really believe that I was another person, who just happened to have all her attributes? Did you?'

'I did. I trusted you.'

Victoria shook her head. 'Sweet! I suppose. But your colleagues didn't. They've been suspicious of me since the start. Bitches! Let's see the rest of the film.'

After a while Neil passed out. The glass dropped from his hand and bounced along the floor. Victoria got a syringe from the pouch in her bag, leaned across the table, opened the fly of his trousers, and injected him in the groin. She pulled out the syringe and put it back in her bag.

'Nice, eh?' she said.

'I don't understand.'

'Naturally! But I'll help you. I injected a hundred micrograms of nicotine. Sixty micrograms should have been enough, but I didn't want him waking up and wanting more.' She laughed. 'I'd hate him to have nicotine cravings. And do you know the beauty of it all?'

Stevie shook her head silently, looking at the gun, which Victoria had placed on the table under a handkerchief. Could she grab it before Victoria? Almost as she had the thought, Victoria leaned over and pulled the gun back to her side of the table, still talking.

'Traces of nicotine deteriorate as the body decomposes. What was left in the bloodstream would be accounted for by the e-cigarette. Not that I really thought anyone would bother to investigate the death of a homeless man. And of course, that stupid old father,' she blew out her lips, 'well, if he even knew Neil was dead, he wouldn't give a stuff. Hadn't seen his son since Mummy died.'

On the TV, the film had now moved to Victoria cleaning up. She wiped her glass clean of fingerprints and put it in her bag. She left Neil's glass where it fell but she took his hands and stroked them up and down the bottle, mushing the fingerprints. Then she started cleaning anything she had touched.

Stevie was struck by a memory. 'So, that's why there were no fingerprints on the car that crashed into Wild Garlic. You cleaned them off? But why?'

Victoria snorted. 'I really am too clever for you. Without the fingerprints the police would soon lose interest. They'd put it down to a domestic, and, well, they have plenty of other things to do.'

Stevie frowned. She found she didn't quite believe that, but she stored it for later thought.

'But why did you crash into Wild Garlic? What was the point?'

Victoria smiled. 'I discovered your agency was looking at Wild Garlic, and I knew it would be only a matter of time before something led you to Neil's death and to me.

Better to be in first so I could set the agenda. And I did. And we would have been fine, except for that fucking Amy and her stupid husband. They led you to me.

She was living in Wild Garlic when Neil died there, you knew that, didn't you? You knew it and you didn't even consider she might have killed him. Which she did: in all apart from the final blow.'

Stevie shivered. Looking out of the window she could see the clouds gently moving; a perfect day for flying the Tiger Moth.

'Is that why you did it then?' asked Stevie. 'Twenty years later. Amy was living there and you thought you could pin it on her. But why bother? You had a new life. You'd made a success of yourself. You were a brilliant nightclub owner, a businesswoman. Why jeopardise that for revenge from the past?'

Victoria hit the arm of her chair in fury. Stevie jumped nervously.

'You don't understand, you really don't! It wasn't just that my body is always in pain. Although that is true. I could live with that. But my whole family were pilots. There was no other career. I was the only failure, and it was not my fault, it was Neil's.'

She paused and her face grew tired.

'I saved him. I got him off the streets. I cleaned him up and even got him flying again. And what then?' Her shoulders drooped and she turned her head away. 'He went off with Amy. Amy! That ham-fisted zero. Anyone but Neil could see she was nothing but a taker, but oh no ... not Neil.'

Stevie looked at Victoria and there were tears in her

eyes. 'He went back to that bitch, and what happened? He was back on the streets within the year. He couldn't even make a success of the very thing he took away from me: the beauty of flight. He didn't deserve to live.

'And you ask why I killed him.'

She looked at Stevie, who stared back at her, her mind blank. She suddenly felt very tired, there was no high moral obligation here, only basic lust and jealousy. Victoria was still talking, her voice high-pitched with resentment.

'I thought it would be obvious to anyone that Amy'd done it. Her house. Plenty of motivation. He nearly killed her in a car crash. You'd think the Rozzer machine would make a beeline for her but what, oh no. They didn't even interview her. OK, she was away on long-haul but all the best killers have a foolproof alibi. They didn't even think she was suspicious! Or perhaps they didn't care. He was homeless. She was a well-connected airline pilot.'

Victoria's eyes glittered and Stevie watched her, her stomach heavy. However, there were still questions.

'So, Anthony,' she said, 'all that stuff about him seducing you … was it true?'

Victoria looked at her steadily. Eventually she said, 'That Miranda must be good as a detective. She's so burdened down with Stupid Stevie and the ghastly old Cat with her *morals*! What do you think? You reckon Anthony has the hots for me? Or did you think he'd like a white lesbo girlfriend? Bit kinky, like? If you're looking for Anthony's misbehaviour I'd look a bit closer home, you know.'

'So why did…?'

'Why did I want to implicate him? Well Amy failed to attract your attention. But who knows? I may still get her one day, even if it's after my death. Then who was left? Anthony.'

'But, Anthony'd been good to you.'

Victoria sneered. 'Think. Outside my family and the medical world no one knows that Bella Chantry is still alive. Even the physios at Hotel du Lac only know me as Miss Victory. The only person there who knew I was still alive was Anthony, and he didn't even know he held the power to hurt me in his hands. But I dealt with him. He won't speak out.'

Victoria moved in her chair.

'But anyway, enough of this light chatter, my darling,' she said. 'I think we will go flying. There is still enough light, and I know somewhere with a lovely Tiger Moth we can use. You have your car outside, so you can drive.'

As Victoria smiled, Stevie felt her body relax: she was going to die, and that was it. She wouldn't have to fight all these feelings that rushed through her body making it hard to breathe: she would die. Dead people didn't suffer.

Her friends and mother would mourn her and then they would all get on with their lives. Or her friends would. But what about her mother? Who would pay for her mother's care if she was dead? They could sell her funny old ramshackle house and that would pay for a while in a care home, but what then? Without her BA money coming in, who would support her old mum? Nobody else cared about her. Cat did. But then, Cat had enough problems of her own, without an extra old woman.

She looked at Victoria and saw that Victoria did not care. She didn't care about Stevie's mother, and she didn't care about Stevie either. She only cared for one person: herself.

Stevie shook her head. What a fool she had been. It was all her own fault that she was trapped here with a killer. She had walked blindly into a trap and never even doubted. She'd failed to believe her friends.

Victoria was observing her closely. 'So,' she said, 'you realise you were a fool. I am right. If you had listened to me from the beginning, we wouldn't be in this hole. Now I have no choice but to kill you, even though I love you.'

Stevie said nothing. She got up. She was stronger than Victoria, she could overpower her. There would be time; she was ready.

'So, my darling,' said Victoria, 'are you ready? You have your car outside, so you can drive. And don't think of trying to overpower me. I may not be able, but I am quick!'

CHAPTER 38
HELL IS OTHER PEOPLE

W hen Cat made an appointment with Anthony's secretary she wondered if the girl would make a connection between her name and that of her daughter, one of Anthony's longest clients, but the discreet woman said nothing to give her any alarm.

Anthony himself, however, was not so assured. When he saw it was Cat who came for an interview, his beautiful face creased with concern.

'Cat,' he said, 'how nice. Do you mind if I leave the door open? It is a normal strategy when interviewing a patient for the first time, as much for your protection as mine.'

She nodded. 'Fine.'

'You told my receptionist you needed to speak to me about something. Is it medical? I don't usually accept a mother and a daughter as patients. Conflict of interest.'

Cat shook her head. 'No, sorry, I should have said. This is nothing to do with Caroline. It's about the video you gave her. The video of Neil O'Banyon. We are trying to find out who killed him.'

Anthony shook his head, relaxing. 'In that case, I might shut the door. That now makes it a more private matter.'

'That's also fine,' said Cat. 'I don't for one moment think you might have designs on me.'

Returning to his chair, he looked up at her sharply. 'Me? Hardly? What do you mean?'

That, Cat thought, was a very interesting response from a man normally so cool.

She said, 'Tell me about your relationship with Neil O'Banyon.'

Anthony leant back into his chair. 'You do know patient confidentiality persists beyond the grave.'

Cat nodded. 'Yes, but this is a murder case.'

He nodded thoughtfully. 'OK, what do you want to know?'

'We know, because Victoria told Stevie, that Victoria had a therapist called Anthony. The names might just be coincidence, but were you Victoria Bell's therapist? Even before you were Neil's?'

Anthony put his hands together in front of his face as though he was praying and rubbed the bridge of his nose thoughtfully. Eventually, he said, 'Cat, I'll have to trust you with this. Victoria Bell was my patient. But if you really think she was involved in Neil's death ... I am conflicted.'

Cat said nothing, waiting.

'OK. Let me talk about a mythical patient, who we might call Victoria, and what might, theoretically, have happened in this theoretical case.'

Cat nodded.

'OK, well, Victoria was in hospital where she was having operation after operation on her back. Her only ambition in life was to get back to flying; everything she did led that way and even when surgeon after surgeon told her it was hopeless, she insisted on going on and on with further work. We can imagine from this case that she is a very strong-willed and dedicated woman, and it was terrible what happened to her.

However, her therapist, for this example we can call him Anthony, could see she would never get better until she accepted that her body had changed irreparably, and her mind needed to do so too.

'Imagine also that Anthony was still a probationer in the therapy world, but he was young like her and he felt that he could help her and asked if he could work with her, and the hospital agreed.'

Cat nodded and he continued.

'So, he suggested that she left home and found somewhere else to live. Away from people who only thought about flying and who lived and breathed aviation. It was her only hope. Especially after her sister got the job she would have had in Hong Kong and moved there.'

'Her sister?' said Cat, frowning. 'Did she have another sister? I thought her sister was dead; killed by Neil.'

'What?' Anthony stared at her in amazement. 'Where on earth did you get that idea?'

'Your video, I mean the one you gave us. Neil said on it that he killed Bella Chantry.'

Anthony hit his head with the palm of his hand. 'Sorry, what a fool I am. I was so used to the idea that Victoria, whose real name is Bella Chantry, was the victim I assumed everyone would know. I thought you would see she was forcing him to say that he killed her, after all she wasn't actually dead and I thought you knew that.

And, of course, the reason she wasn't dead was not thanks to Neil but because a child found her car sinking into the ditch and got her out. He saved her life.'

Cat snorted. 'We had no idea. Victoria told Stevie her office was a memorial for her sister killed in a road accident. Then when we heard the tape it was just confirmation of what she was told.'

Anthony curled his lip. 'They were role playing. He and Victoria. He told me she asked him to read a script saying that he had killed her, and then in the second video it would be revealed that she was still alive and that he had been suffering from guilt all along and that his excessive drinking could be entirely put down to that feeling and he would be cured.

'I told him it was crazy to do something like that, but he felt so guilty about Bella's accident that he would have done anything she asked.'

'But surely he saw making a tape like that gives her a motive for killing him: the death of her sister.'

Anthony gave a spurt of laughter. 'The way she talks about her sister, that would not have given her a motive! *Au contraire*. And I don't think he assumed she would kill him. Why would he?'

Cat frowned. 'I wonder. Where did Bella's accident happen?'

'On the notorious Billington corner, between Billington and Owly Vale.'

'In fact, the place where Stevie came across the "crazy man" and his niece. The man the police called homeless, possibly dangerous. I wonder if that is the same man. Incidentally, was there a second tape? The one that explained that the first was only therapy.'

'I doubt it. Neil missed his next appointment and I never saw him again. It was only when Caroline told me about your investigation into his death that I discovered why he didn't turn up for his appointment thirteen years ago.'

'Why did Caroline tell you about his death?'

Anthony spoke quietly. 'Cat, you must understand that what you do is very important to your daughter. It comes up a lot in our therapy. Obviously, I'm not going to go into specifics but please understand your relationship with your daughter is a very important part of her good health.'

'Oh boy,' said Cat. 'No pressure!'

Anthony raised an eyebrow but said nothing.

'Go on.'

Anthony gave a deep sigh. 'OK. Well, when Victoria had accepted that she would never fly again, her health, mental and physical, began to improve exponentially. She looked around for fields where she could use her expertise to improve people's lives and earn a reasonable income.'

'And came up with the idea of a nightclub,' said Cat dryly, 'an aviation-themed nightclub.'

Anthony stared at her with narrowed eyes, then went on. 'She told me that she bought the place in Clerkenwell with more of her insurance money. Clerkenwell was her choice because it was relatively cheap at that time, and she was able to get the freehold, which isn't always possible in Central London. It was a good purchase, had no listing and could be changed as she wished. It also had underground parking, which she immediately saw was important, given that she was going to make it a safe place for cross-dressers and trans people who, at that time, had no good, safe night-clubs they could use. Considering this was in the 1990s, she was way ahead of her time. And she quickly made it into a thriving business.'

Cat frowned. 'I've looked at her accounts. The club is in debt.'

Anthony sighed. 'Yes, it was much more successful in the 90s and early this century.' He shrugged and took a drink of water. 'Anyway, at that time it was successful and she stopped therapy and I didn't see her again.

'Then, several years later, I was asked to take on a drunk man from the streets. Neil. In our first sessions he didn't say anything about Bella, just that he'd been on the streets for a while moving around between London and Brighton.'

She nodded.

'Then one day he went to sleep in Brighton and woke up in the wood behind Wild Garlic.'

Cat nodded. 'Was that when Miranda met him?'

Anthony raised his eyebrows. 'Did Miranda meet him? I didn't know.'

'Yes, he suddenly appeared in Owly Vale, but he ran away pretty fast. She didn't know how he got there.'

Anthony stroked his cheek thoughtfully. 'I can't say exactly what happened when, but Neil did say on one occasion he went to sleep in Brighton and woke up in a village miles away, with no idea how he got there. He said he got a lift back to London but then the voices started again.'

'The voices?'

'Yes, when he was in London he often heard Bella's voice. Of course he thought she was dead so he thought it was a ghost. She would say things like: "you killed me" and "you ruined my life." The more voices he heard the more he drank. Then he started hallucinating: a woman in a wheelchair, often with distorted features.

Eventually, it was too much and he decided to go to Billington and kill himself with pills and drink, but when he arrived at the station, Bella Chantry was waiting for him in her car.

'At first he thought it was another hallucination. Then he realised she was there in the flesh and not dead, although fatally (as far as flying was concerned) wounded.'

Anthony sighed.

'So she took him to Spinners,' said Cat. 'Cleaned him up and made him want to live again, and then she killed him. Classic!'

Anthony sighed. 'That's the cynical view. Perhaps she genuinely wanted to save him. She had been in love with him once.'

'Really, I thought?'

'You thought she was gay? I think she is everything she needs to be...' He was looking away from Cat and, she thought, avoiding eye contact. Wonder why? What, she asked herself did he know that he wasn't saying?

'Neil was engaged to her sister when Bella was very young. I think the younger sister basically wanted everything her older sister had, and more.'

'Ah, so there is also a bit of sibling rivalry to take into account,' said Cat.

Anthony now looked directly at Cat. 'Plus she hated the fact that he, despite having ruined her life, couldn't take advantage of his own flying ability and was now ruining his own life as well.'

'He did leave the scene of the crime,' said Cat. 'Twice in fact since he did it again with Amy.'

'Yes, I have always wondered if he was suffering from dissociative fugue and had no idea what he was doing.'

Cat raised her eyebrows questioningly.

'It's a form of amnesia, brought on by the fight or flight reflex. I wonder if he had any idea what he was doing ... but then later he discovered what he had done and the guilt washed over him until he couldn't cope anymore.'

'Did Victoria know that Neil was your patient?'

'Yes. He told her.'

'Were you still treating her?'

'Nooo,' said Anthony and the way he said it made Cat look at him sharply. But when he said nothing she decided to leave the issue.

'Was she jealous of your therapy with Neil? She wanted to save him alone?'

Anthony looked at her thoughtfully. 'Possibly, although I hadn't thought of it that way.'

Cat nodded thoughtfully, thinking that Victoria had suggested Anthony might be Neil's killer, but she couldn't for a moment think of a motive. Almost without thinking she asked, 'Did Neil ever meet Caroline?'

Anthony looked at Cat in a puzzled fashion. 'No, I don't think so. Any reason you ask that?'

Cat shook her head. 'Just a sudden thought.'

He pinched the end of his nose. 'Victoria is a very beautiful woman,' he said.

Cat tensed. This man was her daughter's therapist, not just a source. Did she want to hear he was vulnerable to female beauty?

'I don't know how much time you have spent with Victoria, but she is a highly believable person, as well as a beautiful one. The first time she came into my office in her chair she looked so vulnerable, so totally destroyed by life, my heart went out to her. Of course, in some ways she had come from a life of privilege. Her parents were professionals with great jobs, and, for Heaven's sake, their own pair of Piper Cubs: a hobby of travelling all over Europe in their own aircraft, with their two girls. How wild and wonderful is that? But then it was all taken away from her, even when she was going on to excel in the very field her whole family loved, by an accident. A drunk man. Her own trust in another person. She told me that by trying to prevent herself driving when over the limit, by asking someone else to drive her, she put herself in a situation that damaged her irreparably. How could I not feel incredible sympathy for her?'

Cat nodded. So far, okay. She had the nasty feeling Anthony was about to confess and had a sudden vision of a church she visited as a child that had a sign by the confessional: *The priest is very busy. Please just confess your sins and take the penance. Do not try and explain why.*

'You know,' she said, 'Neil told a friend that Bella was trying to drive herself and he stopped her, but then she tried to get on his lap and that was why the car went out of control.'

Anthony stared at her. 'No. I hadn't heard that. He told me he felt totally responsible.'

He rubbed his cheek thoughtfully. After a while he continued. 'But I did feel great sympathy for her.'

'Sympathy?' said Cat sharply. 'You were her therapist.'

'Yes,' said Anthony, 'but I'm also a man.'

I wish Miranda was doing this interview, Cat thought. *Why was I so arrogant? What if he says something awful? Can I tell Caroline not to see her therapist, without explaining why?* Cat blanked her mind and murmured, 'Go on.'

'She blackmailed me.'

Cat stared at him. The words came out so bleakly she hadn't been expecting them. 'How? About what? What had you done? And what did she want?'

'Look,' he said, 'I wasn't completely honest with you. When I said she just stopped having therapy, it wasn't completely true.'

Ah, thought Cat, so her instinct had been right.

'This was back in the 90s,' he said, 'when she'd started Spinners. She thought she had done enough therapy. We both knew our sessions, which had at first been so successful, were turning bad. I wasn't helping her anymore, but I wanted her to move to another therapist. I felt she would benefit from someone else's input. That there were still underlying issues, despite her success. She didn't want to.'

'But she could just quit the therapy? She wasn't sectioned, was she?'

He moved in his chair, leaning forward. 'No, but Victoria is much more cunning than that. Not wanting more therapy was just a ruse. A light thing that neither of us could take too seriously. I was only being asked to make one little insignificant lie. But she wanted more from me. She wanted me in her power. Then, next time, I would do what she needed because I was already her slave!'

Cat felt very cold.

'I'll try and explain.' He was silent for a moment, then he said, 'Why did you do this interview?'

Cat frowned. 'I'm a detective.'

'Why not Miranda?'

This echo of her own thoughts kept Cat silent. Anthony breathed deeply.

'You know, don't you?'

Cat shook her head. 'Know what?' She felt a little curling movement in her stomach. He breathed deeply again and compressed his lips. 'OK, well you obviously know that I have been Caroline's therapist for a long time.'

Cat noticed the room had grown completely still. Silent. Tense. She watched Anthony as closely as her namesake might a mouse.

'A few years ago, Caroline became obsessed by me. She had recently married Rupert and things were not going well. She allowed herself to dream ... anyway, in our sessions she suddenly wanted to know everything about me. Was I married? Did I have children? And so forth. In fact, I'm divorced. My wife left me because she said my clients were more important to me than her, and she was right. But I didn't want to tell Caroline any of that. It is this clinic's policy, for right or wrong, that we do not allow our patients any access into our private lives. It prevents complications.

'However, I had not seen Caroline's tenacity. I had not realised ... Enough to say she started following me.'

'She was stalking you?' asked Caroline's mother, trying to force herself not to accuse Anthony of lying but just to listen quietly and make her own judgement.

He smiled slightly. 'Yes. I work long hours, but even I go home occasionally.'

He stopped and, even though she could see this was a joke to alleviate the tension, Cat could not force a responding smile. She gripped the handles of her bag.

'I live in a flat, on the fourth floor of a block. One evening, I went in, put the lights on, then saw I hadn't got any food in the fridge. So, I popped out the back door of the flats. Usually, I prop the door open so I can get back in, but on this occasion, either I forgot, or someone shut the door, so I had to go around the front. As I got to the corner, I saw someone standing by the lamp-post, looking up at the flats. Of course, I immediately recognised Caroline.'

He stopped again.

'And?' Cat asked.

'I walked up to Caroline gently, hoping we could make this light-hearted. "Caroline!" I said. "What a coincidence. Are you waiting for someone in my flats?"

'And she said, no preamble, nothing, "You. I love you, Anthony. I can't go on with Rupert, he's so ... so ghastly. It's always been you."'

Caroline. Her daughter. Please no. Please, God, don't make this personal.

Anthony went on. 'I made a mistake, then. I should have sent her home, told my manager, and had her changed to another therapist, but I didn't.'

Cat thought she was going to faint. What could be coming now?

'I let her come upstairs with me.'

Cat gasped and his hand immediately shot out, his palm toward her face. 'It's OK! Nothing happened. But I shouldn't have allowed her to come upstairs, to see where I lived. Perhaps I thought it would make her realise I had nothing. I wasn't in her league. I was just a poor man with no prospects and not a suitable mate for Cat's daughter.'

'What?'

'It was a joke, Cat. Steel yourself.'

Cat thought she might well be sick, however, she gave a weak smile. 'Go on.'

'We talked. I told her she would have to change therapists, but she threatened to kill herself if I told anyone, and, either I believed her, or I was so arrogant I thought no one else would be as good for your daughter as me.

'So, I agreed. I said I would say nothing, and she could continue as my patient, provided she didn't repeat her behaviour and tried to make it up with Rupert. Shortly afterwards she told me she was pregnant, and I thought, phew, I did the right thing.'

'OK,' said Cat stiffly, like someone standing on a wall, worried about falling off. 'And?'

'Victoria found out. I don't know how. But Victoria listens in on conversations at her club, her barmen spy for her. She has a network. I suppose it is possible Caroline trusted Victoria and told her herself.'

'Does Caroline know Victoria?'

'I don't know but it is possible.'

'And,' said Cat, 'Victoria stored up the knowledge until she needed something from you.'

Anthony nodded. 'Yes.'

'So, you agreed to let her stop therapy. To sign her off. And you thought the price was so light, that it was worth paying to keep your job.'

Anthony sighed. 'I was a fool. If a patient had asked me what to do, I would have said never give a blackmailer a way in, even if it seems minute at the time. Once they have found your weakness you are theirs. But I didn't take my own advice.'

Cat suddenly relaxed and nearly fell out of her chair. 'But you didn't do anything wrong. Couldn't you have explained the whole thing to your manager? I'm sure all your patients would have supported you.'

Anthony sighed. 'Yes, possibly in the long run. But before then I would be suspended. Even if I was allowed to practice again, I would be put on probation for years. Everything I had worked for would be gone. And I was worried that Caroline would put her threat into practice. I couldn't bear to be responsible for Caroline's death. Since all Victoria wanted was to stop therapy, it seemed negligible.'

Cat sighed.

Anthony nodded. 'Yes. I know you think that is very weak of me. But Victoria is immensely endearing. She brings you to believe in her world even when you know it is not true.'

'And has she ever wanted anything since?'

'No. I moved away from her orbit and made myself inaccessible. Until, that is, Neil arrived on my metaphorical doorstep needing therapy.'

'You think she suggested to Neil he came to you?'

'It is possible.' He paused. 'Has Victoria suggested I made the tape with Neil?'

'Yes.'

'And there will be more steps now. Before long I will be accused of murder.'

Cat looked at him. 'So that was why you gave Caroline the tape to give me? Such a long time after he gave it to you.'

'Yes. When Caroline told me about the investigation, about Stevie's friendship with Victoria, about Victoria's talking about me as her therapist, I felt it would only be a matter of time before she came back to claim the prize. That she had me in a position where I could be the fall guy for her—'

Cat's phone rang.

'Sorry, Anthony, it seems to be Blinkey. Mind if I take it?'

'Go ahead.'

'Blinkey?'

'Cat! There's a woman with a gun forcing Stevie out to the Tiger Moth.'

'What?'

'There's a woman with a gun—'

'Blinkey, are you sure?'

'She's got a stick, and a limp.'

'I'm on my way.'

Cat jumped up. 'Anthony...'

'I heard. I'll come with you.'

'No, you call the police. They may be ages but at least it will be a backup if necessary.' She paused. 'Will they believe you?'

'Oh yes,' he said. 'The word *gun* will get them there in minutes. You'd better go.'

CHAPTER 39
JUMPING SPIDERS

As Stevie drove to the landing strip Victoria sat quietly next to her, the gun trained on Stevie's leg. 'You might,' she said conversationally, 'be able to overpower me, but I will shoot your leg first. I'll smash the bone. You won't be able to fly again.'

Stevie drove on silently.

'OK,' said Victoria suddenly, 'stop just ahead. Pull over to the other side of the road and hover by that postbox.'

Stevie drove across the road and stopped, facing into the oncoming traffic. She didn't bother to point out they could be pulverised by any law-abiding driver on the left side of the road.

'Open the window. Just tell me when the next collection is?'

Stevie looked at the legend. 'In about an hour. It says four p.m.'

'Perfect. I didn't want to miss the post.' Victoria smiled to herself. She passed Stevie an envelope. 'Pop that in, will you, and don't try and be clever by dropping it or anything. I can shoot at distance as well as close range.'

Stevie posted the envelope. It was a bit wide for the slot, but she forced it in, hoping it wouldn't matter if it was a bit crumpled. Then almost laughed since neither of them would be alive to know.

She drove on, towards her Tiger Moth and her home. *Perhaps*, she thought, *I can make a run for it when she gets out of the car to fetch her chair*.

When they arrived, they sat still for a few moments outside the house. Stevie kicked herself for having built such a nice path down to the hangar. It would be easy to take a chair down there. That was why she had designed it that way, to make it easy for her passengers, even if they were at all challenged.

She looked at the sky. It was clear with a light wind: a perfectly lovely evening for flying the Tiger Moth. A perfect evening for dying? Perhaps. She glanced at Victoria.

Victoria saw the look in her eyes. 'So, now you know why I told you everything?'

Stevie was silent, her eyes staring at the gun.

'Yes, I think you do. And we are going down together. Tonight we will be together ... where, do you think? Warmly in Hell? Greeted by Neil perhaps. Don't think of staying alive by killing me, incidentally. I've left all the information on my phone. The police will enjoy reading it all, I imagine.'

Her hand was completely steady.

Stevie's gaze flickered onto the weapon. 'Pretty pistol,' she said, as though complimenting it might will it away.

'Yup. Let's go.'

Stevie's brain was spinning trying to get ahead of the other woman, but no thoughts were emerging. It slipped through her mind that the pistol might be a toy. But what if it wasn't?

'Up.'

As Stevie got out of the car, she noticed that Victoria was taking the cushion from her wheelchair.

'You won't need that. Although it has bucket seats, I have cushions in the parachute bays.'

'Very thoughtful, darling. Thank you. But this is for my back. With my withered legs it helps to be pushed forward so I can use my muscles more effectively on the pedals.' She giggled. 'I knew you'd be interested in the mechanics of my ability!'

Stevie nodded. It made sense. If you shorten a spring it gets tighter and more powerful, so why not a muscle? How clever the human body was. They walked down the gentle slope to the hangar.

Victoria had brought one of her sticks. She leant on it and her gait was slow, but the gun was still steady in her hand. She motioned Stevie to walk slightly ahead of her. As they passed the house, they saw Blinkey was in her usual place at the window. She waved a hand.

'Who's that?' asked Victoria sharply.

'My mother; she has dementia.'

'Just as well,' she said, waving the gun menacingly.

When they reached the hangar, Stevie pushed the trolley under the Tiger's skid, lifting the light machine with the other hand. She pushed it out onto the concrete apron, while Victoria watched, sitting on the low wall next to the hangar, again something Stevie had built for convenience.

'Did you put this all down yourself?'

'Yes.'

'You really will be a loss to society, won't you? Shame.'

'You'd better sit in the front,' said Stevie, putting the trolley neatly back into the hangar by the wall.

'Phruh! You must think I'm green. I'm sitting behind you where I can see what you are up to. I know there's only a radio in the back, not in the front. Perfect. You won't be able to call for help, and I'm certainly not going to. Now I'm going to show you how brilliantly Bella flies. Even after all this time.'

Stevie said nothing. She waited as Victoria heaved herself into the seat backwards, her pistol still trained on the younger girl.

'Switches on.'

Stevie pulled the prop and the obedient little craft started immediately. Why did it have to be such a good machine? Couldn't it have coughed and refused to start?

She pulled out the chocks, storing them by the trolley, and climbed into the front cockpit. Victoria taxied out to the strip. She must have put the gun into her clothes because she seemed to have two hands free to take off.

Even though Stevie knew Victoria was going to kill her, she couldn't help admiring how straight she kept the Moth, how smoothly she applied power and how lightly they came off the grass and into the air. Victoria hadn't flown for almost thirty years, and her spine was irreparably damaged, but her skill had come straight back. Stevie was impressed.

Victoria began circling, then dived down doing a few low passes over the fields, pulling up sharply and starting her climb to height.

Stevie cricked her neck back to glance at the fuel indicator. They had quarter tanks. If Victoria was planning to fly until the fuel ran out, they would both be cold by the time they died. Neither of them was dressed for a long flight in cooling air.

'I've always wondered,' purred Victoria into the intercom. 'How long can you stay upside down before the fuel runs out of the engine? Haven't you?'

'No,' said Stevie. She knew the answer; as there were no

fuel pumps, the Tiger could only fly seven to ten seconds before the engine stopped.

'Now,' said Bella, 'which way to enter. I think I'll do a loop or two first.'

Stevie said nothing. Perhaps, if you must die young, this was as good a way as any. She hated the idea of a long retirement.

Bella dived the Tiger Moth to increase the speed, pulled up a little too sharply and then eased off too early. Stevie felt the g-forces as it fell out of the loop and slipped to the left stuttering slightly.

'Oh! Lost my touch! One side stronger than the other,' Victoria muttered to herself. 'Didn't compensate enough. Better do it again.'

This time she entered too gently, and the willing Tiger only just staggered over the top and collapsed down the other side.

'Oh, dear!' she said. 'No competition prizes for that one.'

She dived again.

'Right,' she muttered, 'now, somewhere between the two.'

This time she gave just the right amount of back pressure on the stick, managed to keep it central despite her failing legs and the little Moth danced over the top of the loop and came smoothly out into level flight.

'Perfect,' she crowed. 'What a way to go!'

Stevie imagined the huge beaming smile on her face.

'Right, and now, the denouement. Thank you, Stevie, for being my friend. Had life been kinder to me we would have got to know each other, probably spent happy lives together. All I ever wanted to do was fly on silver wings and doing it with you would have been perfect. Isn't it sad that one drunken evening, one drunken man, took that all away from us?'

Stevie said nothing.

Victoria rolled the Tiger Moth upside down and counted.

'One, two, three, four, five, six, seven...'

And then the engine stopped, and Victoria screamed.

But the scream was moving, falling ... going farther and farther away.

Stevie grabbed the front stick and righted the machine. The engine remained silent, but she saw a field below and aimed for it, eyed up the distance and landed just over the wooden fence, bumping down the field. The Tiger felt nose heavy, and Stevie kept the stick hard back and although they had a couple of little leaps, it settled. 'Thank Heaven,' she muttered to herself, 'most of the fuel has been used up, which improved the longitudinal balance.'

Sighing deeply, she brought the Tiger to a halt. In the back cockpit the only noise was the flapping of the seat belt straps.

Stevie jumped out onto the wing. The back cockpit was empty. She stared it. What had she hoped to find? She put her hand in the side pouch and felt something hard: Victoria's phone. As she pulled it out and opened it, a message flashed up.

Entry by thumb print only.
Warning: after three false attempts phone will return to factory settings.

How like Victoria to protect her information in that way: all or nothing. She put her thumb on the switch three times and had the satisfaction of seeing a whirl across the screen as the phone returned to its birth settings.

Behind the pouch was the gun. Tucked into the side between the Irish linen cover and the frame strut, she might have missed it, if she hadn't known it would be there. She pulled it out. "Toy gun," the label read. "Misuse may cause serious injury or death."

She sat down hard on the black walkway of the Tiger's wing and shuddered. Her whole body was shaking so much the Moth started to judder on its wheels as though the wind had suddenly got up.

'Stevie, Stevie!' She could hear voices in the distance. Turning her head, she saw Cat and Miranda were running towards her so fast that Cat was tripping over her feet. They arrived panting.

'Are you OK? Your mother told us...'

'My mother?'

'Yes, she must be in one of her lucid moments. She told me there was a woman with a gun forcing you into the Tiger Moth. Luckily, I believed her.'

Stevie started to laugh and all at once tears were pouring down her face.

'Poor, poor Bella. Poor, poor Victoria.'

Cat investigated the back cockpit and then the front.

'Did she jump?'

'No. Do you remember I said my straps in the back were fraying, so we'd better not do any aerobatics?'

'Yes, of course. I'd forgotten, but now you mention it.'

'She did three loops; two weren't completely positive, which might have put some strain on them, but the real problem was flying inverted. Not good for anything.'

'I'm so sorry, Stevie,' said Miranda. 'I had no idea she was so angry.'

Stevie frowned. She was silent while the girls walked around the machine, as though hoping to find Victoria there.

Finally, Stevie said, her voice breaking, 'Before she fell out, she said: "Isn't it amazing what one drunken evening took away from us?"'

Her face crumpled and she turned away from her friends to the Tiger Moth. She leant her cheek on the calming coolness of the Irish linen and breathed in the smell of the dope and paint.

'Well, honestly, Stevie,' said Cat toughly, 'ignore that. You know there is a girl in America who flies without arms. In comparison, Victoria was fit and healthy.'

Even Miranda thought this a bit too bracing. 'She's not flying for the airlines. It's not quite the same thing, sweetheart.'

'No,' said Stevie, keeping her face away from her friends. 'We still haven't reached the day when you can be an airline pilot without arms. But it will come; when remote flying is more widespread.'

She walked to the front.

'Will you swing the prop, Cat? Or would you rather sit in?'

Cat shook her head. 'No, you get in, I'll swing. Want me to prime it first?'

Stevie clambered into the cockpit. She felt old and tired. For the first time in her life, she didn't want to fly. She wanted to go to bed and curl up, forget that the world existed.

She breathed deeply and nodded. Cat turned the prop backwards a few times, then forwards to get fuel back into the lines.

As Stevie lifted the broken straps to put them on, she saw that they weren't broken. Victoria had undone them. She had decided to die alone.

Stevie swallowed. She needed to fly back. She couldn't break down now. She breathed deeply and spoke, her voice steady.

'Should be OK now, let's see if it starts.'

'Switches on.'

The Tiger started like a dream. Stevie taxied back to the far end of the field. Her friends held the wings as she taxied, turned and while she ran up the engine. They let go and jumped back. She accelerated up the field and took off, easily clearing the trees ahead. Hah, she thought, just like Victoria on the greyhound strip all those years ago.

Turning, she flew home.

Miranda and Cat walked back to where they left the car on the road.

Cat said, 'Do you think she'll be OK?'

'Yes, in time. She's made of tough stuff.'

'Maybe,' said Cat, 'but it is quite something when the person you think you are falling for tries to kill you.'

'Oh, really? I thought that happened to you every day.'

'Love you too!'

CHAPTER 40
MRS D. B. COOPER

'Password,' said Blinkey.

Stevie sighed. 'It's me, Mother!'

'Nice. I might use that one. *Mother*. Like it.'

Stevie walked on to the office where the others were already having coffee.

'So,' said Cat, as she walked in, 'we've solved the house problem: it's had so many viewings Jason had had to employ extra staff, just for this house alone!'

Miranda laughed. 'But, what of the rest? Is Stevie safe from Victoria's post-death retribution? What about those videos she made?'

Stevie moved Victoria's phone from hand to hand. 'Luckily, I have this now. It's blank. Gone back to factory settings.'

'And the police?' said Miranda. 'Won't they want it when they investigate Victoria's death?'

Stevie turned and looked at her colleagues portentously. 'What death?'

Her colleagues stared at her.

'She fell out of the plane,' said Cat.

Stevie spread her hands. 'The police and their helpers spent a week searching the site where she disappeared and no sign of the body. Not a trace.'

'Get out!' said Miranda. 'You saw her fall.'

'I heard her,' said Stevie. 'I was too busy righting the Tiger Moth and landing safely to see her fall, or land for that matter.'

'You mean,' said Cat, 'she could have survived the fall? Without a parachute?'

Stevie shrugged. 'In 1972, Vesna Vulovic, a Serbian flight attendant, did fall from more than thirty-thousand feet without a parachute, but she was badly knocked about.

'The police have been looking in hospitals, just in case, but without any result. There are other cases too, from lower heights but they usually have significant injuries, unless they use a parachute. Although, there was also Juliane Koepcke who fell three-thousand metres without a para-chute, much higher than we were, but then she *did* have three seats fall with her.'

'Umm,' said Miranda, 'I remember the film; they showed how the other seats worked to slow her fall, and she was the only survivor and lived in the jungle for ten days.'

'Well, then,' said Cat. 'Is it possible she had a parachute? Wouldn't you have noticed when she was walking out to the plane?'

Stevie sighed. 'Possibly not. I was always in front of her. I don't know. Although I did wonder what had happened to her stick.'

'Her stick?' said Cat. 'Stick that converts into a para-chute?! Like Mary Poppins?' She lifted up an imaginary umbrella and twirled around. 'You could have invented that yourself.'

Stevie started smiling then stopped. She slapped her head. 'Oh, what an idiot I am!'

'What?'

'The cushion. She took a funny sort of knobbly cushion with her saying she needed it for her back. But perhaps it wasn't a cushion at all; perhaps it was a parachute. What a clot I am!' said Stevie, staring in front of her as though seeing Victoria limping in. 'PPPP. She planned this from the start. She never meant to die. Of course! I should have realised someone like Victoria would never hurt a beautiful historic plane like the Tiger Moth. She knew I'd be able to right the machine. This is just part of a big plan. This is just like the story of DB Cooper...'

Cat and Miranda exchanged glances.

'She might have decided not to kill *you*, or herself,' said Miranda, scratching her arm, 'rather than save that old machine.'

Stevie shrugged. 'But honestly, that isn't the oddest thing about this case.'

'So,' said Cat, 'what is?'

'You remember I had to post a letter on the way to the strip.'

'Yes.'

'Well, Caroline received it a few days ago. Doesn't say much for the post, does it? Took over a week to arrive. Honestly.'

'Caroline? What? My Caroline? She didn't—'

'She didn't tell you,' broke in Stevie. 'That's because she wanted to get it checked first. Before she talked to you.'

Cat wiggled her nose. 'And?'

'It's a contract for the purchase of Spinners nightclub for a hundred pounds to be donated to the disabled flying association and a ninety-nine-year lease on the building. Sold by the Bella Chantry Trust to Caroline Harrington. It's completely legal. Caroline had it checked by Anthony's brother who is a lawyer.'

'Oh,' said Cat. She didn't like the sound of that: Caroline's own sister, Vanessa, was a lawyer, and yet her daughter had chosen to use Anthony's brother, not her own family. She tried not to think why that might be.

'Are you saying,' said Miranda, suddenly paying attention, 'that Caroline is now the owner of Spinner's nightclub? Blimey! Some people have all the luck.'

'Yup, that seems to be the case,' said Stevie.

Cat frowned. 'Not luck really. It's heavily in debt.'

'The nightclub is,' said Stevie, 'but not the building. It must be worth millions. But you notice Caroline doesn't get that, just a short lease. Which suggests to me that Victoria is indeed still alive. If not, why would she bother with all these machinations?'

Cat frowned. 'Yes. Good point. But I don't see why she would involve Caroline whom she doesn't even know, or does she?'

'Don't know,' said Stevie, 'but she did say Caroline came to see her, to tell her to stay away from Anthony.'

Cat blew a silent raspberry. 'What is going on?'

'So,' said Miranda, 'we have solved one case, only to find ourselves another.'

'Yes, but,' said Stevie, 'without a client.'

'So,' said Miranda, 'we'll just have to find one.'

The team stared at each other; not for the first time their desire to solve the mystery battling with the lack of finance.

'The question now,' said Cat, 'is where is Victoria? And what might she do next?'

Miranda's phone rang. She looked. 'It's Amy. Perhaps she knows where Victoria might have gone.'

'Amy?'

'No,' said Jenny's voice, 'it's Graham.'

How confusing, thought Miranda. 'Hi, Graham.'

'Look, Miranda, have you seen Amy?'

'No,' Miranda said. Had she and Amy suddenly become besties or something?

'She didn't turn up for work this morning. Something she just wouldn't do. And, as you can see, I have her phone. Something has happened.'

Miranda was still baffled. 'And you are ringing me because? I mean I don't want to be unsympathetic but there's a whole police force out there who look for lost people.'

Graham made a noise. 'I've reported her missing and they told me to leave it a day. She could be dead by then. It hasn't escaped me that that damn Bella Chantry is on the loose. There must be a connection.'

Miranda listened for a while, put the phone down and turned to her companions.

'We've found a client!' she said. 'All we have to do is find Amy and Victoria.'

'Come on,' said Cat, 'this is ridiculous. Amy is a fit, healthy woman. Victoria is in a wheelchair, and even if she can walk a bit, she still has to use a stick, and she doesn't even have the toy gun anymore. How can she possibly threaten Amy? Why does Graham think she's in trouble?'

'Well, maybe, but the fact is she didn't turn up at work and isn't carrying her phone. Both things that she never does normally.'

'When did Graham last see her?' asked Cat.

'Last night, before Jenny went down to the club. Amy

had an early start, so she didn't want to go with her. And, he said, when she has an early start, she always sleeps in the spare room. That way it doesn't matter what time Jenny comes home.'

'What time did he leave home?'

'Around eight. He was meeting Trixie for dinner in the club. They have a separate dining room.'

'So, the club's still fully functional then, even though it now belongs to my daughter?'

'Yes.'

Cat made a noise.

'Concentrate, Cat! How would Victoria get Amy to leave home and meet her? Graham said there was a missed call on his phone from Amy around midnight, but he had the phone turned onto silent and didn't see it. No message.'

'How about tracking, Stevie?' asked Cat. 'Can you tell where the call was made from?'

'Only in emergencies. And it's difficult to get phone companies to give out that data. I can try if you think it's important.'

'No,' said Miranda, 'as Graham found her phone at home this morning it was much more likely the call was made from there. But the question is, if it was Victoria, how would she get Amy to leave home last night if she had an early start this morning? And without her phone?'

'She wouldn't,' said Stevie. 'But what she might do is get her on the way to work. How about if she made a call sound like it was coming from dispatch and asking Amy to come in an hour early. Then she could sidetrack her.'

'Maybe, but how? What would cause Amy to sidetrack?'

'Possibly,' said Stevie, 'we're looking at this from the wrong angle. What is Victoria good at?'

The others shook their heads.

'She's good at spotting and using people's weaknesses. Look at the evidence: Anthony, too sympathetic to others to spot how he could be blackmailed; Neil, too easily falling for women pilots; Caroline, gave her a debt-ridden business which was apparently successful so she would run it down and cause herself humiliation.'

'We don't know that yet,' said Cat, suddenly maternal. 'She may make a great job of it.'

Stevie waved her hand impatiently. 'And even me...' She blushed. 'She used my naivety and inexperience.' She sighed slightly. 'So, what is Amy's weakness?'

Cat shrugged. 'She's clever and well-prepared; does she have a weakness?'

'Of course, she does!' said Miranda. 'I'd say her vanity. She liked telling me I was stupid to highlight her own intelligence; she likes being well-prepared to highlight other workers' inefficiency. Defo. Her vanity is her Achilles heel.'

'So,' said Stevie, 'how could Victoria use that to get her to heel?' She stared at the passing clouds. 'Miranda, can you ring Graham back and ask if anyone had phoned Amy last night?'

Miranda pulled out her phone. In a few moments she had the answer. 'Amy had two calls last night, both unknown numbers, one at ten o'clock, the second just before midnight. After the second she called Graham on his phone, but, as we know, he didn't pick up.'

'And then she disappeared.'

'We could see if she arranged a meeting at Wild Garlic?' said Miranda.

'We could,' said Stevie, 'but there are so many visitors that she'd have been found already. I suppose...'

'What?'

'The weather was really clear last night. Let's suppose Victoria made both those calls, the first as dispatch, to say the flight was cancelled, and the second as me, inviting her to come for a midnight flight in the Tiger Moth.' She paused and blushed, 'Victoria knew I had never flown the Tiger at night. I told her.'

Cat frowned. 'But wouldn't Amy be a bit suspicious? You're hardly besties.'

'Not,' said Stevie, sighing slightly, 'if "I" said I hadn't flown the Tiger before in the dark and that I needed a more experienced pilot to fly with me.'

Cat shook her head. 'Surely, Amy wouldn't believe that. You've been flying the Tiger since you could breathe. Has she ever flown one?'

'Yes, she has a rating on a Dakota, so she would have had to fly Tigers first, I reckon, as a suitable tail dragger trainer.'

'OK,' said Miranda, 'what are we waiting for? To the hangar.'

As they walked down to the strip Stevie could see a large frame outside the hangar door with a screen hanging from it.

'Wait,' she said, 'you two, stay here. We know now how Victoria likes booby traps. If it all blows up, get help.'

The others stopped and Stevie walked on towards the hangar. As she did so, the screen lit up and there was Victoria's face, smiling with joy.

'Well, who's a clever girl then? I knew you'd work it out, but this is quick. Well done!'

Stevie said nothing, waiting.

'OK,' said Victoria, 'now I'm going to share my screen, and here is a picture of your little friend. I'm afraid you put your hangar inside lighting in rather poor places, so the picture is a little dark.'

A picture of someone hanging in a sling emerged. The sling had been hoisted up to the hangar roof and was suspended from the rafters over the Tiger Moth. A close-up by the camera showed it was Amy and she appeared to be asleep. Her hands were hidden from view, but Stevie guessed they would be tied behind her.

'Nice, eh?' said the remorseless woman in the corner of the screen. 'Even if she survives, she'll never get over having been bested by a woman in a wheelchair. Poor Amy!'

Victoria laughed and Stevie wondered where she was. Someone had to have initiated the Zoom this end, so she couldn't be that far away. And she didn't move fast whether she was in the wheelchair or walking.

'Clever Stevie,' Victoria said. 'You're trying to work it out, aren't you? Can you come and surprise me? Well, before you do that, you little heartthrob, I think you'd better save Amy. She won't last up there for ever!'

The picture went back to Amy in the sling, not moving.

'Sadly,' said Victoria, 'I had to give her a little Rohypnol to keep her calm, so you need to work quickly, my darling, before she wakes up and starts causing herself trouble. I thought there was a nice circular irony to giving her a date rape drug.'

Her cheerfully grinning face filled the screen.

'Now,' said Victoria, 'I want to test your brains or rather your ability to think outside the box. Like the Sphinx I have three questions for you. If you answer them correctly, young Amy floats gently down; if you answer them wrong, well, then poor Amy plunges from the rafters into the Tiger Moth, and both are destroyed. Which would be worse for you, Stevie? That wasn't question one, by the way.' Her laughter propelled out of the screen.

She had to be, thought Stevie, somewhere with Wi-Fi, and she was likely to be close. The office seemed likely. But where was her mother? Oh, and the carer? Stevie went cold thinking that Victoria might have hurt her mother. She waited.

'Right,' said Victoria. 'Here is question one. An easy one for warm up. What is the connection between the Tiger Moth and the Dakota?'

Stevie thought for a long time, then she said, 'The Canadian de Havilland and Dakota were at one time both owned by Boeing.'

Victoria gave a low laugh.

'Well, and I thought you were a simpleton. I would have accepted that they were both taildraggers, but you went one step further. What a clever little girl. OK, watch!'

In the hangar, the sling holding Amy was lowered a third of the distance.

'Now, she won't do so much damage to the Tiger,' said Victoria happily. 'Still get a nasty backache though and you won't be flying this season. Mending a machine takes time.'

Stevie put her phone behind her back and hoping she was pressing the right keys wrote:

Victoria? Office? and sent it to Miranda.

'Now,' said Victoria, 'question two. Not so easy this time.'

Stevie hoped it would be like the *Who Wants to be a Millionaire* questions where often the low score ones were harder than the high score ones.

'Question two: what was the name of the radio-controlled Tiger Moth?'

Stevie sighed; it *was* like *Millionaire*. 'The Queen Bee,' she said.

'Oh, my goodness. She's a clever one.'

Amy and the sling moved down another third.

'And now, my clever little darling, the third question. In what year did I found Spinners?'

Stevie's mind reeled. How could she possibly know the answer to that? Had Victoria told her? Was it the same year Neil died?

'Come on, sweetheart. I'm waiting. And more importantly, so is our little friend. She is a swinger, and a spinner!'

The picture focused on Amy whose sling had now started to wave from side to side, as though preparing to go into a spin.

'Yuk,' said Victoria. 'How long before spinning and Rohypnol make her sick all over the Tiger Moth? That isn't the question, though!'

'Oh course,' said Stevie, 'you didn't! Bella Chantry founded Spinners. It's in her name!'

Victoria laughed and, on the screen, Amy descended safely into the Tiger Moth. Stevie rushed into the hangar.

By the time Stevie had released a groggy and shaken Amy, Miranda and Cat had got into the office. Stevie and Amy could see them moving around across the screen.

'She's not here, Stevie,' said Miranda, her face filling the computer screen where Victoria's had been just a moment before, 'but she was obviously broadcasting from here. Your mother and the carer are shut in another room. They're fine. But Victoria has gone. No wheelchair. No sticks. No car.'

The screen spit suddenly and Victoria's face appeared. 'Why,' she said, 'still can't find me, sleuths! You are going to have to try harder. However,' she said, 'since I want to help you, look in the upper left-hand drawer of the desk: there's a memory stick of brilliant info.'

And she was gone.

Miranda watched the words *The host had ended this call* shimmering on the Zoom screen. She opened the upper left-hand drawer of the desk, and there, sitting on Stevie's neat pile of bank statements was a memory stick.

As they were putting the memory stick into the computer they heard, 'Password?'

Cat smiled. 'No long-term effect on Blinkey, then?'

'No,' said Miranda as Stevie came into the room.

'Amy doesn't want to prosecute,' were her first words.

'What?' said Cat, pausing the video that was about to play. 'But Victoria kidnapped her and could have killed her...'

'And made her look a fool,' said Stevie. 'Graham's on his way to take her home. She doesn't want the police involved but she will employ us to find Victoria; discreetly.'

'And then what?' asked Cat. 'Without police interest we can't do anything to her, can we? And as soon as there is police interest, Amy's case will come up.'

'Let's look at the video she sent and see what she wants us to know,' said Miranda.

Stevie raised her eyebrows but said nothing and the screen filled with Victoria's face.

'This is the story of 1988,' she said, 'when I was a young genius with the world ahead of me.'

She disappeared and in her place were the words: Sussex, 8th March 1988 written across a cartoon of Wild Garlic in Owly Vale.

As an animated version of Victoria appeared the narrator's voice said: 'Look! Legs! In those days I was called Bella.'

The video moved inside Wild Garlic with the Bella figure, stepping over the somnolent figures of previous revellers.

'She,' said the narrator, 'was looking for someone to

drive her home because she was way over the limit and, as a pilot who had just accepted her first job, the last thing she wanted was to lose her licence and potentially her future.'

'Sossy, B,' said her best flying mate, Jerry. 'Shouldn't do it, though I'd love to take you home. My muzzer would love you forever. S'paps we shoz do that ... you come upstairs...?'

He fell into a heap of laughter and Bella swished her long, blonde hair impatiently.

Another good friend was asleep on the sofa. Bella looked at her and passed by. Then, to her surprise, a gnome-like man with a beard came over. He smelt of garlic. He looked at her as though expecting something, but, when she didn't speak, said, 'I hear you are looking for a sober driver?'

'Yes, are you sober?'

'I'd say, as a judge, but we have reservations there, don't we?' He smiled and so did she.

'Where do you live?' he asked.

'Billington. It's only five miles away but all country roads, twists, and turns, not a light in sight. Not an ideal place to drive after one, or two,' she giggled, 'too many.'

'Billington? I think I know it. Near Healy?'

'That's it.'

'Great. I'm staying with a relative in Healy. I could bring your car back tomorrow if that's OK.'

'That would be wonderful, thank you.'

'Nice car,' said Mr Sober as they approached Bella's Citroën. 'I've always liked French cars; they are somehow more soigné.'

She glanced at him. That word triggered something in her mind, but she was too drunk to pinpoint what. Then he was opening the car door and the moment was lost.

He bowed her into the car. She giggled. 'Thank you.'

'A lady should always be treated better than the best,' he said.

Shutting the door, he gave a small wave before moving around to the driver's side.

Bella thought that a bit creepy, but it hardly mattered. He was only driving her home.

They set off towards Billington, and Bella's mind went back to the party. Given in her honour, it was to celebrate her brilliant offer from Cathay Pacific, the top employer. Her first airline job: not only was it Cathay, but she would also be one of their first intake of women! Wow! It was just so cool. Only a handful of airline pilots were women, and she would be a trailblazer in every sense of the word.

Even more, she was going to live in Hong Kong. Start a whole new life, away from her family, whom she loved but could do without. It was so, so exciting. And, although she would never admit it to anyone else, it was particularly satisfying that her elder sister was only on the waiting list while she had been given a job offer. For once, she was going to be ahead of Rebecca. She grinned in the darkness. Life was peachy.

Mr Sober swerved suddenly on a corner, bringing her back to reality.

'Ooh, careful.'

'Sorry, sweetheart,' he said, 'it sheemed to come out of nowhere.'

She heard a little lisp in his voice and her stomach gave a warning leap.

'You haven't been drinking, have you?'

He snorted. 'Well, not as much as you. I saw you knocking back the champers! I only got a glass before it ran out.'

'But you are sober.'

'S'of course. As I said, absolutely, first teetotal judge in history, hey, nonny nay.'

Bella noticed he was swinging through the country lanes rather faster than she liked.

'Slow down, will you? These corners can be brutal.'

He took his hands off the steering wheel and waved them in the air. 'OK, OK, Madam airline pilot. You'll start as a *first officer*, you know. Must have respect for the *captain*.'

Bella was silent. She was sobering up herself. He didn't seem to be as clear headed as she had thought. She didn't want to antagonise him, and he did appear to be slowing slightly.

Then she noticed something else. 'You went the wrong way at the vee. Billington is to the left.'

'Yeah, cool it, I know. I clicked in – Environmental Capture, we call it – started going off to Healy. But don't worry. I'll go back to Billinson from Healy, then I'll know the way home.'

'Billington,' she said unwisely. 'It's called Billington, not Billinson.'

He laughed.

'Billson, Billy's son, Billy's got my son. You are getting my goat. Quit whingeing! You know what the Ozzies call you lot – Whingeing Poms – Pomme de Terre, red-faced buggers … ooh la la!'

As they swung around the next corner, now going, as she could see from the lit speedometer, 60 mph, he laughed and she finally clicked—he was not at all sober, judges or no judges.

'Look, um … why don't you stop, and I'll drive.'

Mr Sober started singing.

'Drive me to Heaven in a Handcart. Take me to Hell in a

Bell ... Come on, Bella ... sing along ... This is fun. You used
to be fun. *Fun!*'

'OK,' she said, the words *used to* vibrating in her ears.
Did she know him? Followed by a moment of realisation.
Memory. She almost screamed but kept her voice level. She
knew him once, long ago. His name was Neil and he was the
jilted fiancé of her sister. How could she have forgotten what
a nutter he was. Mad. Crazy. Drunken idiot.

She breathed deeply and spoke cautiously as you might
to a frightened animal. 'OK, let's stop now ... I know this
area. There is a big corner comiiiiiiiiii...'

Her scream echoed all through the dark valley but there
was no one there to hear it.

The car skidded round the corner and careened into the
left verge before bouncing back and sliding into the opposite ditch where it came to a shuddering halt resting on its
left side.

Neil, now forcedly sober, cursed. 'Just my luck! And I'm
already in debt. Have to go driving a car with faulty steering.
Now I'll have to add car repair to my debts. You should've
warned me.'

He looked over at Bella, grinning. But Bella did not
reply. Her neck was at an odd angle and her eyes were
closed. He froze in his seat, his hands clamping into fists.

'Oh, shit! Are you all right?'

There was no reply from the mangled woman
beside him.

He reached over and shook her shoulder. Nothing.

'Helloo! Can you hear me?'

Nothing. But now he saw a little blood oozing from her
lips.

'Oh, shit, shit, shit!'

He thrust open the door.

'Cheap rubbish!' he muttered, as the broken door fell into the drainage ditch, slowly submerging under the water.

Sliding out of the mutilated vehicle he looked around him. They were in the middle of nowhere. No houses. Nothing. Just a few overhead cables. No one had seen them. No one would know who had been driving. He looked back at the still girl in the car. He shrugged.

'Sorry, Bella,' he said quietly, just in case someone was around. 'But life must go on ... well ... mine that is. No point in ruining two lives, eh?'

He jumped over the hedge and began the long run across the fields to Healy. Behind him the car slowly sank deeper into the watery ditch.

The music of Complicated Minds by Doom thudded through the background but the sinking car remained in the picture. The unconscious Bella trapped inside.

A small boy around seven or eight appeared in the picture swinging a stick and trying to catch butterflies. He saw the car and jumped into the ditch. He jumped back and ran off screen, a few moments later an older woman accompanied him back to the scene. While the music of Doom continued, the boy and the woman pulled Bella out of the car, which promptly sank.

Victoria's face appeared again, no longer smiling there were tears in her eyes.

'He left me there,' she said, 'without Jake, and his mother I would be dead. And you saw yourselves what effect that had on the child. Poor crazy man. You met him, Stevie. Neil ruined his life too.

'Tell me, Stevie, who is the victim and who is the perpetrator? Who deserved to die? You saw for yourself what mayhem one drunken driver caused. Isn't he better off dead?'

And her face faded slowly away.

Cat shook her head. 'Ignore it, Stevie. She killed someone in cold blood. We don't even know if this is the true story. The story Neil told Marianne was quite different.'

'But,' said Miranda, 'he did want to die. And Amy's story of being left in the car and pulled out by a young man would seem to confirm what Bella is saying.'

Both women looked at Stevie. She looked from one to the other but it seemed she was hardly seeing them. 'We need to find her,' she said, her face pensive. 'You know she almost certainly landed near Billington when she jumped out of the Tiger Moth.'

'Yes?'

'Where did she go? Someone has got to be helping her and I think I know who.'

'You do? Who?'

'Think about it. She is doing incredibly well at first, then she starts to get into debt and yet her costs haven't changed and the place is still popular. And she is able to disappear at will. Doesn't that remind you of something?'

Her colleagues shook their heads.

'OK. I'll let you know when I get proof. Until then we leave her. Wait for her to make the next move.'

Cat and Miranda exchanged glances.

'She almost killed Amy,' said Cat, 'and she will kill you too if she can.'

'I think she's done with Amy,' said Miranda pensively, 'now she's humiliated her. It's you she's after, Stevie.'

Stevie nodded. 'I didn't mean we shouldn't go after her. I

just meant that we need to hatch a really good plan to catch her. She'll be watching us, for sure. And we want to make sure we are thoroughly prepared.'

'Ah,' echoed her friends, 'Prior Planning Prevents Piss-ups.'

Continued in Book Four

AFTERWORD

This book is dedicated to a flying colleague, the inspiration behind the story. This is something that might have happened but the book is complete fiction.

We were friends and often used to dine together after work, but as colleagues do we changed jobs and drifted apart. One day, I was at a trade show and another colleague told me he had seen our friend sitting in a doorway drinking from a brown paper bag (in those days it was common for the homeless to disguise their bottle in bags). I went to where he had last been seen, but he was no longer there. A year later I heard he had died and that it had taken months to find any family member to identify him. Perhaps that made him one of the lucky ones: 150 unidentified people died on the streets that year.

I have always felt incredibly sad that I was unable to help him and for a long time I have wanted to write a book dedicated to his memory and to others who find themselves living on the streets. This is that book.

* * *

The last chapter is titled Mrs D. B Cooper. This is a reference that many pilots will know: the story of D.B Cooper.

On 24th November 1971, an unidentified man hijacked Northwest Orient Airlines Flight 305, a Boeing 727, in United States airspace During the flight the hijacker told a flight attendant he was armed with a bomb, demanded $200,000 in ransom (equivalent to $1,338,000 in 2021), and requested four parachutes upon landing in Seattle. After releasing the passengers in Seattle, the hijacker instructed the flight crew to refuel the aircraft and begin a second flight. About 30 minutes after taking off from Seattle, the hijacker opened the aircraft's aft door, deployed the staircase, and parachuted into the night over southwestern Washington. The hijacker was never found but was given the name D.B. Cooper by the press.

ACKNOWLEDGMENTS

I would like to thank Kat Gordon for her editorial advice, Gillian Rodgerson for her copy editing and sensitivity advice, Abbie Rutherford for proof reading and Kari Brownlie for her beautiful cover design. Kari has designed all my covers and given them a wonderful consistency throughout.

Also many thanks to my friends and family for their help and advice, and especially my husband Gerald and the dogs: there is nothing like a dog walk for stimulating the little grey cells!

ABOUT THE AUTHOR

This is Gina Cheyne's third crime novel. The first, The Mystery of the Lost Husbands, came out in 2021. The second, Murder in the Cards, came out in 2022. All three books feature the SeeMs Detective Agency (the agency that looks behind what seems to be true to the reality beneath).

Gina worked as a helicopter and fixed wing pilot for many years, before being injured in an accident and retiring to write books. Of the accident she says:

'knowing that I could have been spending the rest of my life in a wheelchair deepened the way I think. Not only is it clear that so many places are impossible (not just difficult but impossible) for people who are not physically 'normal' but it is also incredibly frustrating how seldom 'different' people are asked for their input and advice on subjects that affect them enormously.

www.ginacheyne.com

ALSO BY GINA CHEYNE

Printed in Great Britain
by Amazon

20799875R00182